"You don't need me to fight your battles," he said

"Well, it would be nice to have *someone* fight them." Anne was accustomed to having to stand on her own two feet. However, what she had just said was something she had recognized since Ian had come to Fenton School to collect her. It *was* nice to have someone on her side. And *at* her side.

"And that is the purpose of everything we're in London to accomplish," Ian said softly.

The marriage mart. Someone to fight my battles for me.

Anne had never thought of what they were undertaking in that light. Despite all her romantic fantasies, she had never really believed she would find a husband at any of the Season's entertainments.

She had already found her champion and, ridiculously romantic or not, she knew she would never want any other…!

Praise for RITA Award winner Gayle Wilson

My Lady's Dare
"…three-dimensional characters and intriguing
plot twists kept this reader glued to the pages."
—*Romantic Times Magazine*

Lady Sarah's Son
"…a moving tale of love overcoming great obstacles,
of promises kept and trust restored."
—*Romantic Times Magazine*

Honor's Bride
"A superbly crafted story…"
—*Romantic Times Magazine*

The Heart's Wager
"This is the well-written, well-plotted, gripping book
that we're always hoping for and don't always find.
I give it my highest accolades."
—*Rendezvous*

Anne's Perfect Husband
Harlequin Historical #552—March 2001

GAYLE WILSON

Anne's PERFECT HUSBAND

HARLEQUIN®

TORONTO • NEW YORK • LONDON
AMSTERDAM • PARIS • SYDNEY • HAMBURG
STOCKHOLM • ATHENS • TOKYO • MILAN • MADRID
PRAGUE • WARSAW • BUDAPEST • AUCKLAND

ISBN 0-373-29152-3

ANNE'S PERFECT HUSBAND

Copyright © 2001 by Mona Gay Thomas

Please address questions and book requests to:
Harlequin Reader Service
U.S.: 3010 Walden Ave., P.O. Box 1325, Buffalo, NY 14269
Canadian: P.O. Box 609, Fort Erie, Ont. L2A 5X3

For Alynn, whose beautiful name might be suitable
for a medieval heroine, but not, alas, for a Regency one.
Although its heroine is named Anne, this story
is still for you, along with my love and admiration.
Hope you enjoy!

Prologue

Sinclair Hall
England, December 1813

"Oh, there's no mistake, Mr. Sinclair. We've examined the terms of the colonel's will quite carefully, I can assure you. It's very clear he intended to leave his daughter in your very capable hands."

The well-shaped lips of Ian Sinclair, former major with His Majesty's forces in Portugal, tightened to prevent another expression of disbelief. It was possible, he supposed, that George Darlington had named him as his daughter's guardian. That was almost as easy to believe as the fact that Darlington had fathered a daughter.

"And the child?" Ian asked.

After all, she should be his first concern. The little girl had lost her father, the only parent she had ever known. Of course, knowing Darlington's history, Ian wondered exactly how often the child could have even seen him, much less how well she had known him.

"She is in a very fine school in the north. The location

is a bit remote, but I believe the family has ties to the region.''

''And relations there perhaps?'' Ian asked, feeling the first dawn of hope since he had begun this interview with George Darlington's solicitor, who had come from London to apprise Ian of the terms of his late client's will.

''Not to my knowledge. Of course, you may know more of the family's connections than we are privy to.''

''Actually, I knew very little about Colonel Darlington,'' Ian said. ''Other than his military endeavors, of course.''

''Comrades in arms,'' the solicitor said heartily.

Ian thought how far from the reality of his and Darlington's relationship that phrase fell, but he said nothing. Whatever the colonel's failings as an officer, and in Ian's opinion they were many, he would not speak ill of the dead.

Not even ill of a man who had, without warning, saddled him with a child Ian had never even met. A child whose very existence he had been unaware of until this afternoon.

''Well,'' the solicitor said, his tone verging on euphoric, ''I have taken up quite enough of your time. And I believe that all of the particulars have now been taken care of to everyone's satisfaction.''

Ian wondered if the man were really that obtuse, or if he were simply relieved that he hadn't been shown the door when he'd revealed the reason for his visit. In truth, he was probably glad to have this poor child off his hands and someone else's responsibility.

''Here is the address of the school. I believe the girl's fees are paid through the end of term.''

''Which should be soon,'' Ian realized, reaching to take the neatly lettered paper from the lawyer's hand. ''*If*

I remember my own school days correctly. And I confess, those ended long enough ago that the details are beginning to blur. I *do* remember being at home for Christmas."

The solicitor's thin lips pursed briefly before he said, "No doubt your memory is excellent, Mr. Sinclair."

Underlying that quite unexceptional statement had been some nuance of tone Ian couldn't read. He studied the man's rather pasty face, trying to decide what had bothered him about it.

"If there are no relations," Ian asked, "then where has this child spent holidays during the years her father has been posted abroad?"

"As far as I'm aware, Mr. Sinclair, she has remained at school. There are always a few who do, you know. For one reason or another."

That had been true enough of his own school, Ian remembered. He had a memory of two or three winter-pale faces pressed against the front windows, watching as their fellow students departed to be conveyed home through the snow-shrouded English landscape.

"I see," Ian said, thinking also about the boisterous excitement of those long-ago Sinclair Christmases. And thinking, despite himself, of a lonely little girl who had perhaps never known a real country Yuletide. At least not in the last few war-torn years of her existence.

"Oh, don't bother to see me out," Darlington's representative said cheerfully as Ian began to push himself out of his chair. "I understand that you're still recovering from your wounds, and I certainly have no desire—"

The solicitor's voice stopped in midsentence. That was undoubtedly the result of the same look Ian had once successfully employed to correct any breach of military discipline among his troops.

It involved a leveling at his intended victim of what he had always considered to be quite unremarkable hazel eyes. He was surprised to find the look apparently as effective as it had always been with his subordinates, despite the fact that he hadn't had cause to use it in more than a year.

Totally ignoring the solicitor's broken sentence, Ian said pleasantly, "I shall be delighted to see you out."

The day had been both wet and bitterly cold, with the threat of snow hovering in the dark, overcast December sky since dawn. Weather such as this always made the lingering effects of his injuries more pronounced, but Ian ignored them as much as he possibly could. As did his staff and his family, of course.

That was a lesson both had learned early in his convalescence. He could hardly blame his visitor, however, for not being aware of his sensitivity to any reference to his health.

"Are you certain I can't convince you to postpone your return?" Ian continued, leading the way toward the door. "I should hate to think of you benighted on the road."

"No, indeed, Mr. Sinclair, although I thank you for your kind offer of hospitality."

"Then I shall wish you Godspeed, Mr. Smythe. And a safe journey home."

When they reached the hall, Ian watched as his butler helped his visitor into his greatcoat. Mr. Smythe then placed his tall beaver over sparse, iron-gray hair. He ducked his shoulder almost defensively when the wide front doors were opened, letting in the sharp, wet chill of the December wind.

"Not a fit day for man nor beast," Williams said, closing the door very quickly behind his master's departing guest.

"I tried to persuade him to stay the night, but he was eager to be off."

"Perhaps he has holiday entertainments awaiting him in London," the butler said. "Anxious to get back to his family, no doubt."

"No doubt," Ian echoed, thinking that this would be the first Christmas he had spent at home without any member of his own family with whom to celebrate.

The youngest Sinclair brother was still with Wellington, fighting the French on the Iberian Peninsula. And having spent three years in those same circumstances, Ian knew exactly how Sebastian would keep Christmas.

There would be wine, if the Beau could possibly manage to procure it. And perhaps a couple of scrawny chickens, stewed until they were almost edible. After dinner, the officers would gather around the fireplace of whatever building Wellington had commandeered as his headquarters to sing carols. They would probably be forced to wear their woolen uniform capes against the damp that relentlessly seeped in through the stones and chilled to the bone.

Ian realized that in remembering those deprivations he was smiling. The warmth of the camaraderie those men shared would help them endure. And at least Sebastian wouldn't be spending Christmas alone.

Nor would Val, of course. Ian's smile widened, although he refused to allow himself to imagine *exactly* how his older brother would be engaged during this holiday season. Ensconced in the Sinclair hunting lodge, Dare and his countess seemed determined to stretch their honeymoon to the full year such milestones had once encompassed.

And Ian would be the last person to begrudge his brother that newfound happiness. Dare had more than earned it in his behind-the-scenes efforts to defeat that same enemy Ian and Sebastian had fought by more conventional means.

Still, he thought, limping back to the welcome blaze of the library fire, it would be a lonely Christmas here. And unbidden came the nearly forgotten image of those small, pale faces pressed longingly against the windows of Harrow so long ago. *A damnably lonely Christmas.*

Chapter One

"I beg your pardon," Anne Darlington said, finally looking up from where she was kneeling on the stone floor, her hands full of the grimy edge of Sally Eddington's woolen petticoat.

She was stitching up the hem of the offending garment so that it wouldn't drag on the ground as the child walked. Her concentration on the task, which she was attempting to perform while six-year-old Sally was still wearing the petticoat, had prevented her from hearing the first part of the message the headmistress had sent.

"It's your guardian," Margaret Rhodes said importantly. "Come to take you home for Christmas."

"How nice for you, Sally," Anne said. She took one very large and hurried stitch and then looped the needle through and tied a quick knot. She broke the thread with her teeth before she added, "I didn't know you were leaving today."

In all honesty she hadn't even known Sally had a guardian. Anne distinctly remembered that the little girl had spent the previous holiday at school. There were only a handful of students who did that, and since Anne herself had always been one of them, she certainly knew who the others were. And most of their stories as well.

The loss of a mother, usually in childbirth with the next, too quickly conceived baby. A father's remarriage, perhaps. Or his disinterest.

Anne supposed she herself might fall into that latter category, but her father's disinterest was something she had stopped thinking about a long time ago. She was actually grateful for the upbringing he had provided her, even if it had never included his presence. And just this week Mrs. Kemp had offered her a teaching position here for the next school year.

Then she would never have to leave, Anne thought contentedly, automatically straightening Sally's skirt and smoothing with her hands the carrot-colored frizz that surrounded the little girl's freckled face.

"But I'm not," Sally said, her eyes round at the thought.

"Not *her,* you big silly," Margaret said. "It's you he's come for."

Anne turned her head, looking full at Margaret for the first time. "For me?" she repeated in astonishment.

"And Mrs. Kemp says you mustn't keep him waiting."

Anne opened her mouth to protest, and then closed it again. After all, whatever was going on, it offered to be different from her normal afternoon routine of wiping noses and hearing lessons.

Either the girls were having a joke or there had been some mistake in who had been called for. In either case, going along would prove more entertaining than what she was presently doing. If it were a prank, then the others would enjoy a laugh at her expense, nothing she was averse to. And if it weren't, the mistake would probably have been straightened out by the time she reached the headmistress's office. Until then...

"Well, of course, I won't keep him waiting," Anne said cheerfully. "Come from London, I suppose."

"I don't know about that," Margaret confided, "but he arrived in a bang-up rig with four of the primest bits of horseflesh I've ever seen."

"If Mrs. Kemp hears you talking like that, my girl," Anne warned, "*you'll* be the banged-up rig."

She lightened the rebuke with a smile and then ran down the wide hallway with the younger girl at her heels. Not setting a good example, Mrs. Kemp would have said, especially for someone about to become a teacher.

Since the headmistress wasn't by to say it, however, Anne didn't see any reason not to run off the excess energy the recent weather's confinement had produced. She would be so glad when spring arrived and the woods and fields were again available for roaming.

She slowed to a sedate walk as she neared the open door of the school's office. Working by feel, she tucked a few tendrils of hair back into the neat coil from which they had managed to escape and straightened the shoulders of her linsey-woolsey dress, brushing her hands over the bodice. Then she cast a quick glance behind her to evaluate Margaret's appearance, knowing that in Mrs. Kemp's opinion it, too, could usually be improved upon.

She was right. The younger girl's flannel pinafore was unbuttoned. Anne turned and, still walking backwards, attempted a couple of quick adjustments to the ten-year-old's attire.

Margaret's widening eyes should have been a warning, but she didn't notice them until it was too late. Anne backed into something quite solid and heard a soft gasp of response.

Someone, she realized belatedly when she whirled around. Someone very tall. And dressed in what even such a provincial as she knew to be the height of fashion, from his gleaming tasseled Hessians to the broad shoulders of an expertly cut coat of navy superfine. Considering the weather, there would no doubt be a multicaped greatcoat and a tall beaver hat residing safely in Mrs. Kemp's office.

"Oh, dear," she said. "I hope I didn't hurt you."

He certainly appeared sturdy enough that she couldn't possibly have done him damage, but that gasp had sounded pained. And there was something in the tightness of the lines around that beautifully shaped mouth that also spoke of discomfort.

It was not until the mouth tilted, destroying that ridiculous notion that Anne looked up and found his eyes. They were hazel, and they were smiling as openly as were his lips.

Smiling eyes. She had read the phrase once in a novel, that strictly forbidden pastime carefully concealed from Mrs. Kemp, of course. She had never quite known what it meant until today. Until now. And her heart began to beat a little irregularly.

"I believe I have managed to survive your charge," he said. "It is customary to look in the direction you're treading, however. Just to prevent bowling over the unsuspecting."

Anne laughed. "Only think how boring it should be to always look where one is going. I confess that I much prefer to back my way through life." She longed to add, *"One meets such interesting people that way,"* but she couldn't decide if that would sound sophisticated or simply fast.

And while she was trying to resolve that dilemma, the

hazel eyes left her face and settled, still smiling, on Margaret's. Anne swallowed her disappointment and turned to look at her young friend as well. Margaret's brown eyes were still stretched. Indeed, they had widened enough to be outright rude as she stared, openmouthed, at the visitor.

"Hello," he said.

"'Lo," Margaret mumbled.

The self-important air of confidence with which she had delivered her message had disappeared. Of course, Anne could hardly blame her for that. They were neither very often exposed to someone who was so obviously Top of the Trees.

"I'm not quite sure how this should be done," the elegant gentleman was saying, "but I have satisfied Mrs. Kemp as to my identity and my legal position as your guardian. She has agreed that we may leave as soon as you're ready. Since I gave you no warning, I should imagine it will take you some time to pack. I hope you will make as quick a work of that as you can, however, because the weather is worsening by the moment."

Margaret said nothing, her eyes and mouth continuing to gape unbecomingly as he talked. When he had finished, and the silence yawned empty for a few seconds, she reluctantly pulled her gaze away from his face to look at Anne.

"It's not *me* you want," she said, pointing a trembling finger. "It's her. That's Anne Darlington."

The hazel eyes followed the gesture, and as Anne's met them, she realized they were no longer smiling. They had widened as much as Margaret's, and even that was attractive, she decided.

"*You're* Anne Darlington?" he asked, his shock evident.

No mistake about the name, then, Anne thought, trying to make sense of this.

"I am," she said, inclining her head in agreement, hoping to add a touch of dignity to the confession.

"Colonel George Darlington's daughter?"

"Did you know my father, sir?" she asked.

Again there was a small silence.

"I served with your father in Iberia, ma'am. May I offer my condolences on your recent loss."

Anne had never in her life been called ma'am. It was rather shocking, but despite that, finally she was beginning to have a glimmer of understanding. Perhaps this man was indeed her guardian. Perhaps when she was much younger, her father had named a military friend to look after her if anything happened to him. And now that it had…

"Thank you," she said softly.

She supposed she had grieved in the abstract for her father, but since she had not seen him in over seven years, and not very often before that, she had quickly recovered from the news of his death, about which she had been informed only two months ago.

"My name is Ian Sinclair, and your father's will asked me to serve as your guardian."

How strange, Anne thought. Not "your father asked me," which is what she would have expected, but "your father's will."

"And you agreed?"

"Colonel Darlington was a…comrade in arms."

Anne wondered about that brief hesitation, but then she knew less than nothing about military matters. Apparently her father had chosen from among his acquaintances a man he felt would be trustworthy to look after her.

She wondered how many years ago that decision had been made. And considering Mr. Sinclair's confusion in thinking Margaret was his ward, she wondered if her father had even remembered how old she was. He had certainly never acknowledged birthdays. In actuality, he had seldom acknowledged her existence.

"As you can see, Mr. Sinclair, I am hardly in need of a guardian," she said briskly. "I shall be twenty my next birthday, and Mrs. Kemp has very kindly offered me a teaching post here. My father was unaware of the offer, of course, which was made after his death."

"Then you were in frequent correspondence with your father?"

The hazel eyes were focused intently on her face, and for some reason, Anne found herself compelled to tell him the truth.

"I was not," she said succinctly.

"I see."

Even living as she had among the female offspring of parents who obviously did not wish to be burdened with hiring governesses and tutors for them, Anne had finally been forced to admit her father's total lack of interest in her was unusual. Most of her schoolmates got the occasional letter or present or visit. In all the years she had been at Fenton School, she couldn't remember receiving any of those things.

"I'm very sorry you have made this journey for nothing," Anne said. "Especially since, as you say, the weather is uncertain."

The fine mouth tightened, and again Anne noticed the deeply graven lines that bracketed it. She wondered at his age, but there was something about his face that defied an attempt to judge it, despite the sweep of gray at the temples of his dark chestnut hair. His eyes, when they were smiling, made him seem quite young. Now, however...

"Actually, I have been dreading spending Christmas alone," he said. And then he smiled at her again.

Anne had not been dreading the holidays. She enjoyed the quieter times they provided. There would be only a few girls left at the school, some of them, like Sally, quite small. Since Anne was the oldest student, and the one who had been here the longest, their Christmas entertainment had always fallen on her shoulders. And she welcomed the task.

There was something about the elegant gentleman's declaration, however, that tugged at her heart quite as much as had Sally's quiet sobbing during the first few nights she had spent here. *And who are you, Anne Darlington, to be feeling sorry for the likes of him?* she chided in self-derision.

"Are you sure I can't persuade you to join me?" Ian Sinclair continued. "I can't tell you how excited my servants are at the prospect of having a guest for the holidays. My existence of late has been far too sedate for their tastes, I'm afraid. They were counting on your arrival to give them an excuse for a full-blown, old-fashioned Yule celebration."

My existence of late. Slowly Anne was beginning to put all the small, yet telling clues together. Ian Sinclair had confessed to knowing her father on the Peninsula. And if he had returned to England while the British forces were still engaged in the war for control of Spain, there could be only one reason. A reason that explained both the lines of suffering in his face and perhaps even that nearly inaudible gasp of reaction when she had careened into him.

If there was anything more likely than a sobbing child

to stir a response in Anne Darlington's heart, it was a creature in pain. If it were not for Mrs. Kemp's strictures, during Anne's years here the school would have become a refuge for every homeless cur or injured squirrel in the district.

In spite of the headmistress's injunctions, it had secretly sheltered a variety of carefully hidden invalids. Unknowingly, and without any conscious intent on his part, Ian Sinclair had issued an invitation that would have been almost impossible for Anne to refuse.

"Then I should hate to disappoint them," she said bravely, "especially in this joyful season."

Not exactly what he had bargained for, Ian thought, as he waited in Mrs. Kemp's office for his ward to pack.

And Anne herself had willingly provided him with the perfect excuse not to take this farce any further. For some reason, however, perhaps nothing more than what he had indicated to her about his staff's excitement at the prospect of a Christmas visitor, he had insisted that she come back to Sinclair Hall with him. He could only imagine their reaction when he returned, not with the child they all expected, but with a young woman in tow.

"...shall miss her dearly, Mr. Sinclair. Not that I would begrudge Anne her chance," Mrs. Kemp said, his name bringing Ian's wandering attention back to the subject at hand. "She is a most intelligent and deserving young woman, with the kindest heart I have ever known. I am delighted she will be able to take her proper place in society. I was so afraid that her father had not realized the importance of seeing that Anne has her Season."

The words were chilling. Ian had left home at dawn this morning, expecting to bring a little girl back with him for the holidays. Suddenly, without warning, he had been propelled instead into the role of introducing a young woman into society. And it was a role for which he could think of no one less suitable.

After all, his contact with the ton had been severely limited by his military service and his prolonged convalescence. He had acquaintances within that elite circle, of course, but the implications of being called upon to provide a proper Season for George Darlington's daughter went far beyond anything he had been thinking when he began this harebrained journey.

Sentimental idiot, Sebastian would have chided. And Dare would have been the first to warn that if he ended up in his grave as a result of driving halfway across the country in a snowstorm, then there would be no one around to see to Anne Darlington's upbringing. Not, Ian admitted, that she needed much "seeing to."

In actuality, she was already a woman grown. Most girls her age were married and producing the requisite heirs for their husbands. Just because this one had been hidden away behind the imposing doors of Fenton School for years didn't mean that society wouldn't consider her a woman.

"Her Season?" he repeated, his mind considering with near-horror what he knew about such things.

It was little enough. He had danced with his share of debutantes, of course. That was expected of every man about town, but he had never had the responsibility of bringing one out. And it seemed that Mrs. Kemp was now suggesting that he should.

"But of course," Mrs. Kemp said. "Her mother's family was quite respectable. Her grandfather was a viscount. And I believe the Darlington name to be equally honorable. Now, Anne's father..." Mrs. Kemp paused delicately, one brow raised in question. "Was he a friend of yours, Mr. Sinclair?"

"An acquaintance," Ian said carefully.

He had determined to keep his feelings about Darlington to himself. Airing them would serve no purpose but to rebound unfavorably on his daughter, who did not deserve that stain.

"Ah…" Mrs. Kemp said softly. "I did not think the two of you…" Again she paused, her eyes meeting Ian's in perfect understanding. "He neglected Anne dreadfully. If it were not for the character of the girl herself, due to his financial neglect I should have been forced to send her away years ago."

"I understood from the solicitors that her fees had been paid," Ian said, feeling another surge of anger at Anne's father.

"Her fees, but nothing else. That poor child has been dependent on our charity for the very clothes on her back."

"I assure you, Mrs. Kemp, that what is owing to you will come first out of whatever estate Darlington has left. However, knowing his penchant for gambling and other…vices, I'm not sure of how much that consists. You *will* be repaid for your kindness, I assure you, even if it comes from my own pockets."

"I don't want the money, Mr. Sinclair. Especially not yours. I do, however, want Anne to have the chance at the happiness she more than deserves. She's a good child, with a warm and generous spirit. I want someone to see to it that she is settled into a situation more appropriate to her birth than we can provide for her here. Will you promise me that you will do your very best to give her that chance?"

Ian had come north on a fool's errand, drawn by sentiment and by the thought of giving a lonely child a festive Christmas. Now he was being asked to make a very different commitment. He might know little about providing a Season for a young woman, but he certainly knew the stated intent of such an endeavor.

Mrs. Kemp was asking him to find Anne Darlington a husband. As her guardian, Ian knew that, in reality, he could do no less for the girl and fulfill the obligations inherent in that post.

''You have my word,'' he said softly.

''Such a chance, Anne. An unbelievable opportunity. You must promise me, my dear, that you will do everything you can to take advantage of it,'' Mrs. Kemp said.

''I'm afraid I don't understand. I mean…it's only a Christmas visit,'' Anne said doubtfully, smiling at her headmistress, who had been the closest thing to a mother she had ever known. Her own had died when Anne was four, shortly before she had been sent to Fenton School.

''Perhaps that was Mr. Sinclair's intention at first, but I believe I have made him see his responsibilities to you run much deeper than that. He is, after all, your guardian. It's up to him to see you suitably settled.''

Anne shook her head, still not sure what Mrs. Kemp was talking about. ''Suitably settled?'' she repeated. ''I thought we had agreed I should have a teaching post here next term.''

''Oh, my dear! That can hardly compare with what is now offered you. I find it hard to believe that your father had the foresight to choose so well. He did, however, and now you must do *your* part.''

''My part in what?''

''To find your place in the world you are entitled to by your birth. We both know that you can sometimes be rather headstrong, my dear. I'm simply saying that you must let yourself be guided by Mr. Sinclair, who has, I assure you, only your best interests at heart.''

''But Mrs. Kemp, you know I am very happy here. Of course, I shall be delighted to visit Mr. Sinclair's home for Christmas. That seems to be what he wishes me to do, but to believe that I shall become a permanent resident there or dependent on his charity, is, I should think, something neither of us would wish for. Whatever life you and he believe I am somehow entitled to, I assure you this is the life I truly desire.''

''You can't evaluate what you've never known. And you are about to enter a world about which you know nothing. It may seem very frightening to you at first, but...'' The words faltered, and Mrs. Kemp's eyes seemed troubled. She put her hand on Anne's cheek, cupping it as if she were one of the younger girls in need of comfort. ''Oh, my dear,'' she said, her voice passionate, ''this is *such* an opportunity. I am simply urging you to make the best of it, whatever happens.''

Which didn't sound comforting at all, Anne thought. She caught Mrs. Kemp's hand and folded the fingers down into the palm. She laid her cheek against the back of it a moment before she brought it to her mouth and pressed her lips against the raised blue veins that were visible under the thin skin.

''I shall,'' she said, smiling at the old woman. ''I promise you I shall, Mrs. Kemp. Headstrong or not, I shall endeavor to do whatever Mr. Sinclair thinks is best. I promise you.''

It was not until she was actually in the coach, her portmanteau secured on the top and her feet and legs covered by a thick fur rug, that Anne realized what had happened.

Mewed up in an institution run by rules and discipline, she had fantasized about adventure often enough, especially during her adolescence. Nothing about her previous existence had prepared her, however, to undertake one.

Yet here she was, riding inside a carriage with a man she had only just met, heading to a destination about which she knew nothing at all. Mrs. Kemp's assurance that she had seen the solicitor's papers and her obvious excitement over the prospects offered by Mr. Sinclair's interest had been reassuring enough while Anne had been in the safe and familiar confines of the school.

Now that she was truly alone with her "guardian," however, the Gothic tales of abduction she had read with such shivering delight seemed all too real. And not a little frightening.

"Comfortable?" Mr. Sinclair asked prosaically, smiling at her from the opposite seat. The question certainly dampened that particular flight of fantasy.

"Of course," she said truthfully.

The coach was not only elegantly appointed, but very well-sprung. And despite the cold outside, the interior was every bit as cozy as her room on the third floor of Fenton School. Perhaps even more so. However, that was a room which she missed more and more with each mile they traversed.

"Good," he said.

He had removed his hat and set it on the seat beside him. After they had traveled a short distance in silence, he leaned his head back against the seat and closed his eyes, tacitly giving Anne permission to study his features again in the less flattering light of day.

It was obvious she had been correct in her earlier surmise. Ian Sinclair had undoubtedly been invalided out of service and was not yet fully recovered. She could not help but notice his limp as they had walked to the coach.

Dark smudges lay like old bruises under the long lashes. His face was too thin, and beneath the natural darkness of his skin was a tinge of gray. His mouth was tight, as if set against a pain she could almost feel.

And yet, given all those, it was a face that was undeniably appealing. The nose was as finely shaped as his mouth, the brow high and noble, and the jaw strong. Whatever his age, and Anne was no nearer guessing that than she had been from the first, Ian Sinclair was a very handsome man. *And he was her guardian.*

She wondered if, at nineteen, such a guardianship were even legal. She had little knowledge of the law, of course, so she must trust that her father's solicitor and Mrs. Kemp were more knowledgeable about such matters than she. Neither seemed to have expressed any reservations about the arrangement.

She turned her head, looking out at the passing landscape. The snow that had been threatening for days had finally begun to fall in earnest, and she wondered again that Mr. Sinclair had made this journey, given the uncertain state of his health.

She could not imagine what had prompted him to embark on this foolhardy venture for the sake of a girl he had never met. Duty, she supposed. And a sense of obligation to her father, who had been his friend.

He said they had been comrades in arms. She would have to ask him about her father's service. Perhaps Mr. Sinclair could help her to finally understand the man who had fathered and then abandoned her. At the very least, he would be able to tell her more about her father than she knew now. She could not even remember what he looked like.

She knew she took after her mother. She couldn't remember who had first told her that, but she had known it all her life. As she had grown into adulthood, the face in her mirror did indeed grow to match the one in the gold locket she still wore about her neck. It was the only thing she had of her mother's.

She touched it now, wrapping gloved fingers around its small, familiar shape. At least *something* would be familiar when they reached their destination, she thought, her eyes deliberately focused on the landscape they crossed rather than on the handsome, pain-etched face of Ian Sinclair.

Chapter Two

"I'm afraid it's no use, sir," the coachman said. His voice sounded hollow and distant as it echoed from beneath the carriage. "It's the axle. Damaged beyond our abilities to make repairs here, I can tell you. Someone must ride and get help."

Ian's lips tightened against the curses to which he longed to give utterance. He had learned long ago that cursing fate was an exercise in futility. And that painful lesson had been reiterated more times than he wished to remember during the past fourteen months.

"All right then," he agreed. "I'm afraid that expedition will have to be up to the two of you," Ian said, including the groom in his instructions. "Unharness the leaders and see if there's a house nearby which looks decent enough to shelter Miss Darlington. If not, then ride on and bring back a conveyance of some kind from the nearest posting inn."

"On this stretch of road the inns will probably be our best bet, sir," the coachman said. He had crawled out from beneath the carriage and was beating muddy snow off his knees with his gloved hands. "I can't remember passing any dwelling likely to offer a proper shelter for the young lady.''

"If the storm hits, I suppose any dwelling will be proper. Better than the coach at least."

"I can ride," Anne said.

Ian looked up to find her standing in the open door of the carriage, her breath creating a small white fog around her face. He thought about warning her that she would do better to stay inside and keep the cold out. No matter how well-constructed the vehicle might be, come nightfall it would be vastly uncomfortable, even with the rugs.

There *were* four horses. Ian briefly debated whether to send Anne off with the coachman. Given the rigors of the day, he was frustratingly sure of his own inability to stay astride for any distance at all. The cold and damp had already taken its toll, although he was loath to make that admission, even to himself.

Riding was another of the pleasures that had been taken from him when he had been wounded. And of course, it was one of the things he missed the most.

"I think we should do better to stay with the coach," he said aloud, smiling at her as if this were simply a minor inconvenience. "It won't take long for help to arrive, and the interior of the carriage offers protection from the cold which being on horseback won't afford."

"I assure you, Mr. Sinclair, the ride won't make me ill. I believe I am made of sterner stuff than that," Anne said, returning his smile.

Obviously she was, Ian thought. She hadn't dissolved into a fit of vapors or made any complaint about the delay. For that he was eternally grateful. He had quite enough to deal with right now without adding hysteria to the mix. She would probably handle the ride with aplomb as well, despite the temperature.

That was not the reason he had opted to keep her with the coach. *He* was the problem. Not Anne.

He knew he could trust her to John Coachman's care, if he sent her off on the third horse. However, if there were no suitable houses on the road and they had to seek shelter at a posting inn, Ian also knew he would be endangering her reputation and possibly even her physical safety. He couldn't ask or expect his servants to guarantee either of those. As Anne's guardian, that was his duty. And the demands of duty were something with which Ian Sinclair was very familiar.

"I think we'll do better to wait here. And better not to allow the cold into the carriage," he added.

Her eyes met his, widened a little, as quick color stole into her cheeks. She had interpreted that last as a rebuke.

Perhaps it had been, Ian admitted. Or maybe it had simply been the result of the deep ache in his leg that grew more painful each minute he stood in the middle of this infuriatingly empty road trying to decide what the hell to do with his ward. A young woman who had been thrust into his life by the very man—

"Of course," Anne said.

She stepped back inside, closing the carriage door after her. Closing it hard enough that the entire vehicle shook. Ian heard and ignored the groom's quickly muffled snort of laughter. Reluctantly, his own lips aligned themselves into a less grim aspect, and he met the coachman's sympathetic eyes with resignation in his.

"I can't manage the ride," he confessed, finding the admission difficult to voice. "And I think that since I am Miss Darlington's guardian, she should stay here with me. But it's going to get damned cold when darkness falls, John, and that's going to happen soon," he judged, looking up through the snow at the lowering clouds. "Be as quick as you can, man."

He pulled a small sack of coins out of the pocket of his cloak and opening it, spilled the contents into the palm of his leather glove. "If this is not enough, promise them the moon, but get someone out here before night-fall."

"We won't fail you, Mr. Sinclair," the groom said.

"I'm counting on that," Ian said, slapping him on the shoulder and smiling.

Major Sinclair had known very well how to get the best from his troops. This situation was little different. Lives depended on these two men accomplishing the task they'd been given as quickly as possible.

"We'll get someone, sir," John said. "You stay inside the coach, Mr. Sinclair, and you'll both be right as rain. We'll be back before you'll even know we're gone. Surely there'll be a house within a couple of miles. And if not, there'll a be a posting inn only a few farther."

Ian nodded, wishing he were half as confident as the coachman sounded. Of course, being able to take action always made one more positive about the outcome of any venture. Ian had an intimate if enforced acquaintance with prolonged inaction, however, and he would have to deal with it, just as he had for more than a year.

"Off with you then," he said. "And good luck."

He turned and limped back to the closed door of the coach, his lips lifting, despite their predicament, at the remembrance of the bang with which it had been shut. He resisted the urge to knock, opening the door instead and using his cane and the strength of his right arm to pull himself up the steps.

Thankfully, instead of watching that awkward maneuver, Anne Darlington was rather patently engaged in looking out the window on the opposite side of the carriage. Since there was nothing there but snow-covered trees and shrubs, their shapes darkened by the early-descending twilight, her concentration on the scenery likely had less to do with its attractions than with her anger or embarrassment over his supposed rebuke.

"They're off," he said, settling himself with gratitude on the seat.

He stretched out his leg, stifling the small groan the resulting relief evoked. Despite the fact that Anne had opened the carriage door for those few minutes, the interior was still far warmer than the frigid air outside. And they were sheltered from the wind.

He turned his head, studying her profile. She still hadn't looked at him, and right now he felt as if her displeasure were a blessing. It had given him a few seconds to recover from the cold and the climb up into the carriage, as well as a chance to compose his features.

Just as he thought that, Anne turned, her eyes examining his face. As he watched, they seemed to change, the spark of temper fading to be replaced by an expression of sympathy. He found that he much preferred her anger to her pity.

"I'm sorry I opened the door," she said. "I didn't think that we might be forced to spend some hours in the coach."

"Hopefully, it won't come to that. There will surely be some house nearby that can offer us shelter."

"And if there isn't?"

"They'll bring a carriage from the nearest inn. It shouldn't take long. I think we shall manage to keep warm enough in the meantime," he said.

"And you? Are you going to be..."

The soft words faded. Perhaps his frustration was visible in his eyes. Or perhaps she read there his reluctance to discuss his health. In any case, she held his gaze only a second or two, and then she turned hers once more to the window, pretending to contemplate the rapidly darkening woods.

After a moment spent regretting his surge of anger and her resulting withdrawal, he turned his attention to the window on the other side. And twilight faded into night, as Ian Sinclair awaited the rescue he had confidently promised his ward.

The temperature had fallen with each passing minute, and Ian's anxiety had risen proportionally. When he finally heard the muffled sound of horses' hooves approaching on the snow-covered roadway, his relief was almost physical.

At least until he realized that's all he had heard. No carriage. No sounds at all that might be interpreted as emanating from a coach or even a wagon. In the darkness, he heard Anne, who had been dozing off and on, begin to stir. Ian reached out, touching the rug that rested over her knees.

"Shh," he cautioned, his ears straining to follow the noises outside, which were coming nearer and nearer.

Ian couldn't have said what had first kindled his uneasiness. Perhaps because there had been no hail or salutation from John or the groom as they approached. Whatever the reasons for his apprehension, as the hoofbeats neared, it had gradually increased. Ian fumbled in the side pocket of the carriage, which held the ever-present traveler's pistol.

Although highwaymen abounded on English highways, or at least tales of them did, Ian doubted this weapon had ever before been removed from its pouch.

He could only hope that John had been diligent in making sure it was loaded and ready.

Despite that worry, Ian felt a swell of confidence as his fingers closed around the shape of the pistol. He hurriedly unwrapped it from the oilskin in which it was kept, the weight of it reassuringly the same as the one he had carried on the Peninsula. And he had always been accounted a good shot.

There had still been no shout of greeting, although the horses were now very close. And no talking at all, Ian realized. He eased nearer the door, turning his body to face it and laying the pistol in his lap, his right hand resting over it, although the darkness would certainly conceal that it was there.

With his left hand, he reached out and found Anne's arm. Without speaking, he applied pressure, trying to signal her to move over behind him on the seat he occupied. If he could position her there, with his body between whoever was outside and hers, he could offer her even more protection than the pistol alone would afford. After all, he would have only one shot.

His every sense was trained on what was going on beyond that closed door. With the fall of night, Ian had pulled the shades down over the windows, hoping to keep out some of the pervasive chill. That was a move he now regretted.

There was a soft jingle of harness, quickly muted, probably by a gloved hand. Ian pulled Anne's arm again, more urgently this time, and finally she understood, slipping silently onto his seat and pressing close behind him. He took a breath in relief.

As he did, the door he was facing was jerked open and a torch was thrust into the carriage. It came so close to his face that Ian felt a searing heat, and the sudden flare of light blinded him. He recoiled automatically, to escape both its brightness and the flame, which seemed directed at his head.

He felt Anne's intake of breath against his spine, and he steeled himself, expecting her scream to follow. Apparently she was, as she had claimed, made of sterner stuff. George Darlington might have been a coward, but his daughter was not.

"What have we 'ere?" the voice behind the torch asked. "Lookee, mate. It seems we've got ourselves a couple of passengers in this 'ere *deserted* coach."

As the man talked, Ian's eyes gradually adjusted to the light and his face came into focus. The sight was not reassuring. Despite his years with His Majesty's army, never noted for attracting the cream of the underclass to fill its ranks, Ian doubted he had ever seen a more villainous visage.

It was obvious by the man's comment that there were at least two of them. Ian's gaze flicked to the darkness beyond the blaze of the torch. He could barely make out another figure behind the one who was doing the talking. He could tell little about the second rider, however, and he quickly brought his attention back to the nearer of the two.

"And one of them's a woman," the torch holder said.

There had been a subtle shift in tone with the last word. The possibility of violence had been there since the door had been flung open without warning. Now the threat seemed more purposeful and more clearly directed. And Ian's blood ran cold, lifting the hair on the back of his neck.

None of that fear was allowed to show in his features. They were as imperturbable as he had always determined they would be when facing battle. Then he had made sure of his control in order to give his men confidence that he knew what he was doing. Now he tried to use that same control as a form of intimidation.

"We are awaiting our outriders," he said calmly. "They should be arriving at any moment."

"Outriders?" the torch holder questioned, throwing a quick glance over his shoulder. "We didn't pass no outriders."

"Perhaps you came upon the coach from the opposite direction," Ian suggested logically.

The snow-laden wind whipped in through the open door. The flame of the torch reacted to its rush by leaning inward, as if reaching toward the occupants of the carriage. The acrid smoke from the pitch-soaked rag, which had been wrapped around a broken branch, tainted the air around them.

"Mayhap we can fix whatever's gone wrong with your vehicle," the torch holder said. "Why don't the two of you step out, and we'll take a look."

Ian debated the suggestion, but he could see no advantage to them in being outside. As it stood now, these two would have to go through him—and the pistol—to get to Anne. He could be rid of at least one of them by using the gun. He'd have to take his chances that he could knock the second one out with his fists, but thankfully control wasn't the only thing Ian had learned in his years with the army.

Of course, there might be more than the two he could see. Which could present a problem to his schemes, he thought, fighting the urge to grin at his presumption of planning any kind of extended defense, given his very limited resources.

However, they couldn't both rush him through the narrow opening the door presented. The pistol would take care of the first, and his fists the second, he reiterated mentally, preparing himself for that sequence of events.

He only regretted that while he had had the chance he hadn't thought to instruct Anne to get out through the opposite door as soon as they made their move. Maybe she would be wise enough, or frightened enough, to do that anyway.

"Thank you for your kind offer," he said aloud, those decisions having been reached in a matter of seconds, "but I'm afraid it is quite beyond repair. I've sent for another coach."

"From the inn?"

The man in back spoke for the first time, drawing Ian's attention to him again. There had been some nuance of amusement in that question, and Ian hesitated, wondering what these two knew about the inn. Obviously, if they even knew its location, they knew more than he did.

"From a friend's house," Ian lied. "He lives only a short distance away."

"And what be your friend's name?" Torchbearer probed.

"I can't see how that could possibly be of any concern to you," Ian said, injecting into his tone the freezing censure he had heard often in the voice of his father, the late earl.

"Don't want her ladyship to get cold, now do we?" The man's eyes slid past Ian to examine the girl he sheltered behind him.

"Then I suggest you close the door and be on your way," Ian said. "Our friends will be arriving at any time."

"Nobody on the road," the man denied. "Maybe you ain't telling the truth about what's going on. Maybe you be carrying this young lady off from the loving bosom of her family. Maybe a little rescuing is in order 'ere. And I'm just the man to be doing it,'' the nearer of the two boasted.

He started forward and Ian raised the pistol, both gloved hands wrapped around it, holding it steady, his finger on the trigger. He pointed the weapon directly at the man's midsection, and the sight of it stopped his motion. Ian was thankful to see that the barrel didn't waver, despite the cold.

''We don't need you here,'' Ian said. ''I suggest the two of you remount and go about your business.''

''No call for the popper,'' the man said, taking a step backward, away from the muzzle of the pistol. Some of Ian's tension eased at his retreat. ''We was just trying to help.''

''We don't need your help. Be on your way. Both of you.''

The man's eyes locked on his, holding there for perhaps half a minute. He was obviously trying to gauge Ian's strength of purpose. Or his courage.

Ian resisted the urge to let his finger tighten around the trigger. Unfamiliar with the mechanism, he had no way of judging at what point it would discharge. Actually, he acknowledged, he had no way of knowing it would discharge at all. He blocked that possibility from his mind and concentrated instead on convincing the villain before him of his willingness to shoot.

''They had a fire at the inn,'' the man said unexpectedly. ''Could be a long time 'afore your servants get back.''

''I told you they have gone to borrow a coach from a friend.''

There was a sound from the other one, a noise suspiciously like the snort of amusement that had come from the groom when Anne had slammed the door. And suddenly, with that sound, everything fell into place.

These two, typical of those who frequented the public rooms of the scattered country inns, had probably overheard John or the groom asking about a carriage for hire. Obviously that request had been denied due to the unsettling effects of the fire or perhaps even because it had been the livery stable itself which had burned.

In any case, these scavengers must have heard enough to figure out the location of the stranded travelers on whose behalf his servants were inquiring. Or they had heard enough to know in what direction to search for the disabled coach. Then they had hurried here on horseback, beating the rescue party.

It was quite possible that they loitered at the posting inns, hoping for just such a situation. Ian wondered how many other travelers had fallen prey to their schemes.

"We'll be on our way then," the man with the torch said. "Since you won't be needing our services."

His eyes again shifted to Anne. He smiled at her, revealing the blackened hole of a missing front tooth, before he stepped back, lowering the torch. He began walking toward the horses and his companion, the wavering light he carried revealing both as Ian watched from the still-opened door of the carriage.

Just before he reached his mount, the leader threw the torch into the side of the roadbed. The flaming arc it made through the night drew Ian's eyes. Unconsciously they followed its flight and landing. The fire sputtered and sizzled a moment in the snow before it went out, plunging the area into darkness.

Ian's gaze refocused quickly on the place where the two men had been standing just before the scene had faded into the surrounding black. As he waited for his vision to adjust, he strained to keep track, by sound alone, of what they were doing.

There was almost no noise, however. At least none he could follow. Gradually his eyes had adjusted to the lack of light, other than what little moonlight found its way through the obscuring clouds. The horses were still there, exactly as they had been before the torch had been extinguished, but the two men had vanished as if they had never existed.

Ian turned on the seat, throwing his left arm in front of Anne and pulling her toward him. He shoved her behind his left shoulder. As he did, the two movements simultaneous, he brought the pistol around, pointing it at the rear door of the carriage.

He wasn't disappointed. The door burst open and something came hurtling through it from the outer darkness. Ian delayed for half a second, unsure whether this was something the two had thrown into the carriage to make him fire. He was well aware that he had only one shot. And then, judging the bulk of the object to be man-sized, he knew he couldn't take the chance that it was not one of the scavengers.

He squeezed the trigger, and the noise of the shot filled the coach, along with a smell as acrid as that from the make-shift torch. He had time to think that he couldn't possibly have missed at that range before a body sprawled across his knees. He pushed the man to the floor with the hand that still held the empty pistol, just as another shape scrambled into the opening. It was the second man, who had a hand on either side of the frame of the door to pull himself in.

Ian reversed the pistol, holding it by the barrel and using the wooden stock to strike at the man climbing into the coach. The second highwayman put up his forearm, deflecting Ian's blow, which had been aimed at his head.

Ian felt Anne begin to struggle beside him, but it took him too long to understand what was happening. The intruder wasn't concerned with entering the coach. He had instead gripped Anne's arm and was pulling her toward the open door.

Ian tried to get to his feet, hampered by the body on the floor and by his damaged leg, which had stiffened from the cold and an hours-long inactivity. Although he managed to lurch upward, the leg gave way, spilling him onto his knees on top of the body of the intruder, which had fallen between the two seats.

"Let me go," Anne demanded, her small fists rising and falling as she flailed at the man who held her. Although she was struggling fiercely, she was being drawn inexorably to the door.

Ian reached for her and caught the sleeve of her coat between his fingers. Either they, too, were numb with the cold or his purchase had not been secure. The fabric was ripped from his hand as Anne was pulled forward and out of the coach.

He heard her outcry when she hit the ground. Whether it was an expression of pain or of fear, Ian couldn't be certain, but the thought that the bastard might have hurt her infuriated him.

Discarding the useless pistol, Ian pushed himself upright. He lunged forward, stepping on the dead man. He stood poised a moment in the doorway of the coach, trying to decide which of the forms on the ground below, starkly highlighted against the white snow, was Anne's. Then a foam of a pale petticoat amid the dark material of the girl's skirt settled the question.

Knowing that his mobility was going to be limited no

matter what he did, Ian simply dove out of the door on top of the man who was attempting to drag Anne to her feet and into the woods. A grunt of surprise and a whoosh of expelled breath as the man hit the ground indicated the accuracy of Ian's landing. It also jarred every place in his body where a piece of shrapnel had embedded itself more than a year ago and especially those places where bits of metal still lodged deep in muscle and bone.

Now or never, Ian thought, ignoring the agony. He used the advantage of shock and his superior position to begin pounding the man's head with his fists. The leather gloves he wore offered some protection, but his hands were so cold that each blow felt as if it might shatter his knuckles. He could only hope that the bones of the man writhing in the snow beneath him were experiencing that same punishment.

His opponent somehow managed to get his legs up. He fitted his knees under Ian's stomach and threw him off. The blow to Ian's midsection, which still harbored one of the fragments the surgeons had deemed too risky to remove, was nauseating.

Now he was no longer the one in the superior position. No longer the one raining blows on his opponent's head. Ian put his arms and his hands up, protecting his face as well as he could, as he simply endured the onslaught of pain.

The other man fought with the brutal tenacity of a street brawler, which was undoubtedly where he had acquired his skills. Ian could smell him, a rank, fetid miasma of perspiration that surrounded him despite the bite of the cold, fresh air.

Finally Ian managed to jam his elbow into his opponent's throat. The move was accomplished more by luck than design, but it distracted those punishing fists for a heartbeat, as the man raised both hands to grab at his injured windpipe.

Ian rolled to the side to free himself of his opponent's hampering weight. The maneuver was at least partially successful. Then the ex-soldier attempted to take advantage of that success by putting his knee on the ground and pushing himself upright. Instead, his knee slid sideways in the snow, throwing him forward. His forehead met that of his opponent, who was at that instant attempting to sit up. The force of the hard contact between their skulls was enough to thin the air around Ian's head, and he felt himself slipping into unconsciousness.

He fought the surging blackness, using his hands to hold himself off the ground. Moving as uncertainly as a drunkard, he pushed his body up, swaying on his hands and knees over his equally stunned assailant. Then, with every ounce of strength he possessed, he pushed off the ground and staggered to his feet. He pulled draught after draught of icy air into his aching lungs.

However, the man on the ground also seemed to be recovering from the blow to his head. He, too, began to struggle to his feet. Unlike Ian, however, he didn't make it. There was a crack of sound, like a rotten branch makes when it breaks under an accumulation of snow, and he fell back as if he'd been pole-axed.

Not sure what had happened, Ian lifted his head and found his ward standing like an avenging angel over the fallen man. She held a piece of deadfall, and it was obvious by her posture that she had swung it like a club against the villain's head.

"I'm sorry that took so long," she said apologetically, "but you were too close to allow me to strike before. I was afraid I would hit you instead of him."

She was apologizing, Ian realized. Apologizing that

she hadn't defeated his opponent more quickly. He laughed, unsure whether that laughter was born of relief, admiration or sheer giddiness. The sharp sting that it caused in his cut lip, however, cleared his head, and he began to understand the debt he owed Anne Darlington. He couldn't imagine another woman of his acquaintance having the courage to do what she had just done.

Anne's eyes had fallen once more to the man on the ground, who appeared to be still unconscious. Apparently reassured, she looked up again at Ian, as she lowered the broken limb.

"Are you all right?" she asked anxiously.

Despite the darkness, Ian could see how pale she was, her fair skin drained of color. Tendrils of damp red hair hung about her face or were plastered to it by the snow. Her clothing was undoubtedly as wet as his own, Ian realized, feeling for the first time the cold moisture seeping through his sodden greatcoat and soaking the garments beneath it.

Unable to find breath with which to answer the question he should have been asking her, he nodded. He was beginning to believe he really was all right, despite the exertions of the fight. And then, with an unexpectedness that was shocking, his knees gave way. He fell on them to the ground, reaching out just in time to catch himself with his hand. Ian watched his glove sink into the slush and then begin to slide forward, leaving a shallow trough to mark its passage.

He was almost disinterested in the process, although on some level he knew that he was about to end up face-down in the snow. He wondered idly if he were dying. Suddenly a pair of strong young arms slipped around his midsection. Steadying him. Virtually holding him up.

Still on his hands and knees, he turned his head and looked into Anne Darlington's eyes.

"I'm all right," he said, lying through his teeth.

He looked back down at the ground, watching blood drip onto the snow, staining its white with pink. He closed his eyes, not because the sight bothered him, but in order to will strength back into his body. Every inch of it ached, which was probably why he had no idea where that slow drip of blood was coming from.

"Let me help you up," Anne offered.

He opened his eyes, turning his head again to face her. Obediently, he pushed against the ground, and with her aid managed to get to his knees. And knew with stunning clarity that he wasn't going any farther. Not for a while.

"If I could rest a moment..." he suggested, still breathing through his mouth, trying to assess the severity of his injuries, all of which were making themselves heard in a disharmonious clamor of pain.

"Of course," she said.

He swayed slightly, and felt her arms tighten comfortingly around him. She was very close, her body pressed against his. There was no false modesty in the way she held him. And no more embarrassment than Dare or his valet might have felt in offering him their help.

Ian closed his eyes, allowing himself to lean against her strength. He was infinitely grateful for it, as improper as what they were doing might seem to anyone else. They had been through a terrifying experience, and she was, after all, his ward.

She is also a woman. A very desirable woman.

The thought was shocking, given that until he had seen her brandishing that branch, he had been thinking of Anne only as George Darlington's daughter. As a schoolgirl. She might be the former, but despite the circumstances in which he had discovered her, she was definitely not the latter. Unbelievably, his battered body was forcibly reminding him of that.

It had been a long time since Ian Sinclair had held, or been held, by a woman. And a very long time, therefore, since he had felt this rush of pure physical reaction. It unnerved him, not only because it was so unexpected, but because of its intensity.

And because, of course, that of all the women to whom he might legitimately have felt such an attraction, Anne Darlington was the most forbidden. She was his ward, given into his care by her father. Even if it had been without Ian's consent.

And other than that consideration, Ian was the last man on earth who might make any claim on Anne Darlington. The least suitable man she would ever meet to offer her his heart or his hand.

Since he could not in honor ever do either of those things, he had no right to touch her, even in a situation that had begun as innocently as this one. And so, despite the lingering weakness, Ian put his arm over Anne's slender shoulders, and again relying her strength, struggled to his feet.

As soon as he had, he stepped away from her embrace, creating the necessary distance between them. A distance he had never anticipated crossing.

"Thank you," he said.

Nothing of what he had felt during those brief moments they had knelt together was revealed in his eyes or in his voice. And again, he had reason to be grateful for the control he had learned on the Peninsula, as well as for the lessons of duty and honor.

What had just happened would be forgotten, the memory of it destroyed by his determination to destroy it. And by his determination to carry out the responsibility he had been given.

The responsibility of finding Anne Darlington a husband. And that man could never, of course, be Ian Sinclair.

Chapter Three

"Amazing how quickly it can strike, even in the best of families," a deep voice ventured lazily.

Ian had opened his eyes, and became aware of his surroundings for almost the first time in six fever-ridden days. Hearing that sarcastic comment from the man sitting beside his bed, he fought the urge to shut them again and pretend delirium.

"Insanity, I mean," the Earl of Dare added, closing the leather-bound volume he had obviously been reading from as Ian slept.

Despite the way he felt, Ian's mouth lifted into a reluctant smile, which was quickly answered by his brother's.

"How do you feel?" Dare asked.

"Foolish," Ian said, surprised to find how much effort was required to form that one-word answer.

"As you bloody well should. Whatever made you think you could go tearing off across the country—"

Ian raised his hand, its palm toward the earl, putting an end to that pointless castigation. After a moment, he let it fall to the counterpane, but his eyes held on Dare's, which, below the outrage, were filled with concern.

"No lectures, I beg you," Ian said.

"I'm to let you kill yourself at your leisure, I suppose."

"Hardy a fitting argument coming from *you.*"

"The risks *I* took were always for a good cause," Dare said. "This, however..." The earl shook his head, his expression rich with disgust.

"I trust you will at least admit I had no reason to expect a broken axle or an attack by highwaymen," Ian said.

"It's your sanity in undertaking the journey I question. As well as your sanity in undertaking this so-called guardianship."

"I see Williams has been talking."

"Everyone from the groom up has been talking, mostly about your gallant and heroic rescue of your new ward."

The final word was full of sarcasm, and given what he had felt that night, Ian wasn't sure it was misplaced. He ignored Dare's tone, however, choosing to reply only to the rest of his brother's statement.

"I fell out of the coach on top of the bastard. Hardly a gallant rescue."

"Your admirers disagree. As I'm sure will your dear charge."

"My *dear* charge, as you call her, knocked her attacker out with a well-aimed blow to the head. If anyone deserves accolades for that fiasco, it is she."

"A well-aimed blow to the head? How charming," the earl said sarcastically.

"She *is* charming. Have you met her?" Ian asked.

"Darlington's brat." Dare fairly spat the words. "For that coward to have foisted his daughter on you is beyond enough. He must be laughing his head off in Hell. What

I can't understand is why in the world you accepted the responsibility?''

''Those were the terms of his will. What would *you* have done?''

''I should have paid her fees for the next thirty years and left her in that school where Darlington had her safely hidden away.''

''She's nineteen, Val. Nearly twenty. And she's *been* in that school almost her entire life.''

''And what is that to you?''

''Nothing, I suppose,'' Ian said, almost too tired to deal with his brother's caustic tongue, even though he understood Dare had only his best interests at heart.

''You are too noble for your own good,'' the earl said.

''Noble?'' Ian repeated, surprised into laughter, which resulted in a prolonged fit of coughing.

After a moment, Dare got up from his chair and poured a glass of water from the pitcher on the table beside the bed. Then he sat down on the edge of the mattress and lifted his brother's shoulders to place the rim of the tumbler against his lips. Ian drank the water gratefully and finally the coughing subsided, leaving only a burning ache in his chest to remind him of the danger of responding to his brother's compliments in the manner he usually employed.

''You could have told the solicitor no,'' Dare said, lowering him to rest again against the pillows.

''I thought she was a child. I was imagining a lonely little girl, forced to spend Christmas in a deserted boarding school.''

''And when you saw her?''

A more difficult question, Ian admitted. With a more complicated answer—especially after the events of that journey. He might admit the answer to his own conscience, but he would certainly not offer it for his brother's consideration.

"Her headmistress suggested that it's my responsibility to find her a suitable husband," he said instead.

Dare's lips pursed, and then he stood, putting the glass back on the table before he looked down on his brother again. "And how do you intend to go about that? Anyone who served with you knows what Darlington did. None of your friends will even be civil to the girl."

"Including you?" Ian asked. "Rather Old Testament, Val."

"Good God, you don't anticipate that I should have to meet her, do you?"

"Like it or not, she *is* my ward," Ian said simply. "You are my brother, and the head of this family. I don't see how you should avoid meeting her."

"I shall avoid it by the simple expedient of refusing to meet the daughter of the coward who almost cost my brother his life."

"She doesn't know any of that," Ian said.

"And you don't intend to tell her," Dare guessed.

"Would you?"

The silence stretched a moment, and finally, Dare turned away from the bed and seated himself again in the chair. "Then what *do* you intend to do?" he asked. Both the sarcasm and the anger had been wiped from his voice.

"I intend to find her a suitable husband."

"Does she have any assets that make her marriageable?"

Ian thought about the girl he had brought back from the north, picturing her in his mind's eye. And as he did so, he attempted to divorce his unexpected and highly improper physical response from his judgment.

There was no doubt she was lovely and unspoiled. Unsophisticated as well, he acknowledged. And courageous beyond any woman he had ever known, with the possible exception of Dare's Elizabeth. Having avoided London society for the last few years, Ian wasn't sure, however, if any of those qualities, other than the first, would be considered an advantage there.

"Ian?" Dare prompted.

"Money, do you mean? Very little, I would imagine. The solicitor is still investigating the estate, but whatever Darlington had he usually gambled away."

"Looks?"

"She's…pleasant enough, I suppose," Ian said carefully, remembering that pale face in the moonlight, framed by strands of bedraggled hair. He had thought her incredibly beautiful at that moment, but then she had just saved his life, so he supposed he could not be considered entirely unbiased. "I'm not sure what type of beauty is currently in vogue."

"And what type does she possess?" Dare asked, his voice for the first time holding the familiar amusement with which he normally confronted the vagaries of life.

"She's tall. And rather slender. Her hair is…auburn." At the last second, Ian had avoided his original choice of words. As out of touch with the beau monde as he might be, even he knew that redheads had not managed to take the town by storm in his absence.

"Her eyes are fine. Very speaking," he finished lamely, meeting the earl's equally fine eyes, which were, without any doubt, also speaking. And Ian wasn't entirely sure he liked what they were saying.

"Good luck," Dare said.

"I shall need more than luck, Val. I shall need your help," Ian said doggedly.

This was not a duty he had sought, nor one he wanted,

but he could not fault the girl for her father's sins. He knew the narrow world to which they both belonged would, however, if that story got out. It was a world whose membership was determined strictly by birth, which Anne Darlington did possess. And it seemed that might be the only attribute she could claim that would have any meaning there.

"My help to do what?" Dare asked, the amusement gone. "Surely you don't mean my help to find her a husband?"

"To launch her into society, at least. I promised her headmistress she should have her chance."

"You promised her headmistress," his brother repeated disbelievingly.

"She *should* have her chance to make a proper marriage, one commensurate with her birth. And the only place that may be accomplished quickly, and at this late date, is in London."

"The Season."

"Of course," Ian said.

"And what do you believe *I* can do for her there?"

Again there was silence in the room. By virtue of her own birth and title, Dare's countess certainly belonged to the world of the haute monde. Normally it would have been under her auspices that any young woman sponsored by the Sinclair family should be brought out.

However, the Countess of Dare had forfeited her social standing in a cause as noble as the one her husband had undertaken. A cause which had cost Elizabeth her reputation. And the scandal that had erupted within the ton when Dare married her had not yet died down.

"If you are determined to embark on this venture, you may have the London house, of course," Dare said, apparently answering his own question. "And whatever funds you have need of, if only to get her off your hands."

"I don't want your money," Ian said, "but I'll accept the offer of the town house. *If* you are serious."

"I am never serious," Dare denied, "but you are very welcome to the house. Remember, however, that by using it, you may face guilt by association. Association with Elizabeth and me," he added, a trace of bitterness in his voice.

"I consider myself honored by that association."

"They won't," Dare said bluntly.

"You have seldom cared what 'they' think. Why begin now?"

"Wait until next year," the earl advised, ignoring the comment. "By then, the scandal will have died down. And perhaps..." He hesitated.

"And perhaps I won't be such a crock," Ian finished the unspoken thought, smiling up into his brother's eyes, which had suddenly become far too serious to suit him.

"What can it hurt to wait?"

"Miss Darlington will be twenty by the time *this* Season begins. Her age will be a strike against her, of course, and if I wait another year..."

Again Dare's lips pursed. "We could buy her a husband."

Ian laughed, relieved to believe Dare's good humor had been restored. "Except she has no fortune."

"I'd be willing to dangle enough money to interest some worthy cit. Or even a needy younger son."

"I think she should probably prefer to choose a husband for herself," Ian said, remembering that flash of temper in Anne's brown eyes. Speaking, indeed, he thought, amused by the memory.

Dare laughed. "Have you been talking to Elizabeth by any chance?"

"I beg your pardon."

"My wife has some rather interesting notions about the marriage mart. You must ask her about them sometime," Dare said, his smile lingering.

There was something in the earl's eyes that created an unexpected frisson of envy in his younger brother, who had never before envied Dare any of the things he possessed by virtue of his earlier birth.

"I shall, if you wish," Ian said. "Is Elizabeth with you?"

"I didn't trust the roads."

"I wish I had been as wise," Ian said, and was glad when Dare was kind enough not to comment again on that ill-advised journey north.

"So you want to arrange a suitable marriage for Darlington's brat *and* make it a love match," the earl said. "Why don't you arrange for the defeat of the French while you're at it?"

Not a kindness, then, Ian thought, but simply an attack from the flank. "You think it's an impossibility?"

"If her father's actions become known. Especially since he named you as her guardian."

"No official inquiry was ever held," Ian said, trying to reassure himself that this would not become a *cause célèbre*. "An officer can't be charged on the basis of how he *should* have behaved in an action. Only if he failed to obey a direct order, which was not the case. Besides, most of the men who knew about Darlington's cowardice are either dead or are still fighting in Portugal. And perhaps the fact that I am now Anne's guardian will quell any gossip that might reach London. At least until she has had an opportunity to make a suitable match."

"An improbability, then," Dare amended. "Considering that she has no fortune and nothing to recommend her beyond red hair and, I believe the phrase was, speaking eyes."

"I didn't say she has nothing to recommend her."

"You didn't have to. I've had enough of that sort thrown at my head through the years."

"She isn't 'that sort,'" Ian denied, with perhaps too much emotion.

He realized his mistake as soon as he saw his brother's face. Dare knew him too well not to have noticed that unaccustomed vehemence. The earl's head cocked slightly and one dark brow lifted in question.

"I see," he said softly. A small twitch, quickly controlled, tugged at the corner of his lips. His tone, when he spoke again, was briskly impersonal, however. "If you are determined on this, then I shall have them make the town house ready. And you'll need the name of a good dressmaker. I can recommend someone if you wish."

"Of course I wish. I shall need all the help you and Elizabeth are willing to offer. And Val," Ian added, "don't be angry that I feel I must do this."

"Angry with you?" Dare asked. "I am *never* angry with my brothers. That's your office. But if you let anything happen to you, my noble pigheaded gallant, while you are trying to find the perfect husband for this bothersome girl, I promise you I shall strangle her *and* her headmistress. And then I shall seek Darlington out in Hell to have a go at him."

"I believe you would at that," Ian said, laughing again, despite his resolve not to let Dare provoke him.

The coughing the laughter produced this time was thankfully of shorter duration. And when it was over, he looked up to find Dare's blue eyes focused on his face, their customary amusement again missing.

"I *would* go to Hell to prevent your suffering any more than you already have. And I swear, Ian, if you let this chit hurt you, she'll be sorry Darlington ever produced her."

"Hurt me?" Ian repeated in bewilderment. Dare could not possibly be aware of what he had felt as Anne had knelt beside him in the snow that night.

"Dealing with her has already put you in bed for a week."

"You can hardly blame her for that."

"No, nor for that harebrained journey north in the midst of a snowstorm. That was your fault."

"It wasn't snowing when we set out," Ian said, smiling. "And John brought help as quickly as he could, despite the stable fire. Nothing that happened was her fault. It was simply a combination of unfortunate events."

"And somehow I have a feeling you are about to embark upon another series of those."

"I?" Ian asked in astonishment. "I assure you, Val, my life is most circumspect. By necessity, perhaps, but I'm beginning to consider the possibility that I am simply boring by nature."

"Good," Dare said. "Until your health is fully restored, I intend to see that you continue to be thoroughly bored. And boring. Now, go back to sleep," he ordered, picking up his book.

And after four or five minutes of watching Dare studiously pretend to read the same page, Ian felt his eyelids begin to droop. He briefly fought their heaviness, and then finally succumbed to the lure of a world where there were no worries or concerns. Particularly no concerns about a lively redhead, whose assets in the husband hunt were as meager as Dare had suggested.

He would deal with that when he had to, Ian decided, just before he drifted back into the invalid's world of exhausted sleep.

"Believe me, Mr. Sinclair, I truly wish I could disagree with the opinions of your surgeons. I'm afraid, sir, I must concur with what you were told on the Peninsula. Your lungs were irreparably damaged. They will always be prone to infections. That, in and of itself, however…"

"It is the 'however' that concerns you," Ian Sinclair said.

While he was again being prodded and poked, this time by the man many considered to be the finest physician in England, he had determined that whatever the outcome, this would put an end to it. Whatever McKinley told him, he would accept. And he would live his life, whatever remained of it, exactly as he had lived it before—to the best of his ability.

"The largest piece of shrapnel within your chest is indeed, given its location, impossible to remove. The attempt would kill you outright. Frankly, I can't understand why it didn't kill you immediately when you were hit," McKinley said. "However, if there is anything I have learned through the years, it is that the human body is a remarkable instrument, frequently quite capable of healing itself. *If* we doctors could let well enough alone," the physician added, smiling.

Ian returned the smile, recognizing what the Scottish-trained doctor was trying to do. And it wasn't that he didn't appreciate the effort. It was simply that he preferred his truths unvarnished. Even if the varnishing was intended to make them more palatable.

"Are you suggesting that if we leave it where it is…" Ian began cautiously, knowing this was the only question that mattered. For reasons he chose not to examine right now, it seemed to matter more than it had when he had first been given this same diagnosis more than a year ago.

"It may stay in place for the next forty years, and if it does, you will die an old man, peacefully in your own bed. Or it may shift tomorrow and pierce your heart. In that case…"

He paused, and Ian finished it for him. "In that case, I *won't* die an old man, peacefully or otherwise."

McKinley let the silence build a moment, but he didn't deny the truth of what his patient had said.

"I should advise you to avoid the kind of physical exertion you recently engaged in. That may not be the life you would have chosen for yourself, Mr. Sinclair, but it *is* life," the doctor said. "And much preferable to the alternative, I should think."

"I appreciate your honesty," Ian said, fighting the disappointment of a ridiculous hope he hadn't even realized he had been harboring.

"I take it your brother doesn't know."

"I prefer that he never does. What good would it do?"

"He is very anxious about you. Since you have not told him the truth, he quite naturally feels that your convalescence has been unnecessarily slow."

"And no doubt certain that your well-known skills could remedy the situation."

"I would that they could, Mr. Sinclair," McKinley said.

"So do I," Ian admitted with a smile. "However, since they can't… And not one of us is guaranteed even one more day, of course. That is a lesson I saw demonstrated quite effectively in Portugal. I have simply received notice to live each of mine as well as I can.''

"I have no doubt that you will. What do you wish me to tell the earl?''

"That he isn't rid of me yet," Ian said. "It is, after all, nothing less than the truth.''

"I'm sure he'll be relieved," McKinley said. And then, as his patient reached for the bell on the table beside the bed, "Don't bother the servants. I can see myself back to the parlor. If you have need of my services in the future, do not hesitate to send for me.''

As the door closed behind the physician, the eyes of Ian Sinclair focused on the fine plaster ceiling above his head. The verdict had been nothing he hadn't known, he told himself.

There were things in his life he regretted, but the actions that had led to his being wounded were not among them. And he would therefore deal with the consequences of them without complaint. It was better, however, that he deal with them alone. He had always known that. Better for him. And much better for his family.

Chapter Four

It had been a very lonely Christmas, Anne thought on the bleak, snowy morning following that equally bleak holiday. Whatever Ian Sinclair had intended when he had brought her to his home, she must believe it had not been this.

Of course, there had been a formal Yuletide dinner last night, which had included all the traditional dishes of the season and which she had eaten in solitary splendor in the dining room. The whole house was decorated quite beyond anything she was accustomed to at Fenton School.

What she was *unaccustomed* to, however, and the lack of which she had felt most severely, was companionship. She missed the girls. She missed taking care of the younger ones and she had worried about them. She also missed having someone to talk to and with whom to share games and cherished holiday pastimes.

If, as her guardian had indicated, his servants had been looking forward to providing a festive Yuletide celebration for his ward, Anne had not, during the long, lonely days she had spent in his home, been able to detect any sign of that intent. They had probably been disappointed that she was not the child they expected. And it was apparent they held her responsible for Mr. Sinclair's illness. She didn't blame them. She, too, considered his condition to be her fault.

The doctor, identifiable by his bag, had come and gone several times during the past eight days. From her bedroom window, worried and anxious about the cause of each visit, she had watched him arrive and depart. And her new guardian's older brother, the Earl of Dare, had stayed for several days before finally departing this morning.

Neither of them had spoken to her, of course, although she was perhaps the person most in need of information. After all, no one doubted that Mr. Sinclair had been made ill as a direct result of his rescue of her. A rescue that must surely satisfy every longing for adventure she had ever felt.

A longing she would never feel again, Anne vowed. She saw, thankfully only in memory now, the face of the man with the torch, missing tooth revealed by that ghastly, leering smile, and she shivered. And if it hadn't been for Ian...

For Mr. Sinclair, she corrected. It would not do to presume, even in her thoughts, which had centered, almost exclusively, throughout these long days and nights, around her guardian. And some of those thoughts—

There was a discreet knock on the door, and Anne scrambled off the high bed across which she had been sprawled in unladylike abandon. She straightened her dress and then her hair, tucking in tendrils before she hurried across the room. She even bit her lips and pinched her cheeks to give them some color.

It was not until she was halfway to the door that she realized this visitor could not possibly be her guardian.

And she couldn't imagine for whomever else in this household she might be concerned about her looks. The acknowledgment that she would wish to appear attractive before Ian Sinclair was a clear affirmation that she had spent too much time daydreaming about him in the last few days, she told herself sternly.

She opened the door and was confronted by the disapproving features of Mrs. Martin, the Sinclair family housekeeper. Unfamiliar with the protocol governing the servants in such a large house, Anne wasn't sure if she should invite the woman in or converse with her standing in the hall.

"Mr. Sinclair wishes to see you, miss. Mind you now, no matter what he says, I won't have you tiring him out," the housekeeper warned. "Ten minutes and no more. You understand?"

"Has he been so very ill?" Anne asked, the fear she had lived with through these lonely days rising to block her throat.

"Mr. Sinclair allows no discussion of his health. Those of us who wish to keep our positions in his household learned that long ago. Something for you to remember," Mrs. Martin added.

The housekeeper turned and bustled forward with an important jingle of keys, passing door after door along the long hallway. Anne followed, wondering exactly what her warning had been meant to convey. That if Anne mentioned Mr. Sinclair's health, she would be sent back to Fenton School?

An idle threat, considering that during the past week she had pined for its safe familiarity. She regretted the thought as soon as it formed. Whatever Mrs. Martin meant, Mr. Sinclair had risked his life to save hers. And at last, it seemed she would have the opportunity to tell him how grateful she was.

Finally the housekeeper stopped before one of the doors. She leaned her ear against it for a moment before she straightened and knocked.

"Come in," someone instructed.

Anne couldn't tell if it had been her guardian's voice, but she wasn't given much time to wonder. Mrs. Martin opened the door and indicated with her hand that Anne should step inside.

Only when she had did Anne realize that the housekeeper wasn't coming in with her. She started to protest, just as the housekeeper stepped away from the door she had opened and started down the hall. Anne drew a fortifying breath and then looked back toward the room she had just entered.

Ian Sinclair was seated in a comfortable chair before the cheerful fire. He was fully dressed, as elegant as the first time she had seen him. Expecting an invalid, perhaps even a dying one, Anne could not have been more surprised had she entered the room and found one of the men who had attacked them that night holding court.

"I understand you have been ill," she said, walking forward.

There was a small, uncomfortable silence.

"And I wonder who told you that?" her guardian asked.

He sounded as if he really wanted to know. Remembering Mrs. Martin's warning, Anne understood why. And despite the servants' coldness, she had no wish to get any of them into trouble.

"After several years of looking after the younger girls, my powers of deduction are well-honed," she said. "You disappeared the night we arrived, and I haven't seen you since. In that time, both a physician and your brother have come to the house, the former on several occasions and the latter for a visit of some days. It seemed rather obvious.''

''I'm sure none of your charges were ever able to put anything over on you,'' Mr. Sinclair said, laughing.

And then his laughter became hard coughing. Lucy Bates had died last year of such a cough. Of course, Lucy had never been very strong to begin with, Anne reminded herself, remembering the fragile little girl, whose arms and legs had been more like sticks than like the sturdy, rounded limbs of most of her girls.

And just because something terrible had happened to Lucy Bates didn't mean anything terrible would happen to Mr. Sinclair. She could not, however, control the surge of anxiety as she listened to the deep congestion the cough revealed.

''Are you all right?'' she asked finally as it faded.

''Of course,'' he said.

His hand was pressed against the center of his chest. However, since Mr. Sinclair preferred it, Anne gave in to the pretense that what had just happened had not happened and that he had not really been very ill at all.

''I have wanted to thank you since that night,'' she began, determined to say all the things she should have said then and had not had the chance to say since.

''I truly wish you would not.''

''I owe you my life, Mr. Sinclair. Or at least…''

She almost said my virtue, but then thought that the expression of that reality might be improper. Although she had had a sheltered upbringing, there had been no doubt in her mind about the kind of danger she had faced.

''You owe me nothing of the kind,'' he said into her pause. ''Quite the reverse, I believe. If you hadn't taken a hand, the outcome might have been very different. You had an uncomfortable journey and a dangerous encounter with a couple of rogues you should never have been exposed to. On top of that you have spent a lonely holiday in a house full of strangers. I can only promise you that was not my intent and apologize profusely.''

"I am not to express my gratitude for your rescue, and yet *you* may apologize for a series of things that were not your fault and were undoubtedly beyond your control?''

"As your guardian, I should never have put you in the position of having to *be* rescued, either from rogues or a broken axle or a snowstorm.''

"And if you had not, I should probably never in my life have seen the outside of Fenton School,'' she retorted.

"I take it, then,'' he said, smiling at her, genuinely relieved, she realized, "that your experiences have not *all* been unpleasant.''

The memory of her arms wrapped around his body while they knelt together in the snow brushed through her mind. She supposed that was not the kind of experience Mr. Sinclair meant.

"Indeed they have not. Your home is very lovely.''

"And the servants have seen to your needs?''

Except for the need of company, she thought, but she didn't say that, either. If he could be gracious, despite his illness, then surely she could manage not to mention that she had indeed been both bored and lonely in his home.

"Yes, thank you. I have been very well looked after.''

"And yesterday was Christmas Day,'' he said, his voice regretful. "I'm afraid I didn't even have an opportunity to shop for a present, but I do have a surprise for you which I hope will help in some way to make up for that lack.''

''A surprise?'' she echoed hesitantly. *Surprise?*

''As you know, most young women your age have already been introduced into society. Since your father was away with the army, I understand you have not yet been formally brought out.''

''Brought out?'' Anne repeated, bewildered by the introduction of this topic. Surely, he didn't mean...

''In London,'' Mr. Sinclair clarified.

Anne swallowed, allowing the images that the very name of the capital evoked to fill her head. Provincial she might be, but even the girls at Fenton School knew about the famed London Season. Several of them had been quite confident of the opportunities that would be afforded them by that experience. And confident that it was in their near future, as soon as their schooling was complete.

Anne had listened to their talk with idle interest, knowing her father would never go to the trouble or expense of arranging for her own coming out. And as far as she was aware, she had no relatives who might be called upon to shoulder that burden.

She had put the possibility from her mind years ago, quite content with the direction of her life. And when Mrs. Kemp had talked about the wonderful opportunities that were opening up for her, this was one which had never even occurred to her.

''The Season starts in a few months,'' Ian continued. ''I'm afraid there is a great deal of preparation required if we are to be ready in time.''

The Season. The words seemed to reverberate inside Anne's head, almost blocking the rest of his words.

"Mr. Sinclair, I assure you that I have no desire to be brought out. I am quite content—"

"I believe it would have been your father's wish, Miss Darlington. After all, it is only what is expected for a young woman of your class. I know it is Mrs. Kemp's wish. She was quite clear on that score. And I have promised her that as your guardian, I should see to it that you were given this advantage."

Anne drew breath, preparing to again refuse, before she remembered her own promise to the headmistress. *Headstrong or not, I shall endeavor to do whatever Mr. Sinclair thinks is best.* She, too, had given her word.

And after all, she would spend the rest of her life at Fenton School. Although she was truly not interested in being presented to society, she was also not sure she was ready to return forever to the only world she had really ever known.

Actually, Anne admitted, she was suddenly reluctant to leave Sinclair Hall, despite the loneliness of the days she had spent here. After all, now that Mr. Sinclair was recovered—

"My brother, who has excellent taste," her guardian continued, interrupting that foolish notion, "has recommended a modiste. On his advice I have sent for her to come here and make the preliminary measurements for your gowns. Of course, we shall be in London in time for the fittings."

"In London for the Season," Anne said faintly, feeling more and more as if she had wandered into some bizarre dream. "We are going to London?"

"Within the month," he said, smiling at her again, "if you are willing to trust me to convey you safely there, considering your first unfortunate journey under my guardianship. I promise to take better care of you in the future.''

She truly doubted anyone could have taken better care of her that terrible night than he had. And he had done so at a cost to himself that he would not even acknowledge. Or allow her to.

"I would trust you with my life, Mr. Sinclair," she said.

And watched his eyes change again, the gentle teasing fading from them as they held a long heartbeat on hers. For the first time since she had entered the room, self-absorbed with what *she* wanted to say, she allowed herself to study his face.

If one looked past the rather obvious effects of the fight, which included a fading bruise around his right eye, and an almost healed gash along his left cheekbone, the marks of his recent illness were there as well. And according to Mrs. Martin, that was never to be a topic for conversation. In truth, Anne could not but admire him for that.

"Thank you," he said with the smile she had learned to value for its kindness, even in the brief time she had known him. "I am delighted by your trust, Anne. May I call you Anne?"

She had never been called anything else, not even by the youngest girls in the school. Given the difference in their ages and his position in her life, it seemed natural somehow that he should call her by her Christian name.

"Of course," she said. "But…should I continue to call you Mr. Sinclair?" And realized belatedly, again by watching his eyes change, that she had made a mistake. "I suppose anything else would be improper. I didn't mean to be forward," she said, stumbling for an explanation. "Perhaps—" She stopped, cutting the words off because it seemed this, too, might give offense.

"Perhaps what?"

"I'm sure that… That is…"

"My name is Ian," he said.

"Then…Uncle Ian?" she suggested hesitantly.

His eyes widened slightly, just as they had when Margaret's trembling finger had identified Anne as his ward.

"Do you know," he said, his voice suddenly full of an amusement she didn't understand, "I really don't believe I should be able to endure it if you do."

"I beg your pardon," Anne said, bewildered and embarrassed.

"Forgive me, Anne. You may call me Ian, or even Mr. Sinclair, if you are more comfortable with that. But when I think of my brother's reaction to your calling me Uncle Ian… Truthfully, I beg you, *that* I am not willing to endure. Not even for my ward."

"Too ornate," the Countess of Dare said, her blue eyes lifting from the drawing in the fashion book she and the dressmaker were perusing, their fair heads very close together. "Something more classic, I think, given her height and coloring."

Anne was still standing where they had placed her, on a stool in the middle of her bedroom, dressed only in her chemise and petticoat. She had been humiliated by the rather threadbare appearance of those garments, especially when confronted with the cool, blond elegance of the Countess of Dare.

Neither she nor the modiste had commented on the patches and darns, however, seeming to be far more concerned with thumbing through the pictures in the books the woman had brought from London. Pictures which

Anne had not yet been allowed to see. It seemed she was merely a bystander to this process.

"This perhaps," the dressmaker suggested, and the eyes of both women surveyed Anne's form again, moving from head to toe.

"Only if the color is changed. And I don't like the trim," Elizabeth Sinclair said. "Braided ribbon is not exactly *au courant.*"

"I couldn't agree more," said the dressmaker. "In green?"

"Of a certain shade. We shall probably have to shop for it in London. There is nothing in the samples you've brought that is quite right for her," the countess said, her eyes falling to the swatches of fabric scattered about the floor and draped over the room's furnishings.

"I have others. Your brother-in-law's message was not suggestive of the scope of what he wants."

"What *does* he want?" Anne asked, hoping to at least be informed as to the occasion on which the dress they were discussing should be worn.

"A wardrobe," Elizabeth explained, smiling at her.

"*Without* any cheeseparing," the modiste said, her pleasure obvious.

"A wardrobe?" Anne repeated. Which seemed to imply… "I am to have several dresses?"

"Dozens," the countess agreed. Her eyes met Anne's again before they fell to the pattern book as she turned the page. "Your father was very fortunate in his choice of guardian."

"I understand they were great friends," Anne said.

When Elizabeth Sinclair's eyes came up this time, there was something in their blue depths Anne didn't understand. Some emotion there that she couldn't quite read. Almost as quickly as it had formed, however, it was controlled.

"Indeed?" the countess said. "I didn't know."

Anne didn't either, of course. She had simply made that assumption, based on the fact that her father had chosen Ian Sinclair to be her guardian. And she couldn't imagine any reason for that other than friendship.

However, whenever she had attempted during the past week to introduce any topic that might lead to a recounting of the days they had served together, she had sensed a reluctance on her guardian's part. She had finally been forced to conclude that he was as reticent to discuss his military career as his health. And probably for the same reasons.

"This?" Elizabeth questioned the dressmaker.

Again both pairs of eyes focused on Anne, whose arms were beginning to grow gooseflesh from being bare so long. She didn't complain, however. She stood where they had placed her, the light from the windows of her bedroom illuminating her every feature, good and bad she supposed, and wondered what she had glimpsed so briefly in the eyes of Ian Sinclair's sister-in-law.

"What do you think?" Ian asked, watching from his chair by the fire as Elizabeth pulled on her gloves.

"I think you are going to need a great deal of help."

"Besides that," he responded with a smile.

"She's completely unspoiled. And quite lovely, of course, but… Frankly, Ian, she hasn't much training in the deportment that will be expected of a debutante."

"If you mean blushing and simpering, then I'm not sure I would view skill in those behaviors as an advantage."

The tone of his reply was sharper than he had intended,

but the implied criticism bothered him. While he had been confined to his room by the maddeningly lingering effects of his illness, he had had almost too much time to examine his feelings for Anne.

Although it was true that he had, of necessity, been celibate since he'd been wounded, he didn't believe that completely explained the strength of his attraction. Nor did his admiration of her courage or of the way her eyes met his with an honesty and openness that was unheard of in a woman of his class.

"She does have a tendency to speak her mind," Elizabeth said, softening her reproach this time with a smile.

"As do you," he reminded her.

"But *I* am not a young girl about to make her come-out."

"You once were."

"And I had been very carefully drilled in how to behave and especially in what to expect. The first rogue who flirts with Anne is liable to turn her head and steal her heart. You may make a dash for the Border to retrieve her before it's all over."

"She hasn't the wealth to make her interesting to the fortune hunters."

"Thank God for that. Do you really want my advice?"

"Of course. I should never have drawn you away from your honeymoon if I had not."

"Find her a husband from among your friends and acquaintances. Don't submit her to that brutal round."

"I thought women enjoyed all that. The parties and the routs and the balls."

"Some of them, perhaps. I don't think Anne will. I'm afraid…" Again, Elizabeth hesitated, her eyes on her gloves, the perfect fit of which she was now merely toying with.

"What are you afraid of?" Ian asked. "Not of speaking your mind to me, I hope."

"I'm afraid she'll be hurt."

"Hurt by whom?"

"By all manner of people," Elizabeth said, exasperation in her voice. "Those who have never forgiven Dare for marrying me may be unkind on principle. And Dare told me about her father's actions in Iberia, which may very well come back to haunt her. But beyond that, Ian, she's a little too different to fit in. They'll break her heart and perhaps even her spirit. And I should hate to see that happen."

Again, Ian felt the stirrings of anger. Not at Elizabeth. She was simply expressing what he recognized as the truth. His ire was directed instead at the society they both knew so well.

There were within the ton those who lived to feel superior to others. Their greatest delight was to offer a direct cut or to make a witty if cruel remark at another's expense. Anne would be exposed to all of them, and Ian knew there was little he could do to protect her.

"I gave my word," he said, regretting now that he had. "And I've already told Anne she will be introduced. Besides, the Season is her best chance of finding someone suitable to marry."

Although Anne's marriage had from the beginning been the acknowledged goal of this exercise, as well as of his promise to Mrs. Kemp, the word seemed to bring home to him for the first time what a difficult task he had set for himself.

Elizabeth's eyes assessed his face a moment before she nodded. "I hope you're right. I hope she finds someone who will love her for the very qualities I fear the ton will fail to admire."

"She isn't really so different as all that," Ian said.

"Perhaps not. Perhaps I am allowing the not-very-pleasant memories of my own Season to color my expectations."

"You were surely a diamond of the first water."

"I was a piece of merchandise on sale to the highest bidder," Elizabeth said with a soft, but very distinct bitterness. And neither of them said anything for a long time.

"I'm sorry if this has brought back painful memories," Ian said finally, regretting now that he had asked for her help, despite how much he needed it.

Elizabeth laughed, her former seriousness determinedly wiped from her eyes. "Dare has now given me enough happy ones to quite make up for all of those, I promise you."

"And *I* promise *you* that Anne won't be sold. That isn't what this is about. She is perfectly free to marry whomever she pleases, provided he isn't a blackguard."

"And you are going to play the dragon slayer and protect her from blackguards, of course."

"*Duenna,* perhaps, rather than dragon slayer," Ian said. "I can't see myself in the role of champion. Merely that of the faithful chaperon. Anne has suggested she call me Uncle Ian. And if you reveal that to Val, I shall never forgive you."

Elizabeth's laughter joined his. "Your secret is safe with me, my dear. But…however did she come up with *that?*"

"Perhaps because I am so much older."

"Most *marriages* in our set involve a difference in age far larger than that between you and Anne."

"Val said you have some interesting ideas about marriage. Do I take it this is one of them?"

"A disgust over the usual gap in ages? Perhaps. Especially when it involves a difference that may be measured in decades. Certainly not something relatively minor like the dozen or so years between you and Anne."

Ian belatedly remembered that Elizabeth's first marriage had been to a man old enough to be her grandfather. Perhaps Anne saw him in a similar light.

"I think she believes I'm older than I am. And who could blame her for that assumption?" he said lightly, smiling to insure that simple statement of fact would not be interpreted as self-pitying.

"And you, of course, haven't bothered to disabuse her of that notion?"

"Why should I? I'm already afraid people will question the arrangement her father made. As you say, the gap between our ages is not so great as that which will be between Anne and some of her suitors."

"I take it you don't consider yourself one of those?" Elizabeth asked, her shrewd blue gaze leveled on his face.

"A suitor? Hardly."

"Why not?" She sounded as if she really wanted to know.

"Because it would be highly inappropriate."

"You can hardly be accused of courting her in hopes of gaining control of her fortune."

"Perhaps not," Ian said.

"And so?" Elizabeth questioned, unwilling, apparently, to let the subject drop.

"I could hardly be considered suitable husband material for her either," he said, meeting her eyes.

"I don't see why not."

Ian smiled, hoping that nothing of his discomfort over the subject she had raised would be revealed in his face.

"Do you not? But you are family, after all, and not strictly unbiased."

"Even if I were not family, I should not understand your reasoning in this."

"Anne is to choose her own husband," Ian said, deliberately avoiding the crux of the issue. "I should think that's what you would wish for her. Considering your own experience."

"Of course it is. I'm simply curious as to why you have taken yourself out of the running."

"Because her inclination is to call me Uncle Ian," he suggested with a smile. "I think *she* has taken me out of the running."

"Only because she doesn't know any better," Elizabeth said.

Or because she has seen me at my worst, Ian thought.

"Perhaps," he said again, the word carefully noncommittal.

"Obviously, you don't wish to talk about this."

He should have remembered that Elizabeth was too clever to be put off with platitudes and transparent excuses.

"If you will forgive me, no, truthfully I do not."

She inclined her head in agreement. "Then, of course, I shall not broach the subject again. I wish you would think about what I've said, however. Both about the rigors of the Season for a girl of Anne's sensitivity *and* about this. I can think of no finer man to care for Anne the rest of her life. She would be very lucky indeed to win your heart."

"But my heart is not a stake in this game," Ian said softly.

The silence between them this time was induced by

her embarrassment, he supposed, as the first had been by his.

"I didn't know," Elizabeth said. "Forgive me for being obtuse. I am not usually."

She thought he was in love with someone else, Ian realized. An unrequited love. Which was as good an excuse as any.

"You are never obtuse," he denied, smiling at her.

"I was about this. Am I forgiven?"

"There is nothing to forgive. I am infinitely grateful for your help."

"But not for my advice," she said.

"I shall always welcome any advice you wish to give."

Except about this, he thought, holding his sister-in-law's eyes and seeing sympathy within them. As he had said, Elizabeth was never obtuse.

Chapter Five

London,
Six weeks later

"And this for the trim," Elizabeth said, holding a strand of very fine silver beads against the white silk they had selected for Anne's first ball gown. "What do you think?"

"I think I cannot bear to look at another piece of cloth or another trimming," Anne said truthfully. "Are you not hungry?"

"Hungry?" Elizabeth repeated, signaling to the hovering merchant with a wave of her gloved hand.

"It has been hours since we had breakfast."

"I am training you to do without food," Elizabeth said.

"Without food?"

"In preparation for your first ball."

"They have suppers at balls. You told me so."

"Indeed they do, but you don't actually intend to be seen eating them, do you?"

"I don't?"

"Of course not. Perhaps only a bite or two. If you don't practice starvation now and grow accustomed to it, how shall you manage to do without food, especially after dancing for hours?"

"You're teasing me," Anne said, laughing as she finally detected the mockery in the countess's words.

"Only partially. It truly won't do to be seen to have a hearty appetite."

"Perhaps you could fatten me up during the next three weeks, as they do geese for Christmas, and I could simply live off the accumulated store."

"And then you should never get into all these dresses."

All these dresses, Anne thought, repeating the unbelievable phrase in her head. So many of them that she had truly lost count. So many that she could not imagine ever having occasion to wear half of them. So many that...

"Is he very rich?" she asked, fingering a bronze satin that she thought evocative of leaves in the fall.

She was surprised when Elizabeth took the fabric out of her hands and unrolled enough from the bolt so that she could drape it across Anne's shoulder.

"You're right," the Countess of Dare said, stepping back to look at the subtle gleam of the material next to Anne's skin and hair. "You have a very good eye for what will become you. Too bad we can't have *this* made up."

"Because it isn't white," Anne said, having by now learned the rules that governed a debutante's dress.

"Or cream or pink or blue. Silver if you wish to be thought very daring," Elizabeth agreed.

"All of which make me look like a death's head."

"Not so bad as that," Elizabeth said, undraping the

satin and rewrapping it neatly around the bolt, "but in truth, this *would* be far more becoming."

"Perhaps we could have it made up into something to wear at home. A dressing gown," Anne suggested hopefully. She ran her fingers longingly over the fabric, almost a caress.

"If you like," Elizabeth said, again signaling the merchant.

"Is he?" Anne asked again as they waited for him to cut the satin and add it to their purchases.

"Is he what?"

"Very rich," Anne repeated impatiently. "I mean Ian *is* buying all of this, isn't he? I can't believe my father made provisions for me to have a Season. Especially since he never made provisions for anything else. So...is he very rich?"

"I believe Ian has money from his mother, which he has invested in the funds. I know Dare made a settlement on both his brothers as soon as he inherited. He didn't want them to have to come to him for pocket money."

"So he is not really rich. Then why is he doing all this?"

Elizabeth hesitated a second, and then she said, "Because he is your guardian. And so that you may have your chance."

"My chance to make a good marriage. Which is supposed to be every woman's dream," Anne said.

"And it isn't yours?" Elizabeth asked, smiling at her.

"I don't know. I've never been married, so perhaps I'm a poor judge. Was it your dream?"

"I am hardly the person to ask *that* question."

"I'm sorry. I had gotten the impression..."

"Yes?"

"That you were happy in your marriage."

"My *second* marriage, and I am very happy. I was *not* happy, however, in the first."

"Then why did you marry him?" Anne asked reasonably, trailing Elizabeth as she began to make her way through the crowded aisles toward the outer doors of the linen draper's shop.

"Because that one *was* considered to be a good marriage," the countess said over her shoulder.

Anne took a breath, knowing that she had not really touched on any of the things she longed to ask. And one of them was, of course, why her guardian was yet unmarried. Considering the uncharacteristic abruptness of Elizabeth's answers, however, this might not be the best time to ask that particular question.

Anne had thought she was quite alone in the enormous ballroom. And then, just as she made what she hoped was a fairly graceful turn, she noticed her guardian leaning at his ease against the wall beside the enormous pocket doors. He had been watching her, and she had no idea how long he had been there.

"Please don't let me interrupt," Ian said. "I am enjoying the performance, but I shall leave if you prefer to be alone."

She had stopped her pantomime as soon as she'd spotted him, hot blood rushing into her cheeks. "It's *your* ballroom," she said. "If anyone should leave, it should be I."

"Actually, it's my brother's ballroom. I don't believe I have even been in it for several years. I'd almost forgotten it was here until I heard you singing."

"*That* must have been an unpleasant experience."

He laughed, not bothering to comment on her self-deprecation. "Practicing your steps?" he asked.

Anne had never danced before in company and certainly not any of the courtly dances which she would soon be expected to perform proficiently. When Elizabeth discovered that appalling situation, she had ordered a series of private lessons.

In a little less than half an hour the dancing master who had been hired to add the needed polish would arrive. Anne had come to the ballroom to prepare for that dreaded lesson, since Elizabeth's comments this morning on her progress—or rather on her lack of it—had been less than encouraging.

It was hard to believe someone who could shinny up a tree as rapidly as any boy and do sums in her head faster than Mrs. Kemp herself couldn't master the steps to a few dances. That seemed to be the case, however, and Anne was determined to overcome that failure, especially since she would be expected to perform flawlessly in only a few days.

"Elizabeth has sent for a dancing master," she confessed.

"I see," Ian said, controlling his lips, which seemed to have a tendency to tilt upward at the corners.

"I have no wish to humiliate myself any more than is absolutely necessary, however, so I came early to practice. Do you suppose if I threw myself on his mercy, he might tell Elizabeth that lessons are quite useless and that she must leave me alone before I succumb to a debilitating fit of vapors?"

"I think it unlikely," Ian said, finally giving in and allowing the grin he had been fighting.

A very attractive grin, Anne thought. Less kind than his smile, perhaps, but it seemed to put them on a more equal footing, like fellow conspirators.

"Unlikely she'll leave me alone?" she questioned. "Or unlikely he will tell her that?"

"Very unlikely that *you* would succumb to vapors. Anyone who can face down a highwayman can certainly endure being led through the steps of a few dances."

"Would you care to guess which I should prefer?"

"It's not so bad as that," he said.

He was obviously amused by her distress, which she found herself exaggerating to keep him entertained. To keep him here?

"You," she said, her tone almost accusatory, "probably mastered these steps when you were a child."

He didn't bother to deny it. "Do you think I could help?" he offered instead.

"Do you mean you'd be willing to practice with me?"

Despite the fact that he was undoubtedly being avuncular again, there was a distinct and by now familiar flutter in the region of her heart at the thought.

"Speaking of unpleasant experiences," Ian said, with a laugh. "Should I try to dance, you would certainly have one, I'm afraid. I told you I haven't been in a ballroom in years. And certainly not of late."

Because of his limp. Disappointment settled in her chest, exactly where that brief surge of anticipation had been only seconds before. She didn't really want him to watch her stumble over her own feet today, she supposed, but she had thought he might dance with her at least once during the coming Season. *After* she had mastered the art.

Actually, she realized she had been counting on it. She had envisioned her guardian leading her, graceful and poised, onto the floor at her first ball. Another romantic fantasy destroyed by reality, which seemed to be happening rather too frequently of late. But then she was too prone to fantasy. That was certainly what Mrs. Kemp would have said. And probably what Elizabeth would say as well.

"However," Ian continued, "I would be delighted to take your hand and let you practice your steps around me. It might make you more confident when the dancing master requires that."

"Will he?" Anne asked in horror.

For some reason she had supposed the master would simply walk her through the dance, standing beside her as Elizabeth had done. The thought of actually having to dance with the man was disconcerting.

"I believe that is how it is usually accomplished," Ian said, his eyes smiling again, although his mouth was once more controlled. "But a little practice will surely make perfect. Not, of course, in my case."

This might very well be the only chance she would ever have to dance with him. And she wanted to. She wanted to very much. His hazel eyes were considering her face, one brow raised inquiringly, so she attempted to keep her excitement from showing.

"I should be very grateful if you would," she said primly.

Ian limped across the ballroom and held out his hand. "Then I should be delighted to be your somewhat immobile partner."

It was certainly not how she had envisioned this moment. However, they were quite alone, with nothing to distract her from enjoying his presence, so it might be even better than what she had been imagining. Smiling, she put her fingers into those of her guardian, and took her place at his side.

"I must warn you that I really am *very* bad," she said. It seemed only fair to prepare him.

"Then we should match quite nicely," he said, unperturbed by her confession.

Taking a deep breath, Anne began to move through the sequence of steps Elizabeth had painstakingly taught her, trying to concentrate on them, rather than on the considerable distraction provided by being so near her guardian.

"Perhaps if I hum it will go better," Ian suggested after a moment. "The melody almost tells you what to do."

Her eyes lifted to his, a blush once more staining her cheeks. His fingers tightened encouragingly around her hand, and then he began to hum in a very pleasant baritone. Obediently, Anne tried to think only about the music. After all, Elizabeth had told her the same thing—to concentrate on the rhythm and flow of it, rather than worrying about what her feet were doing.

She reminded herself that she had *better* enjoy this because the opportunity to dance with Ian might never come again. Of course, she admitted, he wasn't really dancing. He was simply holding her hand as she moved through the formal pattern of the cotillion. He, himself, was moving as little as possible, standing in place and simply turning as she circled around him.

However, given all the hectic preparations and lessons in deportment and the shopping expeditions, Anne hadn't been alone with her guardian in a very long time. And she didn't believe she had been this close to him since the night they had knelt together in the snow, her arms wrapped tightly around his shivering body.

Suddenly she was aware of the same subtle aromas that had surrounded him then. The scents of good soap and fine leather. Of freshly ironed linen. Of clean skin and hair. She breathed deeply of them, knowing those fragrances would always be associated in her mind with the night he had defended her. And now, they would forever be associated with this moment as well.

"Much better," he said, turning with her so that she could begin the next section.

Had they really been on the dance floor, he would have handed her off to her new partner. As it was, he simply allowed her to circle away from him and then caught her hand again as she turned back.

Despite the fact that he wasn't attempting to follow the steps, Ian's confidence in leading her through them showed that he must have been an excellent dancer. Or at least a very experienced one.

"You like to dance," she said, surprised into that observation. He did seem to be enjoying himself, even in this necessarily truncated version of the masculine role.

"I was a member of Wellington's staff," he said. "Like it or not, we *all* danced. It's a skill that, once learned, is never forgotten."

For the first time she thought about how much his life had changed as a result of his injuries. He had never indicated that he missed the things he could no longer do, but surely he must. Dancing, for example. And she knew that he no longer rode. There were probably a dozen other activities Ian Sinclair had once enjoyed which were now denied to him.

"You were frequently called upon to dance with lovely Spanish noblewomen, I suppose," she teased.

"Of course. And as frequently with their mustached grandmothers."

She laughed. "As you may possibly have noticed, I have a tendency to romanticize."

"A common failing of youth. It will pass soon enough, believe me."

"At my first ball," she suggested.

"You'll be a great success. How can you not under Elizabeth's tutelage? And mine, of course."

He turned her again, and then stepped across, pretending to become her next partner. As she completed the circle, she glanced up to find him waiting for her. His hand was held out in invitation, and he was smiling at her again.

Her fingers touched his and something happened in her stomach. Something quite remarkable. To be perfectly honest, she realized, she would have to admit that it had not occurred exactly in her stomach, but rather...

As a result of that realization, she missed the beat, failing to begin the new series of steps at the right time. Totally confused, both by the disrupted pattern and by her reaction to the mere touch of her guardian's hand, she stopped. Surprised, Ian turned his head to look into her face.

"I seem to have forgotten what comes next," she said, her voice little more than a whisper.

"The first rule for becoming a success in society," he said, his eyes smiling, despite his admonishing tone, "is never to admit you are at fault."

"I was at fault."

"Of course not. You have an awkward partner."

"Indeed, I do *not*," she said, laughing. "I have clumsy feet."

Although they were no longer moving through the motions of the dance, he had not released her hand. Not that she wanted him to. She realized she would be quite content to stand here all day, her fingers resting in his.

"You couldn't be clumsy if you tried," he said.

"I hope you will stay and tell Elizabeth's dancing master that whisker."

"You don't need me to fight your battles," he said.

"Well, it would be very nice to have *someone* fight them."

Anne was quite accustomed to having to stand on her own two feet. However, what she had just said was something she had recognized since Ian had come to Fenton School to collect her. And it had only been reinforced by Elizabeth's kindness. It *was* nice to have someone on her side. And at her side.

"And that is the purpose of everything we're in London to accomplish," Ian said softly.

The marriage mart. Someone to fight my battles for me.

Anne had never thought of what they were undertaking in that light. Despite all her romantic fantasies, she had never really believed she would find a husband at any of the Season's entertainments.

Someone to fight my battles for me. The memory of the night they had knelt together in the snow was again in her head. As was that peculiar sensation, the one which had moved through her body when Ian Sinclair had taken her hand.

And suddenly she knew with startling clarity why she had never, from the very beginning, entertained any hope of falling in love with a handsome gentleman she would meet in some London ballroom. Unknown even to her it seemed, she had already found her champion, and ridiculously romantic or not, she knew she would never want any other.

Chapter Six

The countess had decided that Anne's first foray into society would take place at a small, intimate dinner party given by Lady Laud, who was Ian's godmother. Since Elizabeth could not chaperone Anne through the upcoming Season's nearly endless round of entertainments, Ian was hopeful that his godmother might be willing to assume that role. Both her husband's position with the government and Lady Laud's own reputation would add to Anne's stature in the eyes of the ton, *if* the old woman agreed.

And that, Elizabeth had declared, would depend on the impression Anne made tonight. It was simply another pressure added to all the others Anne was already very well aware of.

Thankfully, the countess had chosen one of the most becoming of Anne's elegant new gowns for the occasion. The color of rich cream, its only decoration was a few ecru silk roses scattered about the hem. There was another smaller rose sewn discreetly at the neckline, its petals touching Anne's skin just above the swell of her breasts.

She wore a matching rose in her hair, whose color for

the first time seemed to complement her clothing rather than war with it. Elizabeth herself had arranged her coiffure, sweeping her curls high on the top of her head and allowing the fine tendrils that always escaped any arrangement to float around her face.

Considering that her expectations had been so very low, Anne had been enormously pleased with the reflection in her cheval glass. And more than pleased with the approval she was now seeing in her guardian's eyes.

Ian, striking in full evening regalia, was standing in the foyer below, looking up as she paused on the first landing of the grand staircase of the London town house. And despite her nervousness, Anne was certain of one thing: she could not have wished for a more handsome escort.

Of course, she reminded herself, Ian was her guardian and not really her escort. There was nothing, however, which said she couldn't pretend. Her lips lifted into a reminiscing smile as she remembered long hours of her adolescence spent imagining just such a moment as this. And no one, not even her guardian, would ever know what she was imagining tonight.

The harmless fantasy would help her through the evening that lay ahead. She had told herself again and again that she must guard her tongue and remember all the silly rules Elizabeth had so patiently explained. After all the trouble and expense the two of them had gone to on her behalf, it would be a shame not to live up to the standards of the ton on her very first outing.

"What do you think?" Elizabeth asked her brother-in-law. She had pitched the question so that Anne could hear it as she stood above them, waiting breathlessly for his approval.

"I think," Ian said, smiling up at Anne, "that I shall be the most envied man in London."

He held out his hand, and Anne descended the last set of steps to place her fingers in his. As soon as she touched them, there was again that unaccustomed jolt in the pit of her stomach.

If she hadn't already known its cause, she might legitimately have put the feeling down to sheer excitement tonight. After all, this was the moment they had been working toward—the beginning of the long Season that stretched ahead.

Ian's eyes were smiling at her again. And seeing the undisguised admiration in them, Anne began to relax. Whatever apprehension she felt about the success of the evening, her guardian apparently harbored none.

During the last few difficult weeks his unfailing confidence had bolstered hers. And it was rather badly in need of bolstering tonight. Ian tucked her hand into the crook of his arm, placing warm fingers over her cold ones, which were vibrating slightly with nerves.

"You're trembling," he said, sounding surprised by that discovery. "There's nothing to be afraid of, I promise you."

And as long as he was holding her hand, Anne told herself, truly there would not be.

I should have warned her. He had supposed Elizabeth would have explained how the seating would be arranged at such an affair. There was no doubt, however, that Anne had not realized she would not be beside him at dinner.

"Major Sinclair," Doyle Travener said, bowing slightly in response to their hostess's introduction. "I regret, sir, that I have never had the honor of meeting you before. Your reputation among His Majesty's forces can hardly be exaggerated."

The handsome young man who was to take Anne in to dinner had, according to Lady Laud, only recently returned from his own service on the Iberian Peninsula. His sun-darkened skin and fair hair were a becoming contrast to a pair of fine blue eyes, which appeared to be full of genuine respect.

"*You* seem to be doing so quite nicely, I think," Ian said with a trace of embarrassment.

He smiled at the young ex-lieutenant to soften the effect of that admonition. He had not forgotten the pleasure he'd found in the easy camaraderie of his fellow soldiers. Travener's obvious robust physical condition, however, made him feel every one of his thirty-two years. And, Ian admitted, it made him even more aware of the difference between his age and Anne's.

"I assure you, sir, I *could* not exaggerate it," Travener said earnestly before he turned to include Anne in the conversation. "Your guardian was very highly thought of by both his men and his fellow officers, Miss Darlington."

"Of whom my father was one," Anne said. "Colonel George Darlington. Did you know him, Mr. Travener?"

"I don't believe I had that privilege. My misfortune."

Travener's blue eyes had met Ian's briefly before he made that disclaimer. Ian couldn't be sure if the look was meant to convey that he had known Darlington or that he knew of him. Whatever it had indicated, Ian was relieved at the ex-soldier's graceful denial of a personal acquaintance.

Perhaps Travener felt that was simply the best way to avoid any further discussion of Anne's father. Since that was something Ian devoutly wished to avoid as well, he didn't question Travener's comment. After all, it was possible that by the time Travener had arrived on the Peninsula, talk of the infamous incident in which Ian had been wounded had died.

The conversation eventually moved from military matters into other directions more appropriate for the intent of the evening. Although there had been that brief flare of consternation in Anne's eyes when she had understood she wouldn't be seated beside Ian at table, she was soon chatting, seemingly at ease, with her dinner companion. And Travener certainly seemed adept enough in the duties required of him, one of which was to find some topic on which he and Anne could comfortably converse.

Doyle was also the nearest to Anne's age of any of the men here, Ian realized when they had all been seated. It had been a very thoughtful gesture on the part of his godmother, therefore, to pair Anne with Travener, despite Ian's trepidation at having her so far away from him.

Throughout the first two courses, he found himself watching his ward. Since he was also trying to keep up his end of the conversation, the mental exercise was nerve-racking, especially since he had been out of circulation for so long. Travener, however, seemed to be making an effort to entertain Anne, just as he should, and eventually Ian began to relax.

"She's charming," Lady Laud said, inclining her head slightly toward the other end of the table where Anne was seated. "It's really too bad about her father," she added, her eyes coming back to Ian's, a knowing arch to her brow. "You must hope that never becomes public knowledge."

Laud was in the War Office and would naturally be aware of what had happened in Portugal. Ian did not expect that incident should ever become an item of gossip within the ton, however. As he had told Dare, most of the men who had been involved had been killed, either on that day or during subsequent battles. And the others were still engaged with Wellington.

"I see no reason why it should," he said truthfully.

"How strange that Darlington should have chosen you, of all people," Lady Laud continued, her black eyes again assessing the girl at the end of the table.

"The decision was made some years ago, I believe," Ian said. The solicitor had told him nothing to that effect, but he felt it would be better not to feed that particular speculation, not even with someone as friendly as his godmother. "It happened long before...the other."

He had himself wondered often enough about George Darlington's motives. Try as he might, Ian had been unable to come up with any logical reason for what the man had done. He had even thought, more cynically than was his nature, that naming him as Anne's guardian might have been Darlington's idea of some macabre joke. If so, it was one that had been made at his daughter's expense as well as at Ian's.

"How well do you know Travener?" he asked, the question casual, his eyes locked on the interplay between Anne and her dinner companion.

"Very little, actually. I can't remember who recommended him, but he's proven to be an exemplary extra man, something any hostess is in need of during the Season," Lady Laud said with a laugh. "He's only recently come up to town. Sold out due to some family crisis. I can ask Laud if you wish."

"Don't bother," Ian said, not wishing to appear overly curious. "He told me he'd been in Portugal. I was simply trying to place him, but he must have arrived there after I left."

Unconsciously, his gaze settled on Anne again. At that moment Travener leaned close to point to one of the myriad wineglasses, confusingly arrayed before each place.

Anne's fingers touched the glass her partner had indicated. She turned toward Travener, raising her brows, obviously questioning the correctness of her choice. With his nod of agreement, she lifted the wine and brought it to her lips.

There was a surge of anxiety in Ian's chest. This wasn't something they had discussed. Anne was not a child and no longer a schoolgirl, of course, but he doubted she had had much experience with spirits. Not at Fenton School.

Anne's eyes met her partner's over the top of the goblet as her lips closed around its rim. Knowing her as he did, Ian believed the look to be perfectly innocent. Seeing her gaze into Travener's eyes with such a practiced gesture of flirtation, however, caused a flood of heat to scald its way through his body.

Jealousy, he recognized with a sense of shock. And as he continued to watch them, he examined that emotion with the same intellectual detachment he had brought to bear on all the others he had experienced since his return from Iberia.

What he had felt was not protectiveness, not as his concern about the wine had been. Nor was it fear that Anne might be flirting with the wrong man, one of the scoundrels from whom it would be his duty to guard her. What he had experienced as he watched Anne's eyes make contact with Travener's had been pure raw envy that he himself was not the recipient of that look.

His gaze fell, pretending to consider his fingers wrapped around the stem of his own wineglass. *Jealousy.* And that was almost as troubling as the wave of sexual desire which had roared through his body the night that Anne, kneeling in the snow beside him, had innocently pressed her body against his.

He could not afford either of those emotions. He could never allow himself to consider Anne in that light. And despite what he had told his sister-in-law, the reason had less to do with the fact that she was his ward and far more to do with the threat inherent in the souvenir of a Peninsula battle he carried within his chest. A threat he would not be living with now if it had not been for the actions of Anne's father.

My heart is not a stake in this game, he had said to Elizabeth. And it could never be, in spite of what he had felt watching Anne interact with a handsome and eligible bachelor. Something he would have to do for the next several months, Ian realized bitterly. At least until the day he stood beside her at the altar and gave her forever into the keeping of another man.

"But you didn't know Mr. Sinclair," Anne clarified, "other than by reputation?"

"I was in Portugal only a short time before my father died. I was forced to sell out and return to England."

"I'm very sorry to hear of your father's death. It must have been terrible to have received that news when you were so far from home," Anne said.

She tried to imagine what Doyle Travener might have felt. Her feelings about her own father's death were not a reliable guide, since they had never been close.

"I confess it was…unexpected. He had appeared to be in the best of health when I embarked."

Travener's voice caught on the last word, and his eyes fell to the handle of the knife his long, dark fingers were toying with. Her heart touched by his obvious grief, Anne unthinkingly laid her fingers over his, squeezing them slightly.

His eyes came up very quickly to meet hers. It was only then that she realized what she had just done might be misinterpreted, if not by Mr. Travener, then by others who had witnessed her gesture.

She removed her hand, fighting the very natural urge to look around to see if anyone had noticed. Her small faux pas was not really important, she told herself. Not in light of Mr. Travener's loss. She smiled into those beautiful blue eyes and was relieved when his quick smile answered hers.

"You are very kind, Miss Darlington," he said.

"It's obvious you were close to your father," she said. He, at least, understood what had prompted her unthinking gesture.

"Indeed we were. And I had missed him very much while I was away. That is my one regret, that I was away from him during his last months. Of course, with your father away in service, you must understand those feelings without being reminded of them. Do you miss your father a great deal?"

"My father is also dead, Mr. Travener. He died more than five months ago."

"Forgive me, Miss Darlington. When you asked about him before..."

"You thought he was still in Portugal."

"Forgive me," he said again, his eyes darkened with remorse. "I would never wish to cause you pain."

"There's nothing to forgive. Unlike you, I had not seen my father in several years. We were...not close," she said.

"But still..." He hesitated, and then his voice softened

as he added, "It seems we have a great deal in common. More than just our ages."

His gaze swept the table before it came back to her face. There was a decided gleam of amusement in the depths of his eyes. Very attractive eyes, Anne acknowledged with a touch of surprise. They were not hazel, of course, but they *were* attractive. And right now they were alive with mischief.

Her own eyes made the same quick appraisal of their table mates and then returned to his. Although she fought against revealing it, she suspected hers were equally alight with amusement. Because he was right, of course.

"There *is* my guardian," she said, her gaze finding Ian, who was seated beside their hostess at the other end of the table.

His head was tilted toward Lady Laud, who seemed to be regaling him with some lengthy anecdote. Anne had glanced at him several times before now and had found him always engaged in conversation, quite properly of course, with his hostess or another of the guests seated around him.

"I confess I was thinking of Major Sinclair as a contemporary of your father's. I take it he is not."

Anne's eyes came back to Travener, unconsciously examining his features. It was obvious that whatever time he had spent on the Peninsula, his experiences there had not marked him in the same way they had marked Ian.

"He seems older because of what he has endured," she said softly.

"He was severely wounded, I believe," Travener acknowledged. "I'm afraid I don't remember the details."

"And you will never hear them from him."

"You admire him a great deal."

She did, of course, but she hadn't realized she had

made her feelings so obvious. "I *owe* him a great deal," she said, her gaze again unconsciously finding her guardian. "I should not be here tonight if it were not for Mr. Sinclair."

"Indeed?" Travener asked, bringing her eyes back to him.

"No matter what Mr. Sinclair says, I don't believe my father made provision for my Season. I think the idea to bring me out was my guardian's, as were the funds expended to accomplish it."

It was only when she had voiced the last that she realized this was hardly a suitable topic of conversation with a gentleman. Not only was it none of Mr. Travener's business where the money for her Season had come from, it was highly improper of her to have brought it up in the first place.

"Forgive me," she said. "You can't possibly be interested in those arrangements. I'm still a trifle nervous about keeping up my end of any conversation. And I am deeply grateful to my guardian for his many kindnesses. I believe those two things led me to make confidences that would have been better not made."

"I was afraid that what I heard in your voice when you spoke of Major Sinclair might be…something more than gratitude."

"Afraid?" she questioned, a hint of coolness in her tone.

"You see, I was hoping for permission to call on you."

Despite Travener's attentiveness tonight, she was surprised. And she was also flattered, of course. In spite of Elizabeth and Ian's compliments, she had never expected to attract the attention of a handsome gentleman on her first outing. Actually, she had never expected to attract any gentleman's attention, but if someone like Doyle Travener could find her attractive...

Again her eyes sought her guardian. Ian was smiling at something the lady on his left was whispering to him behind her fan. Anne's gaze lingered there until Travener's next question brought her attention back to him.

"Do I *have* your permission, Miss Darlington?"

Permission to call on her. Did she want him to? Perhaps if Ian realized Mr. Travener was dancing attendance on her, he himself would begin to regard her less paternally. Another fantasy, she supposed, but still...

"I believe you must properly apply to my guardian for permission, Mr. Travener."

"But I may tell him that you, yourself, do not object?"

"If my guardian approves, I should be delighted to receive you."

"Then I suppose I must do my utmost to make myself acceptable to Major Sinclair," Travener said with a smile.

"Did you enjoy yourself?" Ian asked on the way home.

After a moment, Anne turned her head to look at him, seeming reluctant to pull her gaze from the darkened streets outside. She was smiling, however, and he thought that in the quality of that smile he could see the effects of the wine she had consumed. It was relaxed, perhaps even contemplative.

Had she been thinking about Doyle Travener as she gazed out the window? His flattering attentions throughout the evening could be cause for contemplation, Ian supposed. And cause enough to turn the head of someone as impressionable as Anne.

"Truthfully, far more than I had expected to," she

said. "Everyone was very kind. Did you enjoy your evening? It looked as if you were debating some very serious topics with Lady Laud."

Did that mean she had watched him? Ian wondered. As he had watched her? For some reason, all his self-strictures to the contrary, Ian felt a sense of satisfaction that she had.

"Not so, I assure you," he said. "One has an obligation not to bore one's dinner partner, after all. Lady Laud and I were usually discussing the next course and the possibilities it might offer for our enjoyment."

Anne laughed. "I wish you would tell Elizabeth that. She believes ladies must profess to have no interest in what they are served at parties and to display no appetite. Do you suppose we can send to the kitchens for something to eat when we get home?"

"We shall forage for it instead, if you like. I confess to being out of practice, but then Dare's kitchens are probably better stocked than the whole of Portugal."

She laughed again, and hearing her laughter, some part of the weight that had settled over Ian's heart when he had realized what a difficult task he had set for himself lifted.

"What about you and Mr. Travener?" he asked. For some reason, he didn't seem to be able to leave the topic alone, as painful as it would be to hear her opinion of another man. "Were the subjects you debated equally weighty?"

"Mr. Travener doesn't strike me as being given to weighty subjects," Anne said. "I heard all about his prime goers and his tailor. Some praise of and complaints about his valet's skills. Oh, and there was mention of a boot-blacking recipe. I should have written it down for you. My apologies."

"I have Dare's. It calls for champagne."

"How decadent. Do you use it?"

"No, but I'm sure Mr. Travener would," Ian said, laughing.

"He asked for permission to call on me."

Ian hadn't been expecting the request, but he should have been. And he supposed he should also become accustomed to the stab of jealousy it had engendered.

Anne was no longer smiling, her eyes on his face. In the darkness, he couldn't read what was in them.

"Did you give it to him?"

"I told him he must ask you. Wasn't that right?"

"Exactly what you should have done. It's one of my responsibilities. Of course, you should have some say in those decisions, provided the gentleman in question *is* a gentleman."

"How will you know whether they are or not?"

"English society is a very small, enclosed world. Everyone knows everyone else. Actually, half of us are related to the other half. The ones I don't know, Dare will. Or if he doesn't, someone of my acquaintance will."

"And if no one does?" she asked with a smile.

"That in itself would be strong grounds for suspicion that the person isn't who or what he claims to be."

"I see," Anne said, seeming to consider the information. "So will you give Mr. Travener permission to call?"

"Do you want me to?"

Ian waited for her answer with a sense of dread. And he knew this was only the first of what would be many such requests. He must find some way to reconcile his growing feelings for Anne Darlington with the reality of their situation.

"He's very good company," she said. "Especially after a glass of wine.'' The last was added with a gleam in her eyes.

''Enough wine, and anyone may seem good company. Do I take that as an affirmative?''

''Do you approve of him? You seem…evasive.''

''I know nothing to his detriment,'' Ian said carefully. ''The fact that Lady Laud invited him gives him credibility.''

''Then yes, I think I should like you to give him permission to call. *If* he does apply to you for it. He may simply have been being kind. I confessed to him how nervous I was.''

''I doubt Travener's attentions have much to do with kindness. You are a very beautiful woman, Anne. And especially beautiful tonight. Your honesty in confiding that you were nervous was undoubtedly intriguing. I shouldn't be *too* honest, however. The ton has rather strict standards of behavior. It won't do to be seen as being too daring or too different.''

''Unless you are *very* different,'' she said. ''Be eccentric to the extreme, and you may become the mode.''

''Generally you'll find those eccentrics have other advantages that overshadow their uniqueness, causing people to look beyond it.''

''I know. Birth and a great deal of money.''

''Elizabeth has taught you well.''

''She tried, but I think that much would be obvious, even if she hadn't. Some people can get away with things others would be ostracized for.''

''The trick is in knowing whether *you* can get away with them or not,'' he suggested, softening that truth with a smile.

''And I couldn't,'' she said flatly. ''At least your lectures are more subtle than Elizabeth's.''

"Contrary to what my brother will tell you, I never lecture."

"Your lessons, if you prefer. I have delivered enough of those, usually couched as yours in terms of suggestions, stories, or analogies, to recognize one when I hear it."

"Did you enjoy teaching?"

"I wasn't a teacher. Not yet, at any rate. I heard lessons and tutored the younger girls, and yes, I enjoyed it very much."

"And you miss it," he said, recognizing that from her voice.

Fenton School was a different world from the one she had entered under his guardianship. She had abruptly been taken away from everything she had ever known and then, in only a few short weeks, thrust into an alien and rather frightening environment.

And he had been the instrument of that change, even if Mrs. Kemp had been the instigator. He wondered if either of them had ever stopped to consider whether or not Anne really wanted to make that transition.

"I miss the girls," she said. "It seems I have a strongly maternal nature. I had thought…"

The words trailed. Although Ian waited, his eyes on her face, which was turned down as she watched her fingers worry the kid gloves she had removed, she didn't finish the sentence.

"I really would like to know," he said softly.

Her eyes came up, looking distant, even a little puzzled, as if she had forgotten what they'd been talking about.

"Your maternal nature," he prodded, smiling at her.

"I had thought I should have to satisfy it by caring for the poor, orphaned Sally Eddingtons of the world."

Although he didn't recognize the name, he understood the implication. Apparently Anne had once thought to devote her life to the girls at Fenton School, and now...

"And now?" he questioned aloud, realizing that he was dreading her response so much because he knew what it would be.

She hesitated, drawing a deep breath before she said, "I wonder if perhaps I won't."

Because she understood for the first time that she could have a husband and children of her own? That realization had no doubt come about because a very eligible gentleman had paid her a great deal of flattering attention. Suddenly Ian remembered Elizabeth's warning. *The first rogue who flirts with Anne is liable to turn her head and steal her heart.*

"Not if you find someone whom you wish to marry," he said. Thankfully, his voice didn't reveal his tangled emotions.

"And that *is,* after all, the purpose of all this," Anne said. "The marriage mart. That's what Elizabeth calls it. As if husbands and wives are bought and sold."

Which wasn't far from the truth. It wasn't so blatant as that, but most marriages within the ton had far more to do with settlements and suitability than with love. It was well and good for him and Elizabeth to be cynical enough to understand that. He wasn't sure that cynicism was appropriate for someone like Anne. Someone who was embarking on her first Season.

"It doesn't have to be that way," he said. "There are love matches within the ton. Elizabeth and Dare's is one. Not all marriages depend on negotiations and financial agreements."

"But most do," she said, holding his eyes.

Although it hadn't really been phrased as a question, he answered it. "Among our class, yes."

"Is that why *you* never married?"

Which made it sound as if she thought he had missed his chance. And he had, of course. For a few moments, in thinking about Anne's marriage, it seemed he had forgotten his reality.

"I never found a woman with whom I wished to spend the rest of my life."

The words echoed with painful irony in his head. That might have been true a month ago, but he knew it no longer was.

"Why not?" she asked.

"Because I was too busy doing other things, I suppose. University. The army."

He expected her to ask why he hadn't found someone in the time since he'd been home from Iberia. When she didn't, he realized, a little amused, that he had been right. She considered him long past falling in love.

"Do you regret that?" she asked instead.

"The army or that I never married?"

"Both, I suppose. They seem to go hand in hand."

And they did, far more than she could possibly know.

"I don't regret joining the army. The cause was just, and I felt an obligation to serve my country."

"No matter the cost," she said softly.

No matter the cost. Until the last few weeks, during which Anne Darlington had lived in his home, Ian had not regretted any aspect of his life. Not even that, except in a distant, almost academic way. Now, however—

"Ian?" she questioned.

He looked up again and into her eyes, knowing that even if he did have regrets, they had come far too late. Expressing them would do no more good than revealing any of the other things he had kept to himself all these months.

"I have nothing to regret," he said, and hoped he would be the only one who would ever know how great a lie that was.

Chapter Seven

"And so, I had hoped to be allowed to call on Miss Darlington, with your kind permission, of course." Doyle Travener let the sentence trail, and his blue eyes waited anxiously.

Ian had been unable to think of a single reason to refuse this request, although he had spent most of a relatively sleepless night trying to come up with one. As far as he could ascertain, other than the fact that Travener was both handsome and charming, there *was* no legitimate reason not to give him permission to court Anne. As much as he might like to turn down the ex-lieutenant's request on the grounds of his personal jealousy, he could not in all honor do so, especially since Anne seemed to enjoy Travener's company.

Ian would have to investigate his background and financial status, of course, especially if Anne seemed to be developing a tendre for him. The fact that his godmother had included him on her guest list, however, even if that had been done on the recommendation of a friend, went a long way in establishing Travener's credentials. No one within the ton would think of making such an endorsement to Lady Laud if he were not acceptable. It simply wasn't done.

"I shall speak to my ward," Ian said finally. "If she's agreeable—" There was a flash of relief in the blue eyes. "As I see you believe she will be," he continued, forcing his lips into a smile that felt stiff and unnatural.

"I'm immensely flattered that Miss Darlington has already indicated she would not be averse to my company."

"I'm sure she won't be then," Ian said.

After his and Anne's discussion on the way home from the dinner party, he *was* sure of that, damn it. *The first of many.* This, then, was the kind of purgatory he had opened himself up to by falling in love with his ward.

"I understand from Lady Laud that she will be Miss Darlington's chaperone during the Season. I should be delighted to offer my escort to the ladies on any occasion on which you find yourself unable to accompany them," Travener said gallantly. And then he spoiled it by adding, "Considering the sacrifices you have made on behalf of this nation, Major Sinclair, I feel that is the least I can do."

"You would consider your escort a form of duty, I take it," Ian said, his smile genuine this time.

He couldn't decide if what the young ex-lieutenant had just said was the most blatant flattery or a sincere expression of his patriotism. Perhaps the fact that Travener's own service had been cut short by family crisis had produced a sense of guilt.

Ian could understand if it had, considering his own guilt-ridden response when he had realized he'd survived that ghastly fiasco of Darlington's making, while so many of his friends had not. In his experience, survivors' guilt was a common phenomenon among soldiers.

"If so, sir, a very pleasant duty, I confess," Travener said, his mouth relaxing into an answering grin. "Actually, your ward confided that you had recently been quite unwell, so I thought you might welcome—"

Travener paused uncertainly. Unsure what his eyes had revealed, Ian fought to control the surge of rage that much more personal offer had engendered.

"What I meant to say is that if there is anything I can do to make all this easier for you—" Travener began again, obviously attempting—and failing—to fix his misstep.

"I quite understand what you *meant* to say, Lieutenant," Ian interrupted. Both the tone and the form of address were those he might have used to a subordinate who had crossed one of the invisible lines of military protocol.

"I meant no offense, sir," Travener said.

"And I took none," Ian lied. He knew that his reaction had far more to do with what he felt for Anne than it did with the awkwardly phrased words Doyle had just stammered.

"Then…I wonder if Miss Darlington is at home, and if I might see her," Travener said, wisely moving away from a topic that seemed fraught with danger. "I had hoped to secure your permission to take her for a ride. I have my carriage outside."

With, no doubt, his "prime goers" hitched to it and ready for a run, Ian thought, remembering Anne's mocking description of Doyle's conversation last night. She hadn't sounded as if she had found either it or the man to be fascinating. And Ian felt an unbecoming, if welcome, satisfaction.

"Even if she isn't free for a drive, I'm sure she would

enjoy seeing you again," Ian said. "I'll send for her. She told me that you were very kind to her."

He pushed up from his chair and crossed the room to the door, limping heavily. Last night had been more taxing than he had realized until he had tried to crawl out of bed this morning. Of course, his primary concern during the dinner party had been Anne and not the undeniable strain of that unaccustomed outing. It wasn't until today that he'd realized what a price he would pay for all the standing he had done last night.

After he had dispatched Dare's butler to ask Anne to join them, he turned and found Travener's eyes on him. Ian wondered if his guest had watched that journey to the door, and if so, whether he was about to be treated to more flattery or even worse, to more unwanted sympathy.

Luckily, however, this time Travener held his tongue about Ian's "sacrifices." They spent a few minutes conversing in idle pleasantries about Lady Laud's party before Anne opened the door.

Her morning gown was the color of the sea where the waters are deep and cold. That muted shade of gray-green set off the pale porcelain of her skin and seemed to soften the red in her curls, which had been dressed very simply today.

"Mr. Travener," she said, with a note of what appeared to be genuine delight in her voice. "How very kind of you to call."

Doyle jumped up from his chair and met her halfway across the room. He eagerly took her outstretched hand, bringing it almost to his lips.

"I told you that I should," he said. "*If* your guardian gave me permission. As he very graciously has, I'm pleased to say."

"Indeed you did tell me. Has Mr. Sinclair been sharing boot-blacking recipes with you?" Anne asked. "He has a very good one from his brother, I understand. I told him you might be interested in acquiring it."

When Anne's eyes touched on Ian's, he realized they were sparkling with amusement. It was exactly as if the two of them shared a private joke—a joke at earnest Mr. Travener's expense.

There was no doubt Anne's teasing was deliberate. And no doubt Travener was aware he was being teased, Ian realized, watching the slow rise of pink above Travener's stiff white collar.

"We haven't become quite that well acquainted yet," Ian said, feeling a brief sympathy for Anne's gentleman caller.

She held his eyes for a fraction of a second before she turned back to give Travener a friendly smile, her natural kindness destroying any isolation he might feel. She gently freed her fingers from his grasp, however, and the blush spread upward into the visitor's cheeks.

"Mr. Travener has his carriage outside," Ian said. "I believe he would like to take you for a drive."

"The grays?" Anne asked.

"You remembered," Travener said happily.

"Of course," she said. "I remember everything you told me."

"Then…"

"With your permission," Anne said, looking at Ian.

He wanted to say no. Actually, he had been hoping Anne would say it for him. And yet there was no reason why she should. This was why he had brought her to London—so that she could meet someone exactly like Doyle Travener.

This was part of the responsibility he had accepted

when he had agreed to be her guardian. He had known that intellectually, of course, but it did not make the reality of sending Anne off on someone else's arm easier to bear.

"Of course," he said.

She smiled at him before she turned her gaze back to her visitor. "I'm afraid it must be a short drive, Mr. Travener. I'm accompanying Lady Laud to a musicale later this afternoon."

"I shall be grateful for whatever time you can spare."

"I'll get my wrap," Anne said. "Perhaps you can convince Mr. Sinclair to accompany us. A quick turn about the park in this glorious sunshine would do us all good."

Ian could imagine Travener's inward response to that suggestion. Whatever Doyle felt about Anne's invitation, however, he hid it well as he quickly turned to Ian and added his second. He even managed to make it sound sincere.

"We should be honored if you would accompany us, sir."

"Not today, thank you," Ian said.

Despite what he had told Elizabeth, he didn't really intend to play *duenna* on Anne's outings. He wasn't perfectly certain he was up to the challenge.

"Perhaps you'll join us one day when you are feeling more the thing," Travener said, his relief almost palpable. "I shall wait for you in the hall, Miss Darlington. I want to step out and make sure my tiger is walking the horses. Major Sinclair," he said, bowing slightly.

"I think since it has been so very long since I *was* Major Sinclair," Ian said, "we might do better without the title."

Whatever Travener's intent, the phrase "when you are feeling more the thing" had grated.

"Of course," Travener said. "Using your title was simply a sign of my respect, sir, I assure you, but if you prefer…"

Ian inclined his head, his mouth tight with suppressed anger. Travener turned, cupping his hand possessively under Anne's elbow. Her eyes met Ian's briefly before she allowed herself to be led out of the room.

Ian waited until the door of Dare's library, which he had commandeered as his own retreat when they had first come to London, had closed behind them. Then he eased down in his chair again, stretching out his aching leg and mentally reviewing every word of the conversation.

Anne had seemed just as she always did. She had treated Travener as a friend rather than a potential suitor. And if it hadn't been for the look she had exchanged with him last night as she drank the wine he'd selected, Ian might have been able to put the handsome ex-soldier out of his mind.

Whatever had been in Anne's eyes when she had looked over the rim of her glass seemed burned into his consciousness, however. And it was still painfully there, as he listened to Dare's butler greet Anne on her return from the ride, something Ian had waited impatiently to hear for more than two hours.

"Ian?" Anne whispered.

She had come back to the library after she had changed to tell him she was leaving for Lady Laud's. She knew that she was cutting the time very close, and she feared Ian's godmother might never forgive her if she were late. She had not, however, been able to resist the impulse to look in on her guardian.

When she had opened the door, she had found Ian in his chair, his head against the back, his eyes closed. She had hovered on the threshold a moment, wondering if she should disturb him or let him sleep. And then, compelled by the same feelings that had caused her to spend too many hours last night thinking about children who would have hazel eyes and kind smiles, she tiptoed across the room to stand looking down on him.

The light from the tall windows highlighted his features. Robbed of their normal animation, they were far more revealing than they had been this morning. *He looks exhausted,* she thought.

Unbidden, there appeared in her mind's eyes the image of Doyle Travener's virile, sun-darkened features. Unconsciously, she contrasted them to these, which were no less handsome, but underlain by both pain and now fatigue. She fought the urge to put the tips of her fingers against Ian's forehead, to soothe away the strain that even sleep could not erase.

Her eyes still on his face, she stooped beside his chair and put her gloved hand on his, which lay relaxed on the arm. His eyes opened slowly to focus on her face, which was now level with his. His long fingers closed tightly around hers. Responding to that pressure, and almost without her conscious direction, her hand caught his, bringing it up so that she could press her lips against the back of it.

The hazel eyes widened. They were more aware now. And she knew with a painful catch of her heart that if Ian had been fully awake when he'd opened his eyes, he would never have touched her hand like that. He eased his fingers from hers.

"Is something wrong?" he asked, his brow furrowed.

"I'm leaving for Lady Laud's. I looked in on my way out and found you asleep. You looked almost *too* peaceful," she said.

She smiled at him, forcing back the surge of emotion she had felt at seeing his vulnerability exposed. A vulnerability he would never have wanted to reveal. Not to her. Not to anyone.

"So I thought, of course, that I would disturb you," she finished, deliberately injecting humor into her voice, which had thickened with the constriction of her throat.

"No rest for the wicked," he said, returning her smile.

"That's no rest for the weary, I think," she corrected, her own brow wrinkled as she tried to remember the correct phrasing.

"How was your drive?"

"Pleasant enough," she said.

She used the arm of his chair to push herself to her feet. The fact that Ian had been forced to pull his fingers away from hers was embarrassment enough. To continue to kneel at his feet could only add to it.

"It could only have been enhanced by a glass of wine," she added, smiling down at him.

His eyes had followed her rise, and at the smile, his mouth relaxed. "I should imagine the same might be said of Italian sopranos."

"I beg your pardon?"

"I understood from my godmother that was to be the afternoon's entertainment."

"Good grief," Anne said faintly, "and to think I gave up wiping Sally Eddington's nose for this."

She smiled at him again, hoping that if they bandied enough nonsense, he would forget the revealing caress of her lips against his fingers. Romantic *and* impulsive, she chided herself. And when you have fallen madly in love with a man who considers you little more than a child and nothing but a responsibility, that could indeed prove a humiliating combination. As it had this afternoon.

"If I don't leave now," she said, "I may miss part of the performance. Are you sure you can't think of some reason to delay me?"

"Have a good time," her guardian said uncooperatively.

"You really have the best of it, you know," she said, looking around the library as she pretended to straighten her sleeve. "What could be better than a pleasant fire and a good book?" Her eyes touched on the leather-bound volume on the table beside him.

"Ah, but *you*..." Ian said straight-faced. "You shall have Mr. Travener *and* the soprano."

"You surely don't think Mr. Travener will be there, too, do you?" she asked, trying to indicate her dismay over that possibility. "He doesn't strike me as being musically inclined."

"Simply opportunistic," Ian said. "I suspect Mr. Travener will begin to appear at whatever occasion you frequent. My godmother likes him. And he's personable enough that he won't have any difficulty procuring invitations to all manner of events. After all, a single man is always a welcome addition."

"The marriage mart," she said, her eyes holding his. "I had forgotten."

Someone to fight my battles for me. And she knew, with more certainty than she had ever felt before, that the only man she would want in that role was the one man in all of London who would probably never consider himself for it.

Not by word or deed had Ian Sinclair ever indicated she was anything to him other than a responsibility. Nor had he indicated that he wanted her to be more. He had certainly not courted her, and it was only now, considering the face before her, forever marked by experiences she could only imagine, that she thought she knew why.

Even if Ian Sinclair found her attractive, he would never reveal that attraction. She was his ward. And as foolish as it seemed to her, he truly believed she should be happier paired with someone as shallow as Doyle Travener.

She had promised Mrs. Kemp that she would be guided by Mr. Sinclair's wisdom. She hadn't promised, however, that when Mr. Sinclair was being so patently foolish, she wouldn't attempt to change his mind.

"I must confess," she said, gathering her courage, "that I should much prefer to spend the afternoon here with you."

His eyes reacted, the dark pupils expanding a little into the rim of color. He said nothing for a heartbeat, and then he smiled. It was the same annoyingly avuncular one he had once bestowed on Margaret Rhodes.

"Only think how disappointed Mr. Travener should be by your non-appearance. Not to mention Lady Laud."

"I doubt either of them would give a fig," she said.

"But Elizabeth should," Ian reminded her. "After all, she has worked very hard to make you a success."

"A success so that I can make a good marriage," she said. "Or is that 'good' marriage in and of itself the success she has worked for?" The edge of bitterness in the words seemed obvious, but Ian's eyes didn't change.

"Of course," he said.

"And what if my idea of a 'good' marriage, a successful marriage, is very different from that which the ton holds?"

"No one will ever force you to marry someone you don't love and want to spend the rest of your life with,"

Ian said. "All Elizabeth and I are trying to do is provide an opportunity for you to meet that man."

And if I have already met him? The words were on the tip of her tongue, and yet she hesitated to voice them. And into the small pause, came the sound of Elizabeth's voice.

"I thought you had gone," the Countess of Dare said.

Anne turned her head and found Elizabeth standing in the doorway. She held a book in her hand, and her questioning eyes moved from Anne's face to her brother-in-law's.

"Am I interrupting?" she asked, her voice puzzled.

"Nothing more serious than a discussion of Anne's newest suitor," Ian said. He sounded slightly relieved at Elizabeth's intervention. "I was telling her that she can probably count on him dancing attendance at whatever events she chooses to attend."

"Well, you shall miss him this afternoon, if you don't hurry," Elizabeth said. "I don't think Lady Laud will like to be kept waiting."

Rebellion flared briefly in Anne's breast. After all, she really *would* rather spend the afternoon here.

She tamped it down, however. Remembering all that these two people had done for her, she knew she couldn't now refuse to follow through. She had been brought to London expressly for entertainments such as this. And she had allowed her guardian to spend an enormous amount of what she now believed to be his own money on her coming out. It would be the height of ingratitude to refuse to go through with it now.

"Of course," she said aloud. "How thoughtless of me. I shall see you both at dinner, I hope."

She glanced again at Ian, but she could tell nothing from his face. His eyes were still fastened on Elizabeth.

And the countess did make a very compelling picture, Anne acknowledged. Coolly elegant and always serene, she was exactly the kind of well-read and intelligent woman who would appeal to Ian Sinclair. Just as she had obviously appealed to his brother.

How did she think she might compete with women like this for Ian Sinclair's interest? Anne wondered.

"Of course," Elizabeth said, seeming surprised by the question. "And now I really must insist, Anne."

She stepped into the room, clearing the passageway for Anne and giving her no choice but to go through it. As she crossed the hall outside, Anne could hear the countess's voice from the library behind her.

"I thank you for your recommendation of the Voltaire, my dear," she was saying to her brother-in-law. "If you have time, I should love to discuss some of his views with you."

"I have nothing but time, Lizzie, as you well know, and there is nothing I should enjoy more than a matching of wits with my erudite sister."

"You make me sound like a bluestocking," Elizabeth said, laughing.

By that time, Dare's butler was holding the front door open for Anne. Heartily regretting that she was not allowed to at least sit and listen as the two of them talked about something far more substantial and interesting than boot-blacking recipes and blood stock, Anne Darlington stepped outside as reluctantly as if the fate that awaited her was far more dire than Mr. Travener and an Italian soprano. At that moment she truly couldn't imagine any fate that might be worse.

"Anne, I should like to introduce you to my brother, the Earl of Dare," Ian said.

Apparently he was becoming proficient at lying because there was nothing about this introduction he liked. He had been dreading it since his brother had made known his feelings about "Darlington's chit." It was not that Ian didn't share Dare's disdain for George Darlington, but in the weeks he had known Anne he had found nothing of the father reflected in his daughter.

"Val, may I present my ward, Anne Darlington."

He held Dare's eyes as he said it, warning him to guard his tongue. Surprisingly, the earl seemed amused as he returned that brotherly look. When his gaze finally focused on the woman standing before him, Dare made a rather pointed assessment of her before he even acknowledged the introduction.

"Miss Darlington," he said. Dare's voice, thankfully, betrayed none of the contempt he had previously expressed.

"My Lord Dare," Anne said, dropping a graceful curtsy and holding out her hand.

"Bravo," Elizabeth said.

Dare's gaze lifted to his wife's face. "A test, I presume. Should I be honored or insulted to be its subject?"

"I was complimenting Anne on handling the introduction so beautifully," Elizabeth said. "It's a shame, my dear, that *your* manners are not so polished."

"Indeed," Dare said, with a small bow in her direction before he turned back to Anne. "I'm charmed, Miss Darlington," he said with an obvious vein of sarcasm.

"The pleasure is all mine, my lord," Anne said, her dark eyes as mocking the earl's. And then she added, "I am sure from your demeanor that it *must* be."

There was a small silence.

"Your kitten has claws," Dare said.

"Be glad you aren't a highwayman," Ian said.

Silently he applauded Anne's refusal to be intimidated by the earl. And if there was anything designed to win Dare's approval, it was a quick wit and someone brave enough to challenge him at his own game.

"You almost make me wish I had been there that night," the earl responded.

"No, I assure you, you do not," Anne said. "I've never spent a more terrifying few minutes."

"I understand from my brother that you saved his life."

"Your understanding is flawed, my lord. Quite the reverse, as a matter of fact. Mr. Sinclair saved mine."

"Since you have been thrust together by the terms of your father's will, I suppose it's only to the good that the two of you are so mutually admiring. But it does makes it difficult for an outsider to ascertain the truth of what happened."

"The truth is that your brother came to my rescue at a cost to himself of which you are very well aware," she said softly.

"Indeed I am aware of it. I wasn't sure that *you* were."

"Believe me, my lord, I am very cognizant of the debt I owe my guardian. My understanding is *not* flawed."

"Are you always so forthright, Miss Darlington?"

"I hope so, my lord," Anne said pleasantly. The glint in her eyes left no doubt that she knew she was being goaded and was determined to give as good as she got.

"Then I'm afraid I have come on a fool's errand," Dare said.

"I am sorry for it if you have," she replied, sounding almost sincere. "With the recent rains, the roads must be a nightmare. What *was* the errand that brought you to London, Lord Dare? Simply to remind me of what I owe my guardian?"

"I had intended to retrieve my missing wife," Dare said.

"Then perhaps *I* should be the one to ask why that is a 'fool's errand.'" Elizabeth said.

"I understood that you were here to prepare Miss Darlington for her entry into society. I had thought that by now that instruction must be complete. I see I was mistaken."

"That's quite enough, Val," Ian ordered, imbuing his voice with an amusement he didn't feel. "Forgive my brother's manners, Anne. Perhaps we can persuade Elizabeth to undertake *his* training in the social graces."

"She has been attempting that since our marriage," the earl said. "I take it you consider that she has failed."

"Perhaps with you, but believe me, Elizabeth's work *here* has been quite successful. The proof stands before you."

Ian had left instructions with Dare's major domo that he should usher Anne into the library as soon as she returned from the afternoon's musicale. She was still wearing the pale blue gown she had chosen for that.

It was a shade that both accentuated and complemented her coloring. Since the dress had been fashioned in the latest style and cut by the master hand of the modiste whom Dare himself had recommended, Ian believed his brother would be hard-pressed to find fault with Anne's appearance.

And despite her willingness to match the earl barb for barb, there had really been nothing about her manners that his brother might legitimately criticize. Anne had held her own without becoming rattled by Dare's obvious attempt to intimidate her.

The earl's eyes remained on Ian's face a long time before he turned back to Anne. The corners of his mobile mouth had moved into a smile, and he gave her the same small half-bow he had just made to his wife.

"My compliments to you all," he said. "Miss Darlington is indeed a diamond of the first water."

"I may forgive you after all," Elizabeth said. "Anne, would you help me pack?"

"Of course," Anne said, smiling at her. "I hope I shall see you again before you leave, my lord."

"Do you? Perhaps you truly *are* a paragon. Please forgive me if I've offended you, Miss Darlington. I confess to being overprotective of my brothers. I only have the two, you know, and both are prone to reckless acts of valor. It's very wearing on the nerves."

"I should never have thought that a nervous disposition was an affliction from which *you* would suffer, my lord. Although I quite understand your concern," Anne said.

For the first time since she had entered the room, she allowed her eyes to rest on Ian's face. And at what was in them, his pulse accelerated. There was no physical contact this time to explain the sudden rush of blood into his groin. Aware of the potentially embarrassing consequences of his reaction, he pulled his gaze away, focusing it on his sister-in-law's face instead.

At the same time, he commanded his mind to concentrate on something else. Anything else. Anything other than what he had just seen in the eyes of his ward.

"We shall miss you," he said, smiling at Elizabeth.

"It has been my pleasure to be of service in this cause, but I truly think my work is done. Anyone who can successfully exchange sallies with Dare is ready to take on the ton. Anne?" Elizabeth said, reminding her of the task that awaited them.

When the two of them had left the room, Ian could no

longer avoid Dare's eyes. And the earl, of course, wasted no time in commenting on what had just happened.

"You're quite right. She *does* have speaking eyes."

Despite himself, Ian laughed. "Anne seems to have taken you into dislike. Do you suppose it could have been because of your rather obvious baiting of her?"

"I wasn't talking about that," Dare said.

Ian should have known that his brother was too astute to have missed the look Anne had just given him. Or his reaction to it. He sincerely wished Dare were not so astute, but his brother had always been able to read him like an open book.

"Gratitude," Ian said tightly.

"I wasn't talking about that either," the earl said.

The blue eyes fell to examine the fit of the skin-tight pantaloons his brother was wearing. Ian could feel a different rush of blood, this one staining his face and neck.

"I can't ever remember seeing you blush," Dare said. "Surely you are a little old for such…schoolboy antics."

"Go to hell," Ian said softly, watching his brother's lips move into the familiar mocking smile. It was not one he usually employed *en famille*, and never, that Ian could remember, to him.

"I thought you were very quick to champion your ward when last we talked. At the time, I put it down to the effects of fever. I see now that your knight errantry has progressed in a rather…interesting direction."

"Let it go, Val," Ian warned, his voice cold and hard.

At the tone, the earl's head tilted. "If you're worried about what I said before, don't be. If Darlington's daughter is the woman you want, I'll make no objection. You know what they say about those who are happily married."

"That they can't resist meddling in things that are none of their concern?"

Ian had never intended for anyone to know how he felt about Anne, but of all the people he would wish to keep this particular secret from, his brother was first on the list. Dare would see through any excuse he might make, and unlike Elizabeth, he was well aware Ian had not previously lost his heart to any woman.

"I think I may claim to have a legitimate concern for your happiness," Dare said, his voice no longer mocking.

"Then I pray you will not bring this subject up again."

"There's no bar to your courtship of Anne Darlington. The fact that she is your ward may cause talk, but I can give you my personal assurance that no matter the gossip you must endure, the rewards of having the woman you love are well worth the cost."

"You are mistaken in what you think I feel, Val. You can be mistaken, you know."

"Mistaken in thinking you are enamored of the chit? Or in saying there is no bar to your pursuing that attraction?"

"Anne is my ward. That's all she is. And that is all she will ever be," Ian said, each word distinct.

His brother said nothing for a long moment, his eyes resting on his face. Ian was determined that his features would not reveal anything except the surety with which he had made that statement.

"Would you like to tell me why?" Dare said finally.

"Not particularly," Ian said.

"I see."

"Leave it, Val," Ian said again, his voice very soft. "There is nothing to be gained by pursuing this topic."

"Six months ago I might have believed this refusal to admit what was in that girl's eyes when she looks at you and what occurred when you saw that look had something to do with the extent of your injuries.''

"Now, however, you know it does not," Ian said, his voice as controlled as his features.

"There are perhaps some lingering effects to your health, but nothing, surely, that should be any hindrance—"

"The hindrance is in my will," Ian said. "That is all you need to know."

And when he spoke again, all mockery had been wiped from Dare's voice. "Forgive me," he said. "You are right. What you choose to do in this matter really is none of my concern."

"I must apologize for my husband," Elizabeth said as they climbed the stairs together. "He *is* overprotective when it comes to his brothers. Especially Ian, who has been through so much."

"Why do I have the feeling you are trying to tell me something?" Anne said, smiling at her friend.

"I am, I suppose. Something I know Ian himself will never tell you. And yet something I believe you need to know."

"About Ian's injuries."

"About their effect, perhaps."

"I don't understand."

"I thought I should warn you."

"Elizabeth—"

"Let me finish, please. I need to say this before I leave. The last lesson I must teach you, if you will. And perhaps the most important one."

They had reached the first landing. Elizabeth turned and held out her hands. Unquestioningly, Anne placed hers within them. "You're frightening me," she said truthfully.

"I don't mean to. And I don't know how deeply your emotions are involved, of course. I do know, because I am not a fool, that your feelings for my brother-in-law are not simply those a young girl might quite rightfully feel for her guardian. Not *just* gratitude and respect. Or am I wrong?"

Anne wondered what Elizabeth would do if she denied what she felt. If she did, however, she might never find out what Ian's sister-in-law thought she ought to be told.

"I should very much like to know what I have done to give myself away," she said.

Elizabeth smiled at her. And then she freed her right hand and touched Anne's cheek. *Offering comfort?*

"Nothing so much. I saw the way you looked at him this afternoon. I have seen that same look in your eyes a dozen times in the last few weeks. Having recently been in love with a man I was sure I could never have, perhaps I am more sensitive to those feelings than someone else might be."

"I'm not—" Anne began, but in the face of the kind understanding in the countess's blue eyes, she didn't continue.

"Ian is a man who is worthy of your love. I was afraid that because of your inexperience you would fall in love with someone who *wasn't* worthy and have your heart broken. And instead…"

Anne didn't question the hesitation, but a small knot of fear closed her throat. It was obvious Elizabeth could have no objection to Ian's character. She could have no doubt, just as Anne had none, that he would always protect his own.

''I never worried that *his* heart might be engaged,'' Elizabeth finished softly.

At first, the words caused a small surge of excitement. It was not until she had coupled them with the pity in the countess's eyes that she understood what they meant.

''Ian's in love with someone else,'' Anne breathed.

She searched her memory for anything, any word that had passed between them, that might have warned her. And despite her question as to why he had never married, there had been nothing. Not one thing. So perhaps…

''I have wondered how to tell you,'' Elizabeth said. ''Or if I even should.''

''I wish you had told me before,'' Anne said, fearing now that Ian, like Elizabeth, suspected how she felt.

''You are very young,'' Elizabeth said softly.

''Don't,'' Anne said. ''I don't believe age has anything to do with what I feel.''

''I know you don't, but perhaps in time—''

''Did she reject him?'' Anne broke in.

''I don't know. Like you, I can't imagine that anyone could, but people very often love where their feelings aren't returned. And it is always possible, Anne, that that was *his* choice.''

''His choice?'' Anne repeated.

''Perhaps until Ian is completely recovered he feels as if he can't offer for any woman.''

''If his injuries matter to her, then she truly doesn't deserve him,'' Anne said.

''Would you ever believe anyone else deserved him?''

''If she loved him, nothing would matter,'' Anne said stubbornly, perhaps because she could not yet deal with the hard reality of what Elizabeth was saying.

''Knowing the Sinclair men as I do now, I have realized that there are some things which will always matter to *them*.''

"You believe he never told her how he felt?"

Elizabeth shrugged. "I don't suppose we will ever know what happened between them. Ian, of course, will never tell anyone. Whatever the reason, I thought it only fair that you should know that Ian is not free to return your affection. As much as he might value it."

"I've been a fool," Anne said softly. "A fool to think that he could ever—"

"No," Elizabeth denied, pulling her close and putting her arms around her. "It's never foolish to love a man worthy of your devotion. It's only foolish if it's the other kind. And it may be that some day Ian will open his eyes and realize how lucky he would be to have your love. However…"

However. They both knew that the feelings she had sheltered so carefully in her heart were far more likely to wither and die unacknowledged, like a shaded flower that is never allowed to feel the warmth of the nourishing sun.

"Thank you for telling me," Anne said. "Thank you for everything."

She hugged the Countess of Dare tightly, and her eyes filled with tears as Elizabeth fiercely reciprocated her show of affection. Then Anne freed herself from that perfumed embrace and turned away quickly before Elizabeth could see her face.

She would do her grieving in private. If her foolishly romantic heart was breaking, it was her own fault. Ian had never led her to believe she was anything to him but his ward. Or that he had any desire that she would ever become anything else.

That had been her stupidity. Her mistake. Another necessary lesson perhaps, and no one except Elizabeth would ever be allowed to know what a very painful one it had been. If Ian Sinclair could hide his broken heart so well that she had never even suspected, then so, Anne decided, could she.

Chapter Eight

"Elizabeth asked me to remind you that you have a fitting today," Ian said. "I suppose that in the rush of packing she forgot to mention it to you last night."

A fitting for her ball gown, and without his reminder, Anne knew she would never have remembered that appointment. There had been too many other things to think about.

She had not gone downstairs again after she had said goodbye to Elizabeth. And she had spent most of last night and this morning with the conversations of the previous evening running endlessly through her mind. To the exclusion of almost any other thought.

"A fitting for my ball gown," she said, willing herself to look up. "I *had* forgotten."

Ian was standing in the doorway, his wide shoulders nearly filling it. He was dressed in a jacket of navy superfine and fawn pantaloons. The sunlight glinted off the highly polished leather of his boots and added highlights to the chestnut hair.

And despite what Elizabeth had told her, seeing him there produced again that peculiar hesitation in the normal rhythm of her heart. She forced her eyes away, afraid of what he might see within them, and focused once more on the letter she had been writing to Mrs. Kemp.

He seemed less tired, she thought, superimposing his features over the girlishly rounded script she was pretending to peruse. At least his face was not so strained as it had been when she had found him asleep in his chair yesterday afternoon.

She hoped that was because *he* had no cause to toss and turn last night. She prayed that whatever had given her secret away to Elizabeth had not been obvious to her guardian because she knew Ian would be troubled by her infatuation.

However, since she had acknowledged the depth of her feelings—which were much more than an infatuation, of course—it somehow seemed harder to ignore them. And more difficult to put him from her mind. Her eyes seemed drawn to him whenever they were in the same room.

"Would you like me to accompany you?" Ian asked. "Since Elizabeth isn't here. She seemed concerned that someone should give final approval of the dress."

"And she didn't trust *me* to do that," Anne said, her eyes still resolutely on her letter.

They treat me like a child, she thought. Of course, they had from the beginning, and nothing was likely to change.

She took a breath, fighting that silly resentment. Because she *was* a child, certainly in terms of experience. If she compared what she knew about life with what Ian and Elizabeth had been forced to learn, she supposed she would have a hard time arguing she wasn't.

"I'm sure that isn't what she meant to imply," Ian said.

"Then what did she mean?" Anne asked.

She finally lifted her eyes to his again and was surprised to see something within them that she had never seen there. Before she could begin to identify the emotion, however, it was gone. Controlled. Or destroyed.

Had Elizabeth betrayed her? she wondered with a stab of anxiety. And then she reassured herself that the countess would never have broken her confidence. Whatever change had been wrought in her relationship with her guardian would have to be laid at her own door, quite possibly because she had so foolishly decided yesterday that she had only to let him know what she felt, and then she had believed he would...

Would what? she wondered. She wasn't sure what she had expected to happen when she had made that decision. In any case, in light of Elizabeth's revelation, it didn't matter now.

"I'm sure she meant nothing more than a reminder of how difficult it is to assess an ensemble given the limitations of a cheval glass. It's much better to have the opinion of someone who can objectively observe the full effect."

Objectively observe. Which certainly seemed clear enough.

"And that is what you propose to do?" she asked.

"Unless you have some objection."

"Why should I? You have the right to oversee your investment."

His head tilted, as if he were considering her tone. "You believe I'm concerned about my...investment?"

"I mean no disrespect, I assure you, but you *have* invested heavily in the success of my Season. It's only natural that you should be concerned with the effect of what you've spent."

There was a small silence, and then Ian said, "If you don't want me to accompany you, Anne, a simple no will suffice. I assure you my offer was not prompted by a desire to make sure I'm getting my money's worth.''

For the first time since she had known him, there was an edge of coldness in Ian Sinclair's voice. And it hurt her to hear it there, although she had deliberately driven this wedge between them. It might be safer for her heart to have it in place, but it was also incredibly painful.

Besides, she knew she had been unfair. Childish. Ungrateful. *And foolishly in love.*

''I should be very glad for your company,'' she said.

The words sounded stilted and a little ungracious to her ears, but the corners of Ian's mouth lifted in response. It was this same smile that had attracted her on the day she met him.

''You're missing Elizabeth,'' he guessed. ''I should have asked her to stay, at least until you have a few more outings to your credit. I must confess, however, that when she told me about the baby—''

He broke off as Anne's mouth fell open to accommodate the quick intake of breath his unexpected announcement had required. ''You didn't know,'' he said softly.

She shook her head, feeling for some reason as if she had been betrayed. Elizabeth was her friend. And she would have expected her to have joyfully shared this news. That she hadn't made Anne feel even more like an outsider.

''Perhaps she thought you already knew,'' Ian said, obviously trying to rectify the countess's omission.

And there had been a dozen small clues, now that she thought about it. Telltale signs Anne had never put together because she had been too concerned with her own dilemma.

''I didn't,'' she confessed, feeling childish again.

"I thought it safer to send Elizabeth home before…" Ian hesitated, forbidden by the dictates of their society from discussing these matters with an unmarried female.

"Before she increases," Anne said evenly.

He fought the upward tilt of his lips, eventually winning the battle, but not before she was aware of his amusement.

"It seemed best," he said.

"I am very glad for them," Anne said, realizing belatedly that she was. She loved children, and she couldn't imagine that someone as kind as Elizabeth wouldn't also. As for Dare… Of course, Elizabeth was very obviously in love with the earl, so perhaps she was judging him too harshly.

"But you are also disappointed that she didn't confide in you," Ian said.

"A little," she confessed, smiling at him for the first time. She had always been able to count on Ian's understanding and sympathy. Those were important assets in a friend. And if that was all he was ever to be to her, then she should cherish them even more. "And that's foolish, I know. I am not family, after all."

"I think she wanted to tell her husband before she told anyone else. If she had sent for Dare herself, he would have suspected something, so the message that brought him was mine. And when Elizabeth asked you to help her pack last night, I thought she was making an opportunity to tell you her news."

It was possible she had been, Anne realized. And then perhaps she had decided, as a friend, that there was something more important to tell Anne in the few minutes they would have alone. Something vital to Anne's well-being. And after the countess had performed that final act of kindness, Anne had run away. There had been no chance for Elizabeth to share the news about the baby.

"I shall write to her and tell her how happy I am for them," Anne said. "Perhaps one day she'll need a governess and remember me," she added with another smile, this one almost teasing.

Ian laughed, seeming relieved that whatever had colored the atmosphere when he had entered the room was no longer between them. And in all honesty, so was she.

Even if she were destined to carry an unrequited love for Ian Sinclair the rest of her days, she fervently hoped that he would never be aware of it. And unless she could pretend that nothing had changed in their relationship, he would be.

"I would welcome your opinion of the ball gown," she said. "If you are sure you won't find such an errand a dead bore."

"Italian sopranos are a dead bore. The beautiful Miss Darlington, attired in a new gown, will be a delight."

"You should give Mr. Travener lessons. His turn of phrase is not nearly so pretty as that."

"Fewer mustached Portuguese grandmothers to charm in his background, I suspect. He doesn't have the practice I've had. I shall see you at three."

He turned and disappeared from the doorway, and suddenly the morning parlor seemed very empty. Anne picked up her pen again, dipping the point into the ink and carefully wiping off the excess. And then her hand hesitated before she applied it to the paper.

After a moment, she laid the pen back on the desk and picked up the letter she had begun. In it she had begged her former headmistress to write to her guardian and request that Anne be allowed to return to Fenton School.

She held it before her, reading the despairing phrases.

Then she rose and carried the letter to the fire. Bending, she slipped it into the flames, watching the paper smoke and curl and finally blacken, obliterating her words.

When they were all gone, she stood, laying her forehead tiredly against the mantel a moment before she turned to survey the sunlit room. She would spend the rest of her life at Fenton Hall and only a few short weeks in the company of the man she loved. And she had found that, despite the outcome, she was unwilling to give up even a single day of them.

Impulsive, romantic, and very, very foolish.

The ball gown had exceeded even her fantasies. Ian, despite his vaunted experience with Portuguese grandmothers, seemed to have been rendered momentarily speechless. By the dress or by the sight of her in it? she wondered. In either case, his admiration was very satisfying and had been salve for her battered heart.

She had preceded him to the door of the shop after they were done with the fitting. When she reached it, she realized that Ian had not followed her, but was still engaged with the modiste. Making arrangement for payment, she supposed, or for having the dress delivered.

The air in the shop was heated and close, almost oppressive. Without thinking too much about the propriety of her action, she opened the door and stepped through it into the street without waiting for her guardian's escort.

The coachman had been instructed to walk the horses while they were inside, and there was no sign of the earl's carriage. She leaned forward to peer along the street in the opposite direction and became aware that something unusual was occurring a little farther along the sidewalk.

There was enough commotion that a crowd had gathered to watch. Judging by their clothing, Anne realized that the people, mostly men, who made up that knot of spectators were not patrons of the neighboring shops. Actually, they appeared to be more like the roughs who frequented the area of London near the wharves than shoppers for this exclusive district.

Anne looked up and down the street again, searching for the reassuring sight of the approaching coach. There was nothing there. Actually, there was very little traffic at all.

She turned, glancing through the glass of the shop's door behind her. Ian and the dressmaker were still conversing. Her guardian didn't even seem to be aware that she had stepped outside.

Just as she had decided that doing so had not been a very wise decision, she heard the scream of a child. High-pitched and distinct, given her background, the cry left no doubt in Anne's mind about her identification of its source.

She looked in the direction from which it had come, realizing that it seemed to originate from the place where the group of ruffians she had noticed earlier were gathered. She had already taken a step in that direction when she heard another scream, this one seeming more despairing than the last. And then another, following in quick succession.

Without stopping to think of her own safety, Anne began to run toward those increasingly frantic shrieks. When she was near enough to peer between the close-packed bodies of the crowd she could see that a man was beating a small boy. The leather strop he was using rose and fell with terrifying regularity and produced a scream from the child each time it landed.

His arm firmly held by the man who was beating him, the little boy was trying to squirm out of the way of the descending lash, desperately dodging away from its blows. His fruitless attempts at evasion seemed to enrage his captor and delight the watchers. They urged the child's tormentor on with catcalls and suggestions.

Furious, Anne began to push her way through the outer fringes of the circle. The element of surprise apparently worked to her advantage because the men parted to let her through, until at last she reached the center. She grabbed at the piece of leather, catching it with her gloved hand just as it was about to crack down again against the boy's narrow back.

The man holding the other end of it looked up, his expression incredulous. It was obvious he hadn't expected any interference with what he was doing, especially not from a gentlewoman.

"That's enough," Anne said, jerking the strap in an attempt to pull it out of his hand.

Despite his shock, the man refused to release it. Instead he turned it once more about his wrist, making his hold more secure.

"Leave off," he said, his face red and contorted with anger, either at the boy or at Anne's intervention on his behalf.

"You cannot beat a child on a public street," Anne said.

"'A course I can. 'E's my boy. I beats him when I pleases." Contempt was strong in his voice.

"Whatever your son has done…" Anne began.

The crowd hooted, as did the man, who seemed not so much amused at her error, but mocking of it. Roughly using the thin arm he held, he pulled the child around to face Anne. "Does this 'ere scoundrel look like he might be *my* son?"

It was hard to tell who the child looked like. His skin

was blackened with soot, which seemed ground into its very pores. His features were twisted as he grimaced with pain at the unnatural angle at which his arm was being held. His face was topped with a stock of badly cropped hair, so darkened by the ash of his profession that it was impossible now to tell its original color.

"I bought 'im. Bought 'im fair and square, and then 'e up and runned away. I got a legal right to beat 'im for that."

He probably did, Anne realized. She wasn't sure about the letter of the law regarding the punishment of apprentices, but young children were forced to backbreaking labor in factories and mines all over England. And chimney sweeps like this poor boy undoubtedly had the very worst of those conditions.

"'E burns me," the boy said, speaking directly to Anne. His blue eyes, the only part of him that had not been affected by his covering of soot, looked up into hers hopefully.

"Burns you?" she repeated, not perfectly sure she had understood the words, given the thick dialect in which he spoke.

"Burns me feet to make me climb the shafts," he said.

Anne's stomach churned. She glanced down involuntarily. The child's feet, as filthy as his hands, arms and face, were bare. Even so, she realized she had no desire to see evidence of his claim. The image his words had produced, of the sweep applying a torch to the soles of those little bare feet to make the boy shinny farther up a narrow flue, was quite vivid enough without any demonstration.

"And is burning a child also legal?" she asked furiously, turning back to his master.

She could tell by the way the man's eyes skated away

from hers that he wasn't any surer of the parameters of the law governing child labor than she was. However accepted by the general populace was the practice the child had just described, it might not be equally condoned by a magistrate.

Pressing her advantage, Anne dropped the strop and took hold of the boy's arm instead. Surprised, either by her boldness or by the fact that such a finely dressed lady was foolishly willing to ruin her kid gloves by contact with the child, the master didn't resist as she pulled the boy away from him.

"Save me, miss," the child begged again, emboldened enough by her defense to lock his filthy hands in the material of Anne's skirt. "'E'll beat me something fierce, 'e will," he said, looking fearfully over his shoulder at his master. "'E liked to 'a killed me the last time I runned away. 'E will kill me now for sure."

"As soon as I gets my 'ands on you," the man threatened, reaching for the child.

Anne backed away, putting her hand on the back of the boy's head and holding him against her protectively.

"What's going on here?" asked a deep voice at her elbow.

Anne turned to find her guardian standing beside her. He looked solidly masculine and incredibly competent to deal with the child's wizened master and even with the spectators to what had turned into a near spectacle.

"He was beating this boy," she said. "I think because he had run away. We have to take him with us."

"Don't let 'im kill me," the boy wailed.

"No one will hurt you," Anne said. "I promise you that."

No matter what Ian said she should do, she knew she could never give the boy back to his master to be beaten again. Not even if that was the law. It seemed, however, that the master had suddenly decided he wasn't willing to wait and see whether Ian agreed with her or not. He grabbed the boy's arm, just above the elbow, and attempted to drag him away.

"Don't no boy run from Bob Thackett. I bought this one fair and square and paid more than 'is scurvy hide is worth. I got the 'prentice papers to prove it."

The child clung so tightly to Anne's skirt that she, too, was pulled forward. Quickly Ian stepped between them, breaking the man's hold on the boy's arm and pushing him away. He then positioned himself between Anne, to whom the sobbing child was still clinging, and the sweep.

Infuriated, the man tried to reach around Ian and take hold of the child again. There were any number of men who had served under Major The Honorable Ian Sinclair who could have told the sweep what a dangerous move that would be. Unfortunately for the boy's master, none of them were at hand.

As he reached for the boy, Ian's fingers closed around the lapels of the rough coat he wore. He held the smaller man away from him at arms' length.

"Leave him alone," he warned, his voice loud enough to carry above the hooting encouragement of the spectators.

"He's my property," the sweep said, twisting and turning as he tried to free himself from those iron fingers wrapped in the material of his coat.

"That's a matter for the magistrates to decide. As are any injuries they might find on the boy's body."

The sweep ceased to struggle, apparently considering the merits of that implied threat. And then his eyes narrowed, seeming to consider as well the caliber of the man who had made it. Since Ian was taller by more than half a foot, he had to look up to make that assessment.

"I got a right to discipline a runaway," he said sullenly. "And no nob need tell me I can't, magistrates or not."

Apparently assuming that his speech would put an end to Ian's objections, he again tried to reach around the ex-major to grasp the boy. Anne stepped back to avoid his hand. The child pushed her even farther back as he attempted to burrow into the perceived safety of her skirt.

It was only then that she realized the sweep's followers had surrounded her and Ian while their attention had been focused on the master. One of the other men, bolder than the rest, grabbed at the boy. Anne turned her back on him, pulling the boy around with her.

As she did, her eyes searched the street, wondering that no one had come to help them. The few shoppers who were about, several of whom had stopped to watch the confrontation, seemed paralyzed by amazement. Although gangs of Mohocks occasionally preyed on those foolish enough to venture unprotected into certain unsavory areas of London at night, it was almost unheard of for people of their class to be accosted in broad open daylight. Especially in this neighborhood.

"Ian," she warned.

He didn't turn to look at her, but he took a step back, putting the child between them again. "Stay close," he ordered.

He was still holding the sweep at arms' length, but the ruffians who had followed the man on his quest to recapture and punish his apprentice had begun to crowd ever nearer, forcing any other pedestrians back. And that had happened with a swiftness that took Anne by surprise.

''Someone call the magistrates,'' Ian called toward the bewildered bystanders.

He had had to raise his voice to carry above the cries of the boy, who pled with heartbreaking sobs for Anne to save him from his master's whip and torch. The voices of the sweep's fellows joined in the growing cacophony, urging him to reclaim his rightful property and not to let any nob come between him and his livelihood. In the hubbub Anne doubted anyone had heard Ian's command.

Their coachman would soon realize what was going on, she told herself, but as yet there was no sign of him. And then, as she looked over the crowd for any indication that a rescue attempt was underway, one of the sweep's supporters began to pull at her arm again.

She wrenched her elbow free, stepping forward toward Ian. Suddenly there was a rush of bodies from the front, shoving Ian into her. She staggered back, the boy still clinging to her skirt like a monkey. He or someone else stepped on the hem of her dress, tearing a portion of her skirt from the bodice.

Just as it seemed she might go down and be trampled, a strong hand grasped her elbow, holding her upright until she had regained her balance. She looked up into a pair of furious hazel eyes. Ian wrapped one arm around her waist, supporting her.

With the other he began to lay about him with his cane, using it like a saber in battle, slashing at the men who milled around them, trying to drive them back. Instead they continued to press nearer, shouting and grabbing at the screaming boy. And above it all, Anne could hear the whistle Ian's stick made as it rose and fell, and even the occasional sound of it striking something.

And he was finally seeing some success, she realized.

The close-packed bodies began to give, driven back by the fury with which Ian was wielding his cane.

Then something struck Ian's chest. It splattered against her cheek, and automatically Anne ducked her head, turning it into the protection of his shoulder. His arm around her waist, Ian lifted her bodily, dragging her off the curb and out into the street, still using his cane to fight off their attackers so that they could escape.

At some point, although she had not been aware of when it had occurred, the child had lost his grip on her skirts and disappeared into the swirling madness. As soon as she realized he was gone, she lifted her head and looked back over Ian's shoulder, trying for a glimpse of the boy amidst the chaos. He seemed to have vanished, although she could see his master at the forefront of the mob, continuing to press his claim.

Another missile landed with a splat on Ian's back. A pungent smell permeated the air around them. Only then did Anne realize that someone was throwing rotten eggs at them. Shielding her face with one hand, she looked up at Ian, seeking reassurance or instruction.

The handsome, familiar features were rigid. His jaw was set, lips flattened and white, as he propelled her, even supporting part of her weight, along the street. This was a man she didn't know, she realized. He was a stern-faced stranger who had been created by the violence that had erupted around them.

Suddenly, Ian stumbled, catching his dragging foot on one of the uneven cobblestones. He fell onto one knee, inadvertently pulling her down with him. Her fall was cushioned by his body, but his had not been. Even from that position, one knee and one hand on the ground, Ian raised the cane as the sweep and his screaming cohorts came rushing after them, like wolves surrounding a downed sheep.

"Run," Ian commanded, releasing his hold on her. "Do it now," he ordered when she hesitated.

Knees trembling, Anne rose in response to the sharpness of that command. Instead of running, however, she put both hands around his upper arm, the one that wasn't raised defensively in preparation for the mob's approach. She pulled, urging him to his feet.

"Go, damn it," he demanded, watching the enemy.

"Not without you," she said stubbornly.

She wouldn't. No matter what happened to her, she wasn't going to leave him on his knees and at their mercy.

"Damn you." The words were uttered under his breath, but the tone of them was vehement. Heartfelt.

As he said them, however, his eyes lifted to meet hers. And seeing the determination within them perhaps, Ian lowered the cane, using it and her support to push himself to his feet. By that time, the howling sweep and his cohorts were on them.

One of them struck Ian with his fist, sending him into her. She braced herself to bear his weight, and he quickly regained his balance, charging the throng, cane slashing. This time, however, his attackers had taken time to arm themselves.

They had grabbed anything they could get their hands on to use as weapons. One held a buggy whip, no doubt snatched from a driver whose vehicle had been blocked by the melee. Another had ripped a length of board loose from somewhere. And far too many of the blows they aimed at the man who was defending her, Anne realized, were hitting their target.

Ian retreated even as he fought, keeping her behind

him and pushing her backwards as he moved, ever vigilant to the next feint, the next blow. She had time to wonder how long he could keep it up, and then he stumbled once more.

He didn't go down this time, thank God. The mob was too close to allow her time to get him to his feet if he fell again.

However, they were being driven inexorably toward the buildings on the opposite side of the narrow street. Deliberately driven? she wondered. Because when they reached it, a matter of only seconds now, considering the fury of the mob, further retreat would be cut off.

"Go," Ian ordered again, reading the situation as she had.

As he turned to hurl the single syllable over his shoulder, he was struck in the chest by that length of wood. He stumbled a step or two, trying not to go down. He didn't, but his backward momentum pushed her into the brick wall at her back.

There was a howl of victory from the mob. She looked up in time to see the sweep grab the cane and rip it from Ian's hand during the split second the ex-soldier had been forced to concentrate on regaining his balance.

Defenseless now against the onslaught, Ian did the only thing he could to protect her. He turned his back to the attackers, pressing her closely against the bricks. He put his hands on the wall above them, and lowered his face so that his cheek rested over the top of her head. The position protected her, but it also prevented her from seeing anything.

Something struck Ian's back, probably the board. The blow was hard enough that the force of it was transmitted through his body to hers. She heard his gasp of pain. Knowing there was nothing else she could do, Anne closed her eyes, her mouth moving soundlessly as she began to pray.

Chapter Nine

A shot rang out. Ian raised his head, probably searching for its source. Her heart in her throat, Anne stood on tiptoe, looking over his shoulder, hoping to see Dare's coachman brandishing the same kind of pistol Ian had used so effectively the night they had been attacked by highwaymen.

Instead, Doyle Travener stood in the middle of the street, aiming the second of a pair of pistols he held at the man who had been lifting the length of board to bring it down on the head of her guardian. With the sound of the first shot, the man had frozen, his makeshift weapon still raised.

"That's enough," Travener said.

So complete was the silence that had fallen after the gunshot, it seemed as if those quiet words had been spoken into a vacuum. The shouts of the angry throng and the screams of the boy were still echoing off the brick of the buildings, but no one was making any sound now.

And then, as quickly and inexplicably as they had appeared on this quiet street of expensive shops, the crowd who had supported the sweep's attempt to retrieve his property evaporated. They ran, each in a different direction, threading their ways through the pedestrians and then disappearing into the maze of streets and alleys.

Within seconds it was as if the mob had never existed. The faces of the shops' other patrons, those who had witnessed the fray, looked as stunned as Anne felt. For a few seconds, none of them moved. Then, seeming to recover more quickly than anyone else, Doyle Travener lowered the second, unfired pistol and began to walk toward her and Ian.

By then Anne had had time to realize she was unhurt. Of course, she wasn't the one who had borne the brunt of that attack. She was the one who had been protected from it, at a cost she was almost afraid to discover. She turned her head, no longer watching Travener's approach. Nor was Ian. He was looking at her instead. Looking into her eyes.

There was a trickle of blood making its way down his lean cheek. Her gaze followed it upward until she found the cut that had been opened above his brow. Then her gaze shifted from the gash to his eyes, trying to read what was in them.

This was what he would have looked like in battle, she thought. This same savage determination in his features. It had been expended on her behalf today, but the will that had made him fight on, despite the odds, despite the blows, despite the seeming futility of his effort, had been forged years ago. It was obvious that no matter what he had laughingly claimed, there had been far more to Ian Sinclair's military experiences than dancing attendance on Portuguese ladies.

"Anne?"

Her name had been a breath, loud enough for her ears alone. And for a moment everything around them faded away. There was nothing but his eyes on hers, his lips whispering her name.

"I'm all right," she said, her throat so tight with emotion it was hard to speak.

Her hand forced itself upward between their bodies. She wanted to put her fingers over the line of his lips. To shape his cheek. To urge his mouth downward to align itself over hers.

She did none of those things, despite the fact that her body was pressed against his as closely as if they were lovers. Still holding his eyes, she put her gloved fingers over the slash above his eye instead, touching it gently.

Ian turned his head, moving it away from contact with her hand. It was not a flinch. It was, rather, a deliberate avoidance. And realizing that, her fingers curled into her palm.

I never worried that his heart might be engaged. It was. And hers were not the fingers he wanted on his face.

"Major Sinclair?"

Doyle Travener's voice was an intrusion, despite Ian's reaction to her touch. Reluctantly, Anne turned her head toward the sound. Travener was standing beside them, and she wondered if he had been close enough to see that small exchange.

After a second or two, Ian stepped away from her, creating a more acceptable distance between their bodies. The movement drew her attention back to him. And she saw, despite Travener's approach, her guardian's gaze had not left her face. It didn't now.

"Are you hurt, Miss Darlington?" Travener asked.

Anne again broke the connection with those piercing hazel eyes and turned to face their savior.

"See to Major Sinclair, if you will, Mr. Travener. I assure you I am not harmed."

"Major Sinclair?" Travener said, more softly this time.

She watched the breath Ian drew, his mouth opening slightly to accommodate its depth. Finally he turned his head to look at the man standing beside them. The pistols with which Doyle Travener had scattered the mob were still in his hands.

"Would you find my coachman, please?" Ian asked, as if that request were the most ordinary thing in the world. As if Travener were someone who might be sent to do his bidding.

"Are you sure you're all right, sir?"

"Perfectly sure, thank you," Ian said formally. "Miss Darlington, however, should be conveyed home immediately. She has had a shock, as you may imagine."

She had, of course, but she wasn't hurt, and she certainly wasn't hysterical. She couldn't imagine why she was not, but then she could never have imagined any of what had just happened.

"Of course," Mr. Travener said, moving away to carry out the assignment he had been given, as if the chain of command that would have bound these two men in Iberia had not been changed by their present circumstances.

When Travener had disappeared, Ian turned his head again, looking down once more into her eyes. He was no longer touching her. There was as much distance between them now as if they were dancing or conversing at some crowded rout.

And yet it seemed as if she could still feel the imprint of each individual muscle of his body on her skin. Her breasts were tight and aching, with fear or excitement or need. And she felt as if she had been burned by whatever incredible current of emotion had passed between them during the seconds-long eternity his eyes had held on hers.

"It seems I once more owe you my life," she said when this silence had also gone on too long.

He shook his head, the movement small, but clearly negative. There was still within his face something of the battle rage she had glimpsed before. Even as she watched, however, his features seemed to be changing, transforming themselves once more into the face of the man she had thought she knew.

"You should have run when I told you to," he said. "You might have been hurt."

"*You* didn't run."

The stern line of his lips softened, not quite a smile. "I can't," he said, touching his thigh.

"I don't think you ever knew how to run from a fight. Maybe that's a lesson I haven't learned either," she said returning the smile. "Obviously Elizabeth's teaching is at fault. Or perhaps I am more my father's daughter than I have believed."

And once more his eyes changed, slowly, gradually, even as she watched. There was again a physical withdrawal, more subtle this time than the actual step back he had taken before. What was happening now was nothing so blatant as that. Perhaps it had been only a shift of his weight onto his good leg. Or maybe a shift of his attention.

She became aware of the arrival of the carriage at the same time Ian turned to face it. The coachman brought the horses as close to them as he could, given the size of the crowd which had now gathered in the street. Anne wondered where all those people had been when they were being attacked.

And then she saw Ian's cane lying in the street between

them and the coach. She brushed past him and walked over to it, stooping to pick it up.

She realized as she did that Mr. Travener was standing beside the coach, holding the door open for her. He had apparently put the pistols away, for his hands were free.

Instead of walking over to the carriage, she turned and carried the cane back to her guardian, who was standing exactly where she had left him. She held the stick out like an offering on her open palms.

His eyes rested on it a moment, and then he reached out and took it from her hands. For a second or two, she stared down at her stained kid gloves, which she had noticed for the first time. She looked up, smiling at Ian to indicate how little she cared that they were ruined, and realized that her guardian's eyes, holding the intensity they had held before, were on her face.

"Thank you," he said softly.

She expected him to take her arm and lead her to the coach. And his support would have been very welcome since her knees had begun to shake. Unaccountably, they hadn't while the attack was going on or even when she had walked that short distance to retrieve Ian's cane.

Now that it was all over, however, she had had time to realize how near to tragedy this had almost been. And time to understand the consequences had Mr. Travener not intervened.

Neither of them had yet expressed their gratitude. She turned and walked toward the coach. As she approached the door beside which Mr. Travener still stood, she held out her hand. Doyle took it, but instead of kissing it, he enclosed her shaking fingers in his, as a friend might have done.

"Thank you, Mr. Travener," she said.

"I only regret I wasn't sooner."

"You were soon enough," she said. "We owe you our lives."

"You owe me nothing, Miss Darlington." His eyes lifted to Ian, who was approaching from behind her. "Major Sinclair was the one who fought them. I simply arrived in time to send the rats scurrying back to their holes."

"You are too modest, Mr. Travener," Ian said. "Your arrival was most fortuitous. You have my gratitude."

"Hardly fortuitous," Travener said, smiling for the first time, and the boyish grin was almost sheepish. "I confess I came today hoping for an encounter." His eyes returned briefly to Anne's face, before they rose to meet Ian's. "*Not* an encounter like this one, of course."

"Hoping for an encounter?" Ian repeated. "You knew we were here?"

"I had invited Miss Darlington to go for a drive. This morning she sent me a note explaining that she would be unable to keep our appointment. She had another, far more pressing engagement with her dressmaker." Doyle turned his head to smile at Anne. "I was hoping to catch a glimpse of Miss Darlington when I set out. Actually, to be honest, I had already driven up and down this street half a dozen times," he admitted with a laugh. "And then, on this particular trip…"

His eyes returned to Ian's face, the fair brows above them arched.

"Lucky for us you are so faithful a suitor," Ian said. "I thank you on my ward's behalf. And on my own, of course. Your intervention was both timely and courageous."

"My fighting days were short, major. My few feats of valor during them nothing to compare with yours. I am very glad that I could have been of service today, but in truth, it was more a matter of being in the right place at the right time than being courageous. *And* a matter of being armed, of course,'' he added with another smile.

He turned to lower the step of the carriage and held Anne's hand as she climbed in. From inside the shadowed interior of the coach, she mentally cringed as he offered that same supporting hand to her guardian. Ian ignored the gesture, using his cane and his hand on the frame of the doorway to pull himself up.

His eyes met hers for an instant as he entered the coach, and then he lowered himself carefully into the opposite seat as Travener replaced the stair and closed the door behind him.

"Good day, Mr. Travener," Ian said through the open window. "Again, please know that you have my most sincere gratitude."

"May I impose upon it then to call upon Miss Darlington tomorrow, sir? Just to see how she gets on?"

Ian glanced at her for permission. Only when she nodded, did he reply.

"We should be delighted to receive your call, Mr. Travener."

And then he tapped on the top of the carriage with his cane, signaling the coachman to move on.

They rode a few minutes in silence. None of the conventional openings for conversation seemed appropriate in this situation. Actually, Anne wasn't entirely sure exactly what the situation between them was.

And she wanted desperately to ask Ian how badly he was hurt. It was obvious to her in some indefinable way that he was. Obvious, too, that he was in pain. About neither of those, however, would Ian welcome questions.

And she certainly couldn't ask him if he, too, had experienced what she had felt as he'd pressed his body protectively over hers. If she ever did find the courage to mention that, he would undoubtedly deny that he had done anything more than put himself between her and a vicious mob. In actuality, that was all he *had* done.

"We are very lucky," she said, echoing the tenor of his comments in the street.

His eyes came up, focusing on her face. "Are you truly unhurt?"

"Not even a bruise," she said reassuringly. "The only lingering effect seems to be a slight residue of sulfur from what I believe was a rotted egg."

Again there was a subtle relaxation of his mouth. "Not so slight a residue, I'm afraid, on *this* side of the coach." He looked down at the mess on his dark coat.

"I wonder what happened to the boy?" she said.

She knew that if she asked Ian to direct the coachman to turn back so that she could look for the child, she would find no sign of him. The boy had wisely fled the scene while his master had been occupied in dealing with her guardian. He was probably far away by now or well-hidden in some dark alleyway.

"How old would you say he was?" Ian asked, lifting gloved fingers to touch against the cut on his forehead. He winced as they made contact with it.

"How old was the boy?" Anne repeated, wondering why it mattered.

The child had been small, his frame slight, but there had been something about his eyes that had made him seem older than either of those might indicate. And despite her years of experience in dealing with children, she really couldn't be sure. Her charges had all been well-fed and well-cared for. They were not abused street urchins, deliberately kept thin and undergrown to allow them to crawl through the narrowest chimney.

"Eight or nine, perhaps," she said. "No more than that I should think."

Ian nodded, his eyes leaving her face to focus on the passing scenery. He shifted on the seat, stretching out his leg. As he did, his gaze came back to Anne in time to discover that she was watching him, the anxiety she felt probably revealed in her face. She dropped her eyes, using the opportunity to pull off the stained gloves.

"Do you think he got away?" she asked.

"He had every opportunity," Ian said.

Actually, the sweep had seemed to forget all about the boy when Ian opposed him. His fury had been directed not against the child so much as against the "nobs."

Of course, there had been a lot of social unrest in the country during the last few years. Perhaps what had happened today had been the result of pent-up frustrations, not so much directed at them for trying to help the boy, but at their class and the excesses for which it was known. The knowledge of those excesses, from those of the Regent down, must be extremely galling to people who had so little.

So little. As that poor child did, she thought. She brushed her bare fingers over the stains the boy's desperately clutching hands had left on her skirt. She could not imagine the senseless brutality to which he had been submitted during his short life. It was a wonder he had found the courage to run.

"If you wish, I shall send the coachman and a groom back to search for him," Ian offered.

She looked up to smile at him. "They won't find him," she said, very sure of that. "Thank you for offering to have them look, but we both know it will be wasted effort. I only hope the men who were helping his master won't be able to find him either.''

"They will no doubt realize the futility as well.''

His long fingers touched the gash above his eye again, wiping at the small, but steady stream of blood it produced. Anne reached into her sleeve and pulled her handkerchief free. She held the scrap of cloth out to him.

"I should ruin it,'' he said, quickly removing his fingers from the cut, almost as if he were embarrassed to have been caught touching it.

"You have just saved my life, Ian Sinclair. And before that, you attempted to save a boy from his tormentors. I think this,'' she said, shaking the wisp of lace to emphasize her point, ''would be a very small price to pay for either of those efforts. Unless, of course, you value my life less than this? I assure you that I do not.''

She smiled at him again, and finally he reached for the handkerchief. It looked absurdly small in his hand, but he used it to dab at the blood. After watching a moment, she leaned forward and took the cloth from his unresisting fingers.

"May I?'' she asked, remembering his earlier reaction to her attempt to stem this flow of blood.

"Of course,'' he said.

He closed his eyes and leaned forward as well. He was near enough that, despite the unpleasant residue of egg on his coat, she could again smell all the fragrances that would forever in her mind be associated with Ian Sinclair.

She didn't know why she hadn't been aware of them in the street. Perhaps because she had been more aware of his body, and of its strength, pressed tightly along the length of hers.

This was the second time he had come to her rescue. And again, just as when her guardian had stepped between her and danger before, she had not found the rescue to be romantic in the least. It had been frightening, rather than thrilling. It seemed that London was determined to teach her the fallacies in all the fantasies she had once enjoyed.

Ian's eyes opened. Brought back to the present by the question in them, she again pressed her handkerchief over the cut. She kept her eyes resolutely on the task, but she was aware that his had not closed again. They remained fastened on her face as she worked. Fighting to keep her fingers steady, however, she refused to meet them.

After all, Ian Sinclair was in love with another woman. And she knew that what she had been imagining was in his eyes as he had leaned against her today had been only that. Only what she had imagined.

"A broken rib, I suspect," McKinley said, lightly touching Ian's back and side. "Possibly more than one."

His fingers pressed more firmly as they worked their way downward. Ian flinched against the pain, trying, as he had from the beginning, not to let any sound escape as the physician made his careful examination.

"I can bind them to give you some relief. The rest of the damage appears to be superficial. The bruising itself will cause some discomfort, but that will become less noticeable after a few days. My best advice is to stay off your feet and allow your leg to heal. This," he said, running his palm along Ian's side, "will resolve itself as you rest the knee."

The worst of the aftereffects from yesterday's confrontation was whatever he had done to his knee. Weakened by the injuries he had suffered on the Peninsula, the leg had been badly wrenched when he had fallen. Today his knee was swollen and so painful he could hardly bear to put his weight on it.

When he and Anne had arrived at the town house yesterday, Ian had dispatched a note to his brother. He had known that Dare would come to town as soon as he could. He hadn't realized, however, that the earl would leave the Sinclair estate immediately upon receiving his message. Dare had arrived in London before dawn, and as soon as he realized Ian had been hurt, he had sent for McKinley.

Had it not been for the doctor's support of Ian's request for privacy, he knew that his brother would have been in the room while McKinley made this assessment. And Ian was very reluctant to have him see the current damage.

"Of course, since you seldom follow the advice of your physicians, Mr. Sinclair," McKinley went on, "I have little hope that you'll give this the time it needs to heal."

"I assure you, Dr. McKinley, I have lived most sedately since we last talked."

"Forgive me, sir, if I beg to doubt that claim. The evidence to the contrary is, after all, before my eyes. Do you mind telling me exactly how you managed to break your ribs and bruise your back in this fashion? That question is simply medical curiosity, I assure you. If you choose to kill yourself, it is really nothing to me."

Ian laughed, and then wished he hadn't. He couldn't prevent a small gasp at the resulting shard of agony in his side.

"It's your brother I am sorry for," McKinley continued, as if he hadn't heard that telltale inhalation. "He has no idea, of course, that if you continue in this fashion, he may lose you. I believe his affection for you to be quite genuine. I've a good mind to tell him exactly what a fool he has for a brother.''

"You will find he is well aware of that," Ian said, smiling as he remembered Dare's comments the last time he'd been injured.

Apparently his voice revealed his amusement about those remarks, for McKinley said stiffly, "It seems that the concern the earl and I have for your continuing survival is not one you share. Rather, it is cause for mockery. I wonder why you would call in a physician if you care so little for your life."

Hearing the undisguised anger in the doctor's tone, Ian feared he had thoroughly alienated the man, perhaps enough to drive him to speak to Dare about the danger of that piece of shrapnel lodged in his chest. And there was nothing, of course, that Ian desired less than that disclosure. Especially now.

"My ward and I were attacked."

The remembrance was certainly enough to destroy any lingering remnants of amusement in his tone.

"Attacked?" McKinley repeated in disbelief.

Using the post of the bed he had been holding on to for balance while the doctor carried out his examination, Ian turned to face the physician, whose features reflected the same shock his voice had just conveyed.

"On a street in this city. A sweep was beating one of his climbing boys, and Miss Darlington, who is both impetuous and courageous, intervened. For some reason, things very quickly got out of hand. The mob that had gathered to watch the sweep's punishment turned ugly."

"And *attacked* you?"

"My ward *was* attempting to take the boy away from his master. There seemed to be some resentment about our interference in his livelihood, and it…boiled over.

That's the only explanation I can make for what occurred.''

"I can't say I would blame her for that attempted rescue," McKinley said. "The way those children are treated is a disgrace to this nation. Still, it would take a remarkable woman to rush to a climbing boy's defense."

"You will find no disagreement from me with either of those opinions, Dr. McKinley."

"And then you, of course, felt compelled to rush to her defense, despite... Despite the risks," the doctor amended, thankfully leaving unsaid the warning he'd made the last time he had examined Ian. "Impetuous and courageous, indeed."

McKinley's eyes continued to examine Ian's face as, still holding to the bedpost, his patient eased his battered frame down to the edge of the high mattress.

"And apparently a lightning rod for trouble," the doctor went on. "This *is* the same ward, I take it, in whose company you were attacked by highwaymen."

"I have only the one," Ian said, his lips lifting into another remembering smile.

"Lucky for you, I should think," McKinley said. "Otherwise, I should indeed worry about your survival."

The doctor had finished and gone, leaving Ian once again to his bed, thoroughly exhausted by the ordeal. At least his ribs were now tightly strapped, and, as McKinley had promised, they were less painful. With the heavy dose of laudanum he had insisted Ian drink, even the agony in his knee was beginning to dull to something bearable.

He had expected Dare's visit from the moment of the physician's departure. Perhaps his brother had accompanied McKinley to the door, asking him the kind of probing questions Ian had managed to avoid for the last year and a half. And he could only hope that the doctor still felt bound by the terms of his original promise not to answer them.

When the door of his bedroom eased open, Ian turned his head to discover his brother looking around it. Finding that he was still awake, the earl walked in, closing the door behind him.

As desperately as he was trying to interpret his brother's expression, Ian found he was uncertain how much Dare had been told. Of course, if McKinley had not kept his confidence, he would be made aware of it soon enough.

"As I'm sure your sawbones told you, I'm still not likely to turn up my toes in the family crypt," Ian said, injecting the kind of gentle raillery into his tone that was customary between them. "You have permission to stop worrying."

His brother crossed the room and stood looking down on him. Ian held up his hand, and Dare enclosed it in his, the grip warm and strong. His expression, however, was still enigmatic.

"I have seen far too much of you in the horizontal lately to do that," Dare said. "McKinley says you have broken ribs."

"He wasn't sure," Ian hedged. "He strapped them in case."

"And your leg?"

"Hurts like bloody hell. Not something I am unaccustomed to, I assure you."

Dare's lips tightened and then pursed, as if he were thinking. "You didn't send for me to offer sympathy. If I know you, and believe me I do, then I should be the last person you'd want hovering at your bedside."

Despite the haze from the laudanum that was begin-ning to steal over his senses, Ian couldn't prevent a smile at the accuracy of that judgment. And feeling the effects of the drug, he knew he wouldn't have long to talk. Not coherently.

Perhaps it would be better to reveal what he had been thinking, as well as the doctor's comment, which seemed to back up his own belief. Then he would give the prob-lem over to his brother's intelligence, trusting him to sep-arate whatever needed looking into from what might be nothing but drug-induced fantasy.

"The sweep's boy seemed old," Ian said.

"Old?" Dare repeated. He leaned closer, apparently trying to make sure he had heard the words correctly.

"Anne thought so," Ian said, knowing he wasn't ex-pressing this well and that it probably made no sense to his brother.

However, the opium was running through his veins in a great roaring wave now. Suddenly, what he had been worrying about since the attack yesterday didn't seem important any more. And far too difficult to explain. Af-ter all, Val was here now, and nothing else would happen.

He closed his eyes, still trying to organize his wayward thoughts. They seemed to be drifting everywhere but where he wanted them to go. He knew there had been something else he needed to tell his brother. Something important.

Perhaps if he had gotten some sleep last night, he would have been able to concentrate. That's what the doctor had told him. The last thing McKinley had said as he walked out the door. *Try to get some sleep.*

And with Val here… He opened his eyes, and found his brother still standing beside his bed.

There was something else he wanted to say, Ian

thought. He couldn't seem to find the right words, however. Maybe if he closed his eyes for a moment, just to rest them, then it would come back to him. Just for a moment.

Dare released his hand and laid it on his chest, pulling the covers over it. Aware on some level of what Val was doing, Ian opened his eyes again, afraid his brother was leaving. He was relieved to see him instead take the chair from beneath the window and bring it to the bedside. As soon as Dare realized he was watching him, the earl smiled at him.

"Go to sleep," he advised. "You can tell me about it when you wake."

Ian wanted to tell Dare that he must stay until he had told him the whole, but it seemed too much trouble to form those words. Besides, he knew his brother. There was no danger of Val deserting him. And he was right, of course. He would be able to think more clearly after he had slept.

Ian Sinclair closed his eyes, no longer conscious that there had been something very important he needed to share with his brother. Something he had believed last night to be important enough to call the earl back to London. Something whose urgency had now been lost in the massive dose of laudanum the doctor had administered before he left.

Chapter Ten

"How is he?" Anne asked the Earl of Dare.

She had been waiting in the hallway outside Ian's bedroom for most of the morning. She had not been brave enough to stop the doctor in order to pose her question. Sometime in the slow hours that had passed, however, her reluctance had been pushed aside by her growing anxiety.

"He's asleep," Dare said.

He attempted to walk around her, probably headed downstairs for breakfast or dinner, neither of which he had bothered with before. Anne took a step to the side, blocking his passage.

Dare stopped, one dark brow raised as he looked down into her face. He was taller than his brother, she realized, and though the family resemblance was clear, his classically handsome features were more finely formed. And right now, his cold blue eyes seemed to be boring a hole through her.

"I really need to know how Mr. Sinclair is, Lord Dare," she said. "Would you please tell me?"

"And why are you so interested in my brother's condition? Guilt, perhaps? I understand you were instrumental in beginning that ridiculous contretemps in which he was injured.''

"Ridiculous, my lord?'' she asked, stung by the accusation. "I don't believe your brother thought it ridiculous.''

She could feel her cheeks begin to flush, this time from anger. Although there was certainly an element of guilt in her concern for Ian, it was not over her defense of the child.

"Did you give him an opportunity to decide whether or not your interference on that boy's behalf was worth his dying for?''

The word chilled her blood. "Dying?'' she whispered.

"He isn't, thank God. No thanks, however, are due to *you* for that. A gentleman has little choice about coming to the defense of a woman in his charge, even if her actions are both ill-advised and foolhardy.''

"The man was beating a child. What would you have had me do, my lord?''

"I would have had you refrain from putting my brother into danger for your own quixotic motives.''

"I see,'' she said tightly. "And it is quixotic to you to attempt to rescue a child.''

"As quixotic as it was of Ian to attempt to protect you from the consequences of your actions. Believe me, I'm thoroughly annoyed with both of you.''

Again he attempted to move past her, and again she stepped in front of him.

"There is little I can do about your opinion of me, Lord Dare,'' she said. *Nor do I give a damn what it is,* she thought rebelliously. "However, I should still like an answer to my question, if you please.''

"I don't please. If you'll excuse me, Miss Darling-

ton..." He offered her a half bow, the gesture far too
polite for the tenor of the conversation they were having.

"You don't like me," Anne said. "And you have
made that abundantly clear. Whatever I've done to inspire that dislike—"

"I don't dislike *you,* Miss Darlington. I dislike the fact
that you endanger my brother. I warned him from the
beginning that this guardianship would be nothing but
trouble. Even I couldn't conceive, however, how right I
should be proven to be."

"From the *beginning,*" she repeated. "And why
would you have believed, even before you met me, that
I should prove troublesome? I can assure you that has
never been my reputation. Nor was it your brother's opinion of me. I wonder why it should have been yours, my
lord."

There was a small hesitation and, if possible, the earl's
eyes seemed to grow colder than they had been before.
"Perhaps I am simply an outstanding judge of character,
Miss Darlington."

"But at the *beginning* of your brother's guardianship,
you had no way of knowing mine."

Dare's lips tightened, as if he had clamped them shut
against the rejoinder he wanted to make. And from what
was in his eyes, there was no doubt he wanted to make
one.

When he finally opened them, he said instead, "You
told Ian the boy was too old. Would you explain to me
what you meant?"

The question was almost incomprehensible because
she had been expecting something very different. Something caustic and bitter. Accusing. His tone had been neither, and that, too, confused her. But the only boy she
and Ian had ever discussed had been the climbing boy.

The one who had started everything yesterday with his cries and his pleas for rescue. What the child's age could have to do with anything...

However, Ian had asked her this same question in the coach. Her mind occupied with worry for her guardian, she hadn't understood the relevance of it then. She didn't now.

"He asked me how old I would judge the boy to be. I didn't see why it mattered. I still don't, but I gave him my opinion."

"Give it to me," Dare suggested.

"Eight or so. It was hard to tell, given the deprivations in his background. He was small and thin, but still..." She hesitated, recreating the urchin's dirty face in her mind's eye. After she had, she could see no reason to change her original estimate. "What difference can it possibly make how old he was?"

"I'm not sure," Dare said. "Ian seemed to think it was important enough for him to attempt to tell me about it, despite the fact that he was half-asleep with the doctor's dosing. I suppose laudanum alone could be responsible for whatever significance he has attached to the child's age."

"Except he asked me this question yesterday. When there was nothing to interfere with his ability to reason."

Dare's lips quirked. "Very astute, Miss Darlington. Perhaps it is your intellect that has so attracted my brother. And all along I had believed it was your speaking eyes."

She examined the words, searching them for any other possible meaning. Any meaning other than the one that seemed to be obvious, if unbelievable.

"Attracted your brother?" she repeated, feeling foolish even as she picked that phrase out of the whole.

"He hasn't told you? How clumsy of me then to reveal his secret. I'm afraid Ian clings to the rather strange idea that because he was injured so severely, he is no longer worthy of a woman's interest. No matter how strongly he is attracted to that woman. I wonder that your intellect has not allowed you to arrive at that conclusion."

No matter how strongly he is attracted to that woman... No matter how strongly...

"You don't mean me, my lord?" Anne said.

"Then I wonder why I would bother to have had this conversation with you, Miss Darlington. I am not yet in my dotage, I assure you, despite the difference in our ages."

"But..."

Again she searched her memory for Elizabeth's exact words. As she did, the remembrance of what had been in Ian's eyes as he had looked into hers yesterday was in her mind as well. And in light of what the earl had just said, that look took on a new and compelling significance, causing her to rethink everything she had believed she understood about their relationship. Although his gaze remained on her face, surprisingly the earl refrained from comment as she reviewed all the things that had caused her to reach that understanding.

"He is in love with someone else," she said finally, realizing that one piece of information was at the heart of what she had been led to believe.

"And who told you that? My so-noble, pigheaded brother?"

"Your wife."

"Elizabeth?" Dare said, a crease forming between the wings of his brows. "I wonder why she should think that."

"Perhaps because your brother told *her?*" Anne said, feeling her pulse begin to increase at Dare's puzzlement.

"If so, I can assure you he did it with a purpose. That ridiculous nobility I was talking about."

"Because of his health?"

"Another quixotic notion. The two of you deserve one another," Dare said mockingly.

"You are mistaken," Anne said, trying desperately to quell the surging hope.

This had been a battle she had believed she was winning. She had been forced to accept that, no matter how she felt about him, Ian Sinclair was in love with another woman. He had turned his head away from her touch because of it.

Or was it possible there was another reason for his reluctance to have her touch him? A reason which she would find far more palatable, of course. *Was* it possible, as his brother had just suggested, that her guardian believed he was unworthy of her love? *Unworthy.* The idea was so ludicrous that she would have rejected it out of hand, except...

She searched the Earl of Dare's eyes, which were no longer cold, she realized. And no longer mocking. They seemed slightly amused and schooled to patience as he watched her adjust her thinking to the idea he had just planted in her head.

Planted. He had deliberately told her this because he had known Ian never would. After all, there was no one who knew her guardian better than did his notorious brother. And if Dare believed this were true...

"Thank you," she said softly.

The finely shaped lips relaxed, that motion very reminiscent of another beautiful mouth moving from the sternness of battle fury into this same enigmatic half smile.

"I am overdressed to play Cupid. And I shall never do so again, believe me. What use you make of this information is up to you. I seldom interfere in my brother's life. However, I have never seen him in love before, at least nothing beyond the calf-love variety of our boyhoods."

"Are you sure, my lord, that... I cannot afford to be mistaken in this."

"Ian is an admirer of courage. Despite the indisputable fineness of your eyes, I suspect my brother's attraction to you had far more to do with that quality than with anything else."

"Are you saying he's attracted to my courage?" she said, her own lips tilting.

Amusement, whether at her or at his brother, had replaced the coldness in Dare's blue eyes. They were almost conspiring.

"Forgive me if I am unable to fully explain my brother's attraction. People fall in love, I have found, for the most astounding reasons."

"And after all, I have nothing else to recommend me," Anne said, smiling at him.

It seemed she was finally beginning to understand Ian's sardonic brother, and perhaps even to understand Elizabeth's love for him. *People fall in love for the most astounding reasons.*

"An open and gallant heart," the earl said, "is the one quality that will always guarantee a Sinclair's acceptance. I pray you will have both in dealing with my recalcitrant brother. And now, if I have your permission, Miss Darlington, I should very much like to partake of my dinner.

I have an unfortunate habit of fainting on stairs. You may ask Elizabeth for verification if you wish.''

"Anne," she said, holding out her hand. "My name is Anne.''

There was a long hesitation as his eyes studied hers. This time she met them fearlessly, however, fighting to control the smile that tugged at the corners of her mouth. Finally Dare took her hand and brought it to his lips, just as he had once before.

And yet nothing was the same about the gesture. He held her eyes as his mouth brushed over the back of her hand. And then he held her fingers in his long dark ones as he considered her face.

"I should want to kill a man who hurt my brother. I feel I must tell you that with all honesty, if you and I are to have any sort of relationship. As for the woman who would hurt him…''

"I suspect you would want to kill her, too. I am undaunted by the threat, my lord. If there is one thing of which I can assure you, it is that I would never willingly hurt your brother. You have my word on that.''

He held her eyes another moment, and then he nodded, freeing her fingers. And when the Earl of Dare brushed by her this time, Anne didn't attempt to stop him. She stood instead where he had left her, her gaze on the closed bedroom door across the hall.

When Ian opened his eyes, it was obvious he had slept the day away. The room was dim, its windows darkened and opaque. He turned his head toward the chair where Dare had been sitting. He didn't really expect his brother to still be there after so many hours, but knowing Val, he would not have been surprised.

He *was* surprised, however, when he identified its current occupant. The low light from the lamp across the room drew copper highlights from the dark auburn hair of his ward. Her lashes shadowed her eyes. It appeared her gaze was on her hands, which were in her lap, the right lying unmoving within the left.

Ian couldn't remember when he had ever seen Anne so still. There was always animation about her features, her eyes alight with humor and mischief. Or with anger, as they had been yesterday.

He wondered if she were asleep, as unlikely as that seemed, given the uncomfortable straightness of the chair. Just when he was about to decide that must be the case, however, she lifted her head, as if she had sensed he was watching her.

He expected her quick smile as soon as she saw he was awake, but her lips remained unmoving. And he realized the familiar planes and angles of her face were somehow different. It was hard to decide exactly what the subtle variance was, but there was a serenity about her features he had never seen there before. A quiet maturity, which had apparently developed overnight.

"You're awake," she said.

It wasn't a question, of course, because she could see that he was. And like whatever he had noticed in her face, her voice, too, seemed changed. It was as soft as the shadows that gathered in the room beyond the reach of the light from that single lamp.

Ian wasn't able to read her tone, and yet he had believed he was becoming quite adept at that. After all, he had tried for weeks to memorize all the subtle nuances of phrase and expression that made Anne Darlington who and what she was.

The process had been slow, and it had also been deliberate. He knew very well that when he had found the perfect husband for the woman with whom he had fallen in love, those memories would be all he would have left. And they would have to sustain him through the empty years that stretched ahead, however few or many that might be.

"How long have you been here?" he asked.

That she should have been the one left to watch over him as he slept was as unbelievable as it was undesirable. He wondered that his brother hadn't understood his feelings. After all, he had already been forced to demonstrate his physical inadequacies before Anne far too frequently during their short acquaintance.

"Since your brother left."

"Val's gone?"

That thought was frightening for some reason, although it was again difficult for his fogged brain to grasp why it should be. He remembered that he had sent for Dare. He wasn't perfectly sure, however, whether or not he had managed to convey to his brother his reasons. If Val were no longer in London—

"Only to eat and to sleep. He traveled most of last night, I believe. He indicated that your note seemed quite urgent."

Ian tried to remember what logic had created that urgency. All he knew was that he had believed Anne to be in danger, and until he was again able to protect her…

Able to protect her. The words jeered at him through the cloud of opium that obscured his thinking. He could no more protect Anne than he could convince himself he wasn't in love with her. The fact that he was flat on his back again made a mockery of both.

"But he didn't explain why you had sent for him," she added.

Because… The reasons, even those he managed to

dredge from his disordered brain, seemed as insubstantial as smoke. Was it because, as McKinley had noted, Anne Darlington seemed a lightning rod for trouble? Or because his own inadequacies had made him exaggerate out of proportion to their significance the two incidents in which she had been endangered? The questions seemed beyond his mental powers tonight. As fighting off those dangers had proven to be humiliatingly beyond his physical ones.

"He is my brother," he said truthfully, "and I am accustomed to depending on him." He lifted his hand and touched the plaster the doctor had put over the gash on his forehead.

"Does your head ache?" Anne asked.

"Not appreciably worse than the rest of me."

He smiled at her and became aware only then of the painful dryness of his lips. Of course, laudanum always affected him that way. That was only one of the lesser of its many side effects, which for him usually included nightmares and tremors.

They had dosed him too heavily when he had first been wounded, certain he would die before he could be transported home. He had resisted taking the drug since he had returned to England, and he wished McKinley had not insisted this morning.

Keeping his wits about him and his emotions in check when he was with Anne had become harder and harder as the days of his guardianship had passed. And after yesterday...

The memory of his body pressed into hers was suddenly too vivid in his brain. It seemed he could still feel the delicate curve of her breasts lifting against his chest as she breathed. And incredibly, given the debilitated state of his body, he was reacting in the same way to that remembrance as he had to the sweet reality. At least this time—

"Why did you ask about the boy?" Anne questioned, bringing his wandering attention back to the present.

He took a breath, trying to gather what little control he had left. It was almost ironic to remember how much he had once valued his self-discipline. His growing feelings for his ward had made a mockery of that, as well as of his determination never to allow himself to fall in love with a woman, considering that he no longer had anything to offer. Not even his life.

"He seemed...too knowing to react as he did."

"Too knowing?"

Ian tried to remember what had bothered him about the child. Thankfully, the longer he was awake, the clearer his mind became.

"He had to know what would happen if he ran away. And he surely knew that by appealing to you, he would not lessen his ultimate punishment. The sweep had every legal right to do what he was doing. And any child who has worked in that capacity very long has experienced the strop often enough to be relatively callous to it."

"*And* to having his feet burned?" Anne asked. "Callous to that as well?"

"But they weren't," Ian said, remembering only now that this was part of what had bothered him about yesterday's incident. "Because of his claim, I looked at them very carefully."

"You couldn't see the soles."

"The practice causes scarring along the outside of the foot as well as on the bottom. It would probably be an impossibility to control the torch so that they would not be burned there as well. The boy's feet didn't bear any evidence of that particular mistreatment. Not even old or faded scars.''

Anne shook her head, her eyes no longer focused on his face. She was obviously trying to reconcile what he had just said with the events of yesterday.

''Then why would he make that claim?'' she asked.

''To evoke your sympathy perhaps.''

She shook her head again, the movement almost unconscious, as if she were weighing that idea.

''Then it worked, I suppose,'' she said finally.

''It would have worked on anyone with such a tender heart.''

She laughed, and the sound moved within him. She had been made for joy. He had known that from the moment her eyes, alight with humor and such an obvious zest for living, had challenged his in the hallway of Fenton School.

''My greatest failing. At least according to Mrs. Kemp.''

''I thought she believed that to be a tendency to romance,'' Ian said, remembering Anne's confession. Of course, it was not surprising that he remembered, since he had treasured every word she had ever said to him.

The laughter faded, first from the mobile lips and then more slowly from her eyes. And still they rested on his face.

''*That's* what you're afraid of,'' she said softly.

His heart stopped and then began to beat far too rapidly, a phenomenon he had experienced previously only on the eve of battle. And this fear was not so far from that. It, too, was the result of the recognition that he was in grave danger.

Because he was not prepared for this. That she knew

what he feared was as unexpected as the sudden confrontation in the street had been.

He tried to think how to meet this attack, wishing that the control that had always governed his behavior had not been weakened by the effects of the drug. And, he admitted, by yesterday's unexpected contact between his hungry, aching body and the young, strong one of Anne Darlington.

Young, strong, and beautiful. And deserving of far more than the shattered remnants of the man he had once been.

Had there been any guarantee of how long the flawed vessel that held his heart would last, he might have been weak enough to offer her that tawdry gift. And given her nature, she might well have accepted it, never even stopping to compare it to her worth.

"I don't understand," he said.

Even in his own ears, his voice was strained. Revealing?

"You're afraid that what I feel for you is the result of my tender heart," she said. "Or of my romanticism."

"What you *feel* for me?" he repeated, injecting a note of disbelief into the repetition.

"At least do me the courtesy of dealing with me honestly," she demanded, her own voice unchanged. "Your brother said that to me—that an open and gallant heart would always win favor with the Sinclairs. I am trying to have both. I hope you will as well."

She paused, holding his eyes as if she expected an answer to that assertion. He found he was incapable of giving one.

He could hear the blood beating in his ears, almost loud enough to drown out the sound of her voice and the truth it spoke. Almost enough.

"Then I shall be open with you first," she went on when he said nothing in response. "I am in love with you. I am not sure when it began. Or even when I was first aware that it had. I had always thought I should immediately know the man I would love. I believed that the identification would come to me like some startling revelation as soon as I had laid eyes on him. And instead—" Her voice broke, and her eyes glazed with tears. She fought them, blinking the moisture away.

"Instead," she went on, speaking so softly he had to strain to catch the words, "it grew so slowly that I was not aware of what was happening until it was far too late. And so I could not guard my heart against the cruel possibility that you would not love me in return."

Again she paused, swallowing to overcome the force of emotion. His eyes traced the movement along the slender column of her throat before they came back to hers.

"So I have no shield at all against what I feel," she said, "but I can tell you with all the honesty and courage I possess that what is in my heart for you has nothing to do with pity."

The silence lengthened as her words echoed again and again inside his head. And had his reason been the one she named, they might have been enough to defeat his determination. But it was not, of course.

He was the guardian of her heart, which had been made for joy and not for sorrow. The decision he had made about her future had nothing to do with her father's will, and everything to do with the deadly legacy Darlington's cowardice had left inside his chest. It seemed as if he could feel it there. The weight of the metal as cold and heavy as the death he knew it would inevitably bring.

"Believe me..." he began, hating himself for what he

was about to do. And yet this self-hatred would be nothing to that he would feel if he were selfish enough to take what she had offered him. "It is not that I do not value your affection."

He stopped because he saw the impact of that rejection in her face. He had thought its lines were more mature, but now he saw it age before his eyes. The soft curve of girlish cheek tightened and thinned. Her lips reshaped themselves, no longer full and expectant.

"Valued perhaps, but undesired," she said, her voice flat.

He wondered if he were capable of that lie, remembering the long sleepless nights during which he had desired her. Dreamed of her. Wanted her with a need so great that his body ached and trembled in the darkness.

"The fault is not in what you offer," he said softly.

"Your brother said you believe yourself unworthy of a woman's love."

"My brother says a great many things," he said, smiling at her again. "Sometimes he thinks he knows more about my affairs than I do. He had no right to speak to you about my feelings. I can only tell you how sorry I am that he has misled you about the reality of them."

"Elizabeth told me you are in love with someone else. If you will tell me that is true, then..." She paused, her eyes on his as she drew a breath. "Then I will never speak to you again about what I have told you tonight."

An open and gallant heart. All it would take would be another lie, and eventually, she would forget what she believed she felt for him. *She is so young,* Ian thought, trying to justify what he knew he must do. Too young, surely, to have formed any lasting attachment.

You're afraid that what I feel for you is the result of my tender heart. Or of my romanticism. She was wrong, of course, for what he really feared, more than he had ever feared anything else in his life, was that it was not.

One more lie, he thought again, his gaze on her face. *At least do me the courtesy of dealing with me honestly.*

"Elizabeth was wrong," he said, and could not bear the sudden flare of hope in her eyes. So he added the words that were designed to destroy it, as surely as he was destroying himself, "But so was my brother."

She said nothing for a long time, her eyes locked on his. And then, when he thought he could not endure their scrutiny any longer, she nodded, the movement small and carefully contained.

She rose and, without looking at him again, left him alone with only the cold, black memory of what had been in her face in response to the lie he had chosen. He had understood before he had uttered it that it was by far the crueler of the two weapons she had placed within his hands. And he had chosen it because it would be, or so he prayed, the more effective.

"You sent for me?" the Earl of Dare asked. He had opened the door wider this time, surer, perhaps, of his reception.

"Come in," Ian instructed, and waited until Dare had closed the door behind him and advanced across the room.

He would not have wished to hold this particular interview in the horizontal, as Val called it, but the things he needed to say to his brother could not wait. There had already been too much damage done by his reticence to speak honestly. *An open and gallant heart* echoed somewhere within his.

"You told my ward that I am in love with her."

He could read the shock in his brother's eyes as easily as he had read the pain in Anne's.

"It seems Miss Darlington wastes no time in going after what she wants," Dare said, controlling the upward slant of his lips.

"She is very young. What she thinks she feels for me is rooted in an unfortunate, and given her age, perhaps natural tendency to romanticize our roles."

"And what *you* feel for *her?*"

"You had no right to speak to her."

Dare raised one dark brow, the arch of it inquiring. "I have a brother's right, I think."

"You bloody, arrogant bastard," Ian said bitterly. "You have no idea what you have done."

"Are you denying that you love her? It won't do any good, you know. I know you far too well."

"You don't know me at all. Not if you believe my reason for hiding what I feel is because I limp. Do you take me for a fool? Or so insufferably vain that I would reject Anne's love because I can no longer dance with her?"

The pupils of his brother's eyes widened minutely, expanding into the rim of sapphire blue.

"You have no idea what you have done with your meddling," Ian continued, emphasizing every word. "Where I choose to love or not is of no possible concern to you. Nor is what I do about those feelings. I am not Sebastian, who does not know his own emotions well enough to control them. I am the Sinclair who is *neither* impetuous nor reckless. How dare you question whatever decisions I make about my life? And how dare you confide my feelings, whatever you believe them to be, to a woman?"

There was an answering fury in Val's eyes. Ian imagined that no one had ever talked to the Earl of Dare like this, certainly not either of his brothers. To Dare's credit he did not respond, and despite his anger, Ian drew in a sharp breath to finish what he had begun.

"You may be the head of this family, but that position gives you no right to interfere in my life. Since I have returned to England, you have persisted in treating me as a child, as if I were incapable of deciding what I am fit or not fit to do. And because I love you, I have endured and even forgiven your unwanted attempts to coddle me. But I swear, Val, I shall *never* forgive you for this."

Still the earl made no response, although the small garnet stickpin that held his cravat shimmered with the force of his breathing. His lips were firmly set, his jaw rigid with the force required to keep them that way. Dare waited, unspeaking, apparently recognizing that there would be more to this tirade.

Did he believe that whatever anger his brother felt would fade once he had expressed it? Ian wondered. Or believe that he had sent for Dare to require his promise that he would never again interfere in his life?

Even anticipating, perhaps, that when he had given it, things would go back to the way they had always been, back to the lifelong camaraderie and friendship they had shared? As the silence lengthened without that request, however, the fury slowly seeped out of the earl's eyes to be replaced by something Ian was not sure he had ever seen in them before.

Seeing it there now, he went on, pressing his advantage, "I would like to ask that you leave this house. I know I have no right to make that request, since it and everything within it belong to you. I assure you that if it were possible—"

He broke the sentence, unwilling to admit that he him-

self was physically unable to leave. He had found that
realization, reached within the hour since his ward had
left, to be the blackest moment of his prolonged convalescence.

What a satisfaction it would have been to slam out of
his brother's home, rejecting both his charity and his concern. Since he was incapable of doing that, the next best
thing was, Ian had decided, to attempt to throw Dare out.
And, judging by what was in those blue eyes, his brother
might be shocked enough by his uncharacteristic anger
to let him get away with it.

"You have my apologies—" Dare began.

"I don't want your bloody apologies. I want you
gone."

There was another silence as the earl evaluated his
tone.

"I was wrong to interfere," Dare said finally, the last
of the lingering anger wiped from the darkly handsome
face. "I shall speak to Anne and tell her so."

"*I* have spoken to Anne. You have no idea of the harm
you have done. If you dare speak to her before you leave,
I swear to you, Val, I shall never see you again. And
whatever has been between us in the past, whatever love
and brotherhood—"

"No," Dare said softly, refusing to allow that particular threat to be articulated.

"Then get out," Ian said relentlessly.

"If I understood—"

"What you must understand is that this is my decision.
Believe me, it is not one I make lightly or without valid
reason. And it has nothing to do with vanity or pride or
any of the petty causes you have assigned to it."

"If you love her—" Dare began.

"If I do, it is none of your concern," Ian said implacably.

Another silence. "You are my concern. Grant me that."

"I am not," Ian said. "I know you are accustomed to thinking of me as a boy in need of your guidance. Perhaps at one time that was true. After Iberia, I assure you it is not."

"I'm afraid—"

"What you *should* fear is the break in our relationship which will occur if you persist in this. Believe me, there is nothing you should fear for me more than that."

"Ian," Dare said softly.

The fear he had seen in his brother's eyes before was expressed in that single word. And hearing it, Ian relented enough to offer what explanation he could.

"Believe me, if there were any way I could make her mine, I would find it."

This time the silence stretched too long, and in it echoed all the memories of what they had meant to one another through the years. And finally, against the force of a stricture neither of them could bear, the Earl of Dare nodded.

"If you ever need me, you have only to send word," he said.

He inclined his upper body in a small and formal half bow before he turned on his heel and crossed the room to the bedroom door. And as Anne had done before him, he did not look back before he closed it behind him.

Chapter Eleven

There was a certain sameness to everything, Anne thought as she moved unthinkingly through the now-familiar pattern of the cotillion. Not only a sameness to the dances, of course, but to all the crowded and exhausting days of the Season, during which she hurried breathlessly from one event to another.

There was usually only enough time to accomplish the required change of costume before she was due at the next function. And despite her initial doubts that she would wear half the gowns that had been ordered for her, she had found herself already rewearing some of them.

The demands of the rigorous schedule Lady Laud had instituted had, however, two much-to-be-desired results. During the round of dinners and routs, where she was introduced to and required to converse with perfect strangers, she did not have time to think about Ian. And at night she was so exhausted that she could almost always fall asleep without weeping. *Almost* always.

With his innate kindness, her guardian had made the days since his brother's departure as easy for her as he could. She supposed she should have appreciated his efforts, but since they consisted of his staying out of sight on the rare occasions when she was at home, she was torn between gratitude and an unspeakable pain.

At first he had used the injuries he had suffered in the street brawl as an excuse to keep to his rooms, freeing her from having to face him during those first few difficult days. And then, as the Season progressed, he was careful not to dine at home on the evenings when she did not have an engagement.

She never asked, of course, about the particulars of where he was on those occasions when Williams declared her guardian to be "out." She suspected, as often as not, he was eating a solitary dinner in his rooms as she ate an equally solitary one in lonely and elegant state in the dining room below.

Had it not been for the Earl of Dare's abrupt departure, she might have suspected her guardian was avoiding her because her declaration had embarrassed him. Instead, she had finally concluded that the break between the brothers had occurred because Ian believed Dare's indiscretion had been painful to her.

He was not wrong about that, of course, but she had never blamed the earl. Obviously he had been mistaken in what he had told her. However, she had been more than willing to grasp his words as the truth because they had fit so well with her own fantasies.

"Some refreshment?" her partner suggested.

The question jerked her out of the familiar cloud of abstraction in which she spent far too much of her time. She realized belatedly that the music had stopped.

"How very kind," she said, opening her fan.

In spite of the pleasant temperature of the night outside, the ballroom was overcrowded and overheated. There didn't seem to be a breath of air stirring within it, despite the fact that all the French doors leading into the gardens were open.

And they looked incredibly inviting, Anne thought, feeling a trickle of perspiration slide downward between her breasts. The darkness beyond the doors seemed to beckon, offering a brief escape from what had become a nightly ordeal of too much heat, too much scent, and too many bodies vying for the same limited space.

She had resorted to marking off the passing days of the Season, as a prisoner might keep up with the slow passage of his sentence. That was almost what it had become, she acknowledged. Something to be endured until she could return to Fenton School and the life she had planned for herself there, long before she had known any other.

And now there would be no other. Nor did she wish there to be. Although she seldom lacked for a partner at any event, she was well aware that she had excited no undying passion in the heart of any of the gentlemen she had encountered. That was, of course, with the possible exception of Mr. Travener, who tagged after her with such remarkable devotion that even Lady Laud had commented on it.

Anne had assured her sponsor that her feelings were not mutually engaged, and indeed they were not. However, Doyle's presence did protect her from the unwanted attentions of those few suitors who were so lacking in town bronze that they didn't realize she had nothing to recommend her—neither beauty nor wealth nor birth. And without some combination of the three, she was, thankfully, unlikely to receive any respectable offer.

She glanced again toward the opening that led to the garden, wondering if she dared evade Lady Laud's vigilance and slip outside. Only a moment…

One of Elizabeth's cardinal rules, however, was never to place yourself in a position where your reputation could be compromised. And venturing any distance from the lights and the crowd had the potential for danger.

She pulled her gaze away from the invitation of the garden to scan the mob again, searching for Lady Laud. Or even for her partner, who should certainly be on his way back by now, refreshments in hand. Seeing neither, and taking that as a sign, she began to make her way through the throng toward the doors across the ballroom.

Only later would she realize that at almost any step on that fateful journey something might have happened to change its outcome. She might have encountered Lady Laud or been approached by either her next partner or her last. The ever-present Mr. Travener might have come to speak to her. As might any of the host of people to whom she had been introduced tonight.

Unfortunately, none of those things occurred. Her eyes still searching the crowd as she hurried across the floor, she bumped into someone instead. An elderly gentleman in outdated evening dress had been escorting his equally elderly partner onto the floor just as Anne had almost reached the safety—and the anonymity—of its other side.

"I do beg your pardon," she said, embarrassed that she had drawn attention to herself.

After all, she realized, the eyes of most of the people in the vast ballroom were now focused on the dance floor, waiting for the music of the reel to begin. And most of those who intended to participate in that lively dance had already assumed their places.

She wished now, of course, that she had edged around the perimeter of the room, but when she had started across the polished parquet, she had believed she had time to make it before the music began. And if there had not been so many people leaving it from the last set and an equal number coming onto it for the next, she might have managed.

She smiled at the old man as she apologized, expecting an equally apologetic response. Instead the gentleman's black eyes fastened on her face.

"Darlington's chit," he said.

An acquaintance of my father's, Anne thought, feeling a sense of relief.

"I am indeed, sir," Anne said, smiling at him again. "Did you know my father?"

As she waited for his answer, it seemed a sudden stillness had fallen over the room. The orchestra was not yet playing. The dancers were in position for the reel, breathlessly awaiting the signal of its first notes. And far too many of the guests were watching the floor in anticipation.

Only a few minutes before, she would have welcomed this lull in the eternal hubbub. Now she was uncomfortably aware that hundreds of pairs of eyes seemed focused on the very spot where she and her father's friend were standing. And as she awaited his reply, the silence in the room deepened.

"I knew your father," the old man said, his voice carrying clearly through that unnatural stillness. "I knew him for what he was—a coward and a murderer. And I have no wish to be in the same room as his daughter."

Anne could not have been more shocked had he struck her. As his words reverberated, she tried to make sense of them. Before she could, and certainly before she could formulate any answer to that incredible accusation, the gentleman deliberately turned his back on her.

Instead of walking off the floor as he had threatened, however, he simply stood there. And it took a few seconds for her to realize what that gesture meant. He was offering her a direct cut, the worst possible insult one person could give another in this setting.

The back of his evening jacket, which hung loosely from thin, narrow shoulders, seemed to be all she could see. And she could hear nothing, enclosed in a soundless vacuum of horror. It seemed that no one in the vast room was saying a word.

His, however, echoed over and over. *I knew him for what he was—a coward and a murderer. I have no wish to be in the same room as his daughter.* Perhaps they sounded only in her head, but if so, they were loud enough there to drown out cannon fire.

Her first instinct was to flee, but Anne Darlington had never run from anything in her life. No matter what else she might be, she told herself, she was not a coward. Her second instinct, coming closely on the heels of the first, was to put her hand on the old man's shoulder and pull him around to demand what he had meant.

As his words continued to beat in her consciousness, however, she realized that somewhere inside she had always known there was something shameful about George Darlington. And in that terrible isolation, alone and yet surrounded by scores of people, a hundred subtle clues she should have put together before now ran through her brain like summer lightning, shimmering and intense.

Ian's lack of response to her questions about his relationship to her father. His strange wording concerning the will on the first day she'd met him. The look in Elizabeth's eyes when Anne had remarked on Ian's supposedly close friendship with her father. And, most tellingly, her guardian's reaction to her comment about taking her courage after her father. *Coward and murderer.*

There had even occasionally been something within

the eyes of a few of the gentlemen to whom she had been introduced. Some emotion she had noticed and had not understood. They had all been her father's age or older—like this man, who stood with his back to her, thin shoulders squared, his head held erect.

As a soldier's daughter, she should have recognized the stance, but Anne had never in her life been exposed to anything dealing with the army. Or with her father's reputation within its ranks.

"Miss Darlington is now the ward of Ian Sinclair, General Mayfield. Perhaps you didn't know."

The calm, familiar voice pulled her back to the present. Doyle Travener was standing before the old man who had deliberately turned his back to her.

Dear Mr. Travener. Who was again prepared to come to her rescue, it seemed, despite the watching eyes of the ton. The riot in the street, during which he had cleverly fired the warning shot that had dispersed the mob, flashed through her head. And now, thankfully, he had had the presence of mind to evoke her guardian's name.

"Sinclair?" the general repeated, obviously surprised by that revelation. "You must be mistaken, sir. Sinclair's brother was one of Darlington's victims. He should be the last person—"

"*Not* his brother, sir," Doyle corrected. His eyes lifted over the old man's shoulder to meet Anne's before they returned to the general's. "The youngest Sinclair is still in Iberia. Miss Darlington is the ward of *Major* Ian Sinclair, who was…" Travener hesitated, his eyes reflecting a reluctance she didn't understand. "Miss Darlington's guardian was the Sinclair who was with Wellington at the time of your son's death."

"I was told he had died from his wounds."

"I believe that for some time—" Travener began.

Hope suddenly stirring in her heart, Anne broke in, not allowing Doyle to finish. If Mayfield had confused Ian with his younger brother, then perhaps he also had confused her father with someone else.

"I'm sure, sir, that since you were mistaken about my guardian's identity, you are mistaken about my father as well."

"There is no mistake about your father's actions," the general said, shooting a glance at her over his shoulder. "I was told, however, that Major Sinclair had died of his injuries. It seems that was not the case, thank God."

His dark eyes, piercing under those bristling white brows, raked her with such scorn that she was silenced. Without apology, he turned back to Doyle.

"Why would Sinclair, of all people, agree to be this woman's guardian?" he demanded.

For several seconds, Travener vouched no answer, although it seemed to Anne that not only she, but everyone in the room, waited for one.

"He was named in Darlington's will. Perhaps the colonel realized Sinclair was the one man respected enough to undertake that task," he said finally.

Anne wondered if Doyle realized that his praise for her guardian was such a condemnation of her father.

"Or perhaps Colonel Darlington knew that whatever his personal feelings," Travener continued, "Major Sinclair would take such a responsibility seriously. As he always took seriously the welfare of the men under his command."

"By accepting Darlington's daughter as his ward, Sinclair abuses the memory of men that coward murdered. Including the memory of my son," the old man added.

There was another long silence, and Anne's heart

begged for Doyle's denial to break it. What he said, however, was not the contradiction she had hoped for.

"However men may fail to react to crises on the field of battle, sir, you and I both are aware that does not constitute murder. The accusation you have made tonight is unforgivable."

"Through his cowardice Darlington murdered my son," General Mayfield said evenly, "as surely as if he himself had put the gun to his heart. How you can defend him—"

"It is not my intent to defend Colonel Darlington. It is simply my intent to protect his daughter from something for which no reasonable man might hold her accountable."

"Then I must prefer *not* to be a reasonable man. I won't be in the same room with Darlington's spawn. Her blood offends me."

"Then regretfully, general, I must inform you that your comments about the woman I hope to make my wife offend me," Travener said quietly, bowing from the waist. "My second will call on you tomorrow."

Without another word to Mayfield, he walked around the old man to offer his arm to Anne.

"Come, my dear," he said.

Despite her shock, she had comprehended Travener's ridiculous declaration that he intended to make her his wife. She had given him neither the right to make such a statement publicly nor to hope for it privately. She had no intention of accepting any offer he might make.

Except this one, she realized. Because the arm he offered represented a means of escape, which she wanted more than she wanted anything else right now. And, suddenly Travener's kind face blurred, veiled by her tears. *They will not see me cry.*

Released from her paralysis by that determination, she was finally able to move, reaching out with fingers that trembled to slip her hand within the crook of Mr. Travener's arm. She felt his close over hers, and she knew that was intended to comfort and give her courage.

She needed both. Because it only got worse. As they began to walk across the ballroom, the silent crowd parted before them as if they were lepers, opening a path to the door.

Anne kept her eyes straight ahead, unable to look at the faces of those around them. However, by the time they had reached the anteroom, still crowded with people coming and going to the ball, she could no longer control her tears.

She took one softly shuddering breath, almost a sob. Doyle turned his head to look down at her. She was aware of the movement, but she didn't dare meet his eyes.

"Not here," he ordered. "Hold your head up until we're outside. And alone."

He increased his pace, not even stopping to collect her wrap. She wouldn't miss it. She longed for the night air, hoping it would cool her flaming cheeks and stop the deep burn of pain and humiliation in her chest.

"Courage, my darling," Doyle whispered as they hurried down the steps. "We are almost away."

She could barely see the steps, forced to trust in his guidance. The tears could no longer be denied, but here in the darkness, with nothing but the flambeaux and the servants to see them, they didn't matter.

There was a carriage at the curb, but it wasn't his, of course. On some level Anne was aware of Travener's discussion with the footman standing attendance beside it. She had no idea what he said to the servant because her mind had begun repeating the general's words over and over, seeking a way past the most painful part of them.

Thankfully, however, it was only a matter of seconds before the door of the coach was opened and the steps lowered. Once more Travener's hand offered support. Using it, she climbed into the welcome darkness and closed her eyes, putting both palms over her face.

She felt the coach dip with Travener's weight as he joined her. Only when she heard the door close behind him did she release the pent-up sobs. And there seemed nothing more natural than to allow herself to be gathered into Doyle Travener's comforting arms. At last, the carriage began to move, carrying them away from that terrible scene.

Despite feeling she should make some effort to compose herself, she instead gave in to the hurt and exhaustion and accumulated tensions of the past few weeks. She sobbed them all out against the broad shoulder that so willingly sheltered her.

Doyle said nothing as he held her. After all, if the general's accusation about her father was true, what possible comfort could he give her? And that was something she had to know, she realized. One of the many things she needed to understand.

Putting her hands flat against his chest, she pushed away from Travener. After a moment Doyle's arms released her, although he seemed reluctant to do so. Did he dread telling her the truth about her father as much as she dreaded hearing it?

Somewhere inside there was still hope that this was all a misunderstanding. A mistake. Something that could be straightened out and the record eventually set straight.

"Tell me about my father," she said, her eyes on his face.

Travener's mouth was set, his eyes troubled. She was unaccustomed to him in the mode, she realized. He was always smiling, never caustic or mocking or moody. Now, however, he cruelly said nothing in response to the hardest question she had ever had to ask in her life.

"Why would he call my father a coward and a murderer?"

She could hardly bring herself to say the word. The other was bad enough, but the last…

"You are not responsible for your father's actions."

"Tell me what he did," she demanded, her voice sharp with frustration. "Believe me, it can be no worse than what I will imagine."

Even that wasn't true. She could not begin to imagine what her father, her own flesh and blood, might have done that was awful enough to acquire those sobriquets. Or to cause the look of absolute disdain in the old man's eyes.

"Your father's actions in battle caused the death of a number of men, one of whom was the general's son."

She examined the words and found them less horrifying than whatever she had been expecting. *Your father's actions in battle…*

She remembered vaguely that he had said something like that before. That it had not been a deliberate murder. *Your father's actions in battle…*

Her heart was beginning to beat again, if not with its normal regularity, at least in some semblance of it. She took a deep breath, which still sounded suspiciously like a sob, and Doyle's thumb traced over the track of an escaping tear, wiping it from her cheek.

His eyes had left hers to watch the movement of his

finger, and when they came back, they were somber. And pitying.

"Your father chose not to bring his command to the rescue of a unit which was under attack and heavily outnumbered."

"*Chose* not to?" she repeated.

"He had not been given a direct order to reinforce them, but..."

"Tell me," she said when the explanation again faded.

"Any other commander would have come to their rescue. Everyone knew that. And because he refused...men died. It was Sinclair's command your father failed to reinforce. His men who were slaughtered."

The resulting silence as she absorbed that blow was almost as deep as that within the ballroom. *I am not a coward,* she reminded herself, as all the telltale clues she had missed paraded mockingly through her consciousness.

Including the sudden memory of Doyle Travener's eyes meeting her guardian's the night they had been introduced. She had asked him if he knew her father, and he had denied it, but his eyes had found Ian's, and within them... Within them...

"My father was responsible for the injuries Ian Sinclair suffered on the Peninsula," she said, speaking the realization aloud as soon as she made it.

The injuries that had crippled him. The injuries that had left him forever vulnerable to the kinds of illness he had suffered in rescuing her from the highwaymen. The injuries Ian refused to discuss were the result of her father's cowardice.

Doyle nodded, the movement slight.

I should want to kill a man who hurt my brother...

Now she knew why the Earl of Dare had told her that.

And it was no wonder he had disliked her from the beginning, even *before* he knew her. He blamed her father for all that Ian had suffered since that day, and like the general, he had transferred that hatred and disdain to her.

"You have known this from the first," she accused.

Doyle's lips tightened, but he told her. "I have."

"How many others knew? How many others here in London besides the Sinclairs?"

"Some of those who were there that day have returned, invalided out of service as Major Sinclair was. A few within the War Office knew of the incident."

"But it was *not* general knowledge within the ton. Not until tonight."

Slowly, he shook his head.

"And now it will be."

He hesitated again before he answered her, but by now he understood she would not be put off until she understood it all.

"There will undoubtedly be...gossip," he admitted.

"Gossip," she repeated softly.

His phrasing was intended as a kindness, she supposed. *Gossip.* The story of the general's actions tonight would certainly be told with varying degrees of horror or relish across a hundred breakfast tables tomorrow. And she realized she truly did not care if it were. That she was ruined in the eyes of the ton was the least of her concerns.

"How could he *not* hate me?" she whispered, knowing this was the answer to so many things she had not been able to understand.

"He lost his only son," Doyle said. "Perhaps it makes that loss easier for him to bear if he has someone to blame."

And lost in grief, Anne did not even bother to correct his mistake.

Chapter Twelve

Williams had taken one look at her face and, despite the lateness of the hour, told her where she would find her guardian. Without even considering whether or not he would welcome the intrusion, she opened the door of the library and stepped inside.

Ian was asleep in the same wing chair where she had found him a few days before. The curtains had been drawn against the night, and a low fire burned in the grate, the only light in the room. She stood unmoving for a long time, watching it play across his face.

His hair, tousled as if he had run his fingers through it, was touched with gold by the subtle firelight. It emphasized the slight hollows in his lean cheeks and the dark shadows that lay beneath the long lashes. And the bone structure that underlay those beloved features was too pronounced, more so than it had been on the day she had first seen him at Fenton School. All indicators of the reality behind the facade of health and vigor her guardian outwardly maintained.

She took a breath, fighting a surge of guilt and the strongest inclination to back out of the room and leave him in peace. *Not a coward,* she told herself again.

There was a book, open and lying facedown across the arm of the chair, as if he had tired of reading and closed his eyes to rest them. A half-empty glass, its liquid ambered by the flames, stood on the table beside him. And she wondered how many nights he had fallen asleep in this cold, dark room.

Seeking escape from things too painful to remember, just as she had done in the endless round of the Season's entertainment? Or dutifully waiting, in spite of his exhaustion, for her to come home? How many nights, she wondered, had she passed this door, never dreaming Ian was here? Listening for her return?

Was that why her father had chosen this man? Because he had somehow known, that of all the men who would despise him for what he had done, this was the one who would be able to put duty before emotion. Honor before any need for revenge.

Ian Sinclair had done both. He had treated her with nothing but kindness and a genuine consideration of her feelings, even when she had been so foolish as to fall in love with him. And more foolish to confess what she felt. Even then—

The man in the chair moved, his head turning restlessly against the fabric of the high back. She had already stepped out the door, prepared to disappear into the hall, when his eyes opened and found her. The paleness of the gown she wore, silhouetted against the darkness, would have drawn them, of course. It seemed, however, that when they had opened, they were already focused on the doorway.

"Anne?"

Too late to retreat. Too late to melt into the shadows of the darkened hall. *Too late.* There was nothing to do but what she had done in that crowded ballroom. Pretend she was not as great a coward as her father.

"I know what he did," she said.

Even in the low light she could see his brow furrow.

"You know what who did?"

"I know what my father did in Portugal. I know what he did to you."

The silence in the room was suddenly as heavy as that which had fallen over the ballroom. And as isolating.

"I'm sorry," Ian said softly.

It was not what she had expected, and yet she could tell by his voice that it was true. He was sorry for *her*. And for the first time, hearing his tone, she understood why he feared her pity.

"Why should *you* be sorry? *You* aren't the one who killed men by your cowardice. You were the victim of that outrage. I, who bear his blood, should be the one—"

"You are not responsible for what your father did."

Which was what Travener had said. The argument was no more convincing from Ian's lips than it had been from Doyle's.

"Do you believe that will make any difference to them?" she asked. "Do you believe it can make any difference to me?"

"To *them?*"

The edge of dismay in the question was clear. He had obviously just realized that what her father had done was no longer a private scandal, but a very public one.

"A man named Mayfield was offended by my presence tonight. Actually, I believe he was offended by my very existence. Publicly offended, I'm afraid. He turned his back to me. Whatever scandal you have hoped to prevent by your reticence about my father's actions will be full-blown by morning."

Ian said nothing for several long heartbeats. She measured them by the sound of the blood beating through her ears.

"Mayfield's son served under my command," he said finally, and she could read nothing in his tone.

"And he died because my father failed him. As he failed you. Why *didn't* you tell me, Ian? Why would you allow me to find out in this way?"

"I had hoped you would never find out."

He had tried to protect her. And in doing so, he had left her far more vulnerable to their cruelty because she had never expected it. All of the pain had come without warning or preparation.

"When you came to find me, to fulfill the terms of my father's will, you thought you were rescuing a child. It seems I am still that child to you. I suppose I shall always be."

"If I could have prevented this, Anne, I would have. That doesn't mean I consider you a child."

She shook her head, her smile almost bitter, and then she turned to leave, knowing there was nothing he could tell her that would ease this hurt. He had known from the first what her father was, and he had tried to protect her from that knowledge. She could not blame him that the story had been too widely known to contain.

"By the way," she said, turning her head to look at him again before she stepped out into the hall. "You should probably expect another visit from Mr. Travener tomorrow. Unless he is wise enough to think better of it after a night's sleep. In coming to my defense, he rather rashly announced his intention of marrying me."

"Travener?"

"Which is remarkable, considering that he has always known the whole. Another noble soul. Not one I intend to wed, however, despite my gratitude. As my guardian, discouraging unwanted attentions from my suitors is your office, is it not? I'm sure that in a month or so, when whatever he believes he feels for me has faded, you will have his undying gratitude. As you already have mine."

"I never wanted your gratitude," Ian said.

Or my love. And now, finally, she understood why.

"As *I* never wanted your noble sacrifice. But then, I suppose few people get what they really want. Or even what they deserve. Only look at my father."

"If you allow it to, what he did will embitter you and destroy who you are."

"I am not his victim," she said softly. "I am his daughter. I bear the same blood. And no one will ever forget that. Not even you."

She held his eyes, expecting a denial. Or at least more comforting platitudes. And she found, surprisingly, that she was infinitely grateful when he offered neither.

At least do me the courtesy of dealing with me honestly. Tonight, at least, it seemed he had.

She had finished packing long before dawn stole through the mullioned windows of her room, throwing barred patterns of pale lemon across the hardwood floor. As she had paced it throughout the long dark hours, the soft kid slippers she had worn to the ball made no sound. None that was loud enough to drown out the voices that echoed endlessly through her brain.

Mayfield's. *I knew him for what he was—a coward and a murderer. I have no wish to be in the same room as his daughter.*

And Doyle's. *It was Ian Sinclair's command your father failed to reinforce. His men who were slaughtered.*

And Dare's, laced with an irony she had not understood then and could not bear to remember now. *I should want to kill a man who hurt my brother. I feel I must tell you that with all honesty, if you and I are to have any sort of relationship. And as for the woman who would hurt him…*

And finally Ian's voice, rejecting who and what she was. *The fault is not in what you offer…*

Not in what you offer. Always the circling thoughts came back to this. The fault is not in what you offer…

What she had offered Ian Sinclair, no matter how pure and sincere, would be forever tainted by what her father had done. Not only to the men who had died under his command, but to him.

Like General Mayfield, how could Ian *not* be offended by the very blood that flowed through her veins? The blood of the man whose cowardice had cost him so much.

I should want to kill a man who hurt my brother, Dare had said. She had known then that the earl spoke the truth, although she had had no idea he was speaking of her father. How could Ian himself feel any differently about that man?

And why, in light of this revelation, had he agreed to be her guardian? Why had he come to Fenton School to find her?

Whatever his intent, and she had no doubt it was noble and honorable, he had unwittingly imposed a punishment on her that was more than fitting for her father's crime. George Darlington had destroyed the life Ian had known. And in return, Ian had made his daughter long for a life which she could never have. One she had never dreamed of before she met him.

I had thought I should have to satisfy it by caring for the poor, orphaned Sally Eddingtons of the world. Once that small enclosed world would have been more than enough. And then Ian Sinclair had given her a glimpse of another.

Not the glittering artificial world of London society. She would turn her back on that with as much satisfaction as the general had found in turning his to her. It was the other possibilities that falling in love with Ian had created that she would grieve for. Possibilities that she *had* grieved for throughout the long night that had just passed.

Because even her ability to fantasize did not extend to believing the man her father had injured and betrayed would ever return her love. Even the man she knew Ian Sinclair to be could not find that much forgiveness in his heart. Nor, in all fairness, should he be asked to try.

And knowing him as she now did, she had begun to divine finally a reason for what he had done. In bringing her to London, Ian had found a way to atone for the hatred he had quite naturally felt for her father. He had fought its corrosive power by treating the daughter of his enemy with the same consideration he would give to the child of a beloved friend. That was the only explanation that made sense. And it fit with the character of the man she not only loved, but admired above all others.

She had known from the first that it was ridiculous for a woman of her age to have a guardian. She had allowed herself to be carried along by his and Mrs. Kemp's surety that this Season was what her father had intended. That this silly carnival was how a woman of her class should live her life.

Now, of course, there could be no doubt that neither of those things was true. And no doubt that it was past time for her to assume control of her own destiny.

She walked across to the bed and touched the fabric of the dress she had laid out on it last night. It was one of the few garments she had brought with her from Fenton School. Only in comparing it to those she was now accustomed to wearing was she aware of the cheapness of its sturdy fabric and of how shoddily it was made.

Eminently suitable, however, for kneeling on cold stone floors as one commanded small, reddened noses to blow. She smiled at the image, even as her eyes glazed again with tears, blearing the faded pattern of the cloth that rested under the tips of her fingers.

One more favor to ask her guardian and then she would put this entire episode from her heart. One more chance to see him, to be with him, and then she would never again allow herself...

Even as the words formed in her brain, she knew them for a lie. She would fill the years that stretched ahead with substitutes for his children, which she had once foolishly hoped to carry beneath her heart.

But she would never forget Ian Sinclair. She would think of him often. And always with love.

"How dare you put my ward in such a position," Ian said, putting both hands flat on his brother's rosewood desk and leaning over it toward the man he was addressing. "Who the bloody hell do you think you are?"

For a long moment the man on the other side of the desk said nothing, his handsome face tightened with suppressed anger. And then, blue eyes earnestly fixed on Ian's, Doyle Travener began to explain.

"Someone had to defend Miss Darlington's honor," he said, "and since you were not there—"

"You decided to take it upon yourself to issue a public challenge to General Mayfield."

"My cousin called upon him this morning, acting as my second. It was all quite properly done, major, I assure you."

"And *I* assure *you,* Mr. Travener, that calling out a man old enough to be your grandfather can *never* be properly done."

Ian pushed away from the desk, taking a step back. He was afraid that if he remained within striking distance of Doyle Travener's pale, determined face, he might be tempted beyond his raveling control. *Of all the insufferable jackasses.*

"May I remind you, sir," Travener said, his own tone coldly formal now, "that with your kind permission, I am a suitor for Miss Darlington's hand. I have every hope of making her my wife. I could not stand by and see her maligned and insulted."

"And has she agreed to this match?" Ian asked, hiding his anxiety as he awaited an answer he had thought Anne had already given him.

"I have not yet approached her," Travener said stiffly. "In none but the most general terms. I assure you, however, that she is in no doubt about my feelings. Not after last night."

"Perhaps you should explain exactly what you mean by 'not after last night,' Mr. Travener, before I am forced to call *you* out. I would remind you that I am accounted to be a very good shot. And *my* aim will not be affected by failing eyesight and a palsied hand."

An unbecoming blush stained the cheeks of the young ex-officer, and despite himself, Ian found some satisfaction in Travener's discomfiture.

"I only meant that I comforted Miss Darlington after the incident and then escorted her home. She did not seem averse to my attentions, and there was nothing improper about them, I assure you. I resent your implication, sir.''

"Resent and be damned," Ian said softly. "Are you really too stupid to understand that by proposing this absurd duel you are making matters worse for her?"

"I see nothing absurd about defending the honor of the woman I love."

"The only honor impugned last night, at least until you stepped in, was George Darlington's. I don't suppose you are defending his?"

There was a thread of sarcasm in the question, and Travener's blush deepened.

"It won't do, you know," Ian said, modifying his tone through an enormous effort of will. "You can't challenge Mayfield. He said nothing about Anne's father that was not the absolute truth."

"Whatever her father did, she should not be made to suffer for it," Travener said stubbornly, his blue eyes determined.

"Except that is the way our world works. And you are certainly old enough to be aware of it. That the sins of the father will be visited upon the children is not a new concept. Nor is it one this society invented."

"Miss Darlington has done nothing wrong. Until last night, she didn't even know about her father."

"And you undertook to explain everything to her, I suppose."

"The general said enough that—" Travener broke the sentence at Ian's snort of disgust. "As a friend, Miss Darlington begged me for the truth. I had no choice but to tell her what happened in Portugal. What would you have had me do?"

"I would have had you behave like a gentleman, although apparently that is too much to hope for. You should have found Lady Laud and handed Miss Darlington into her care. And then you should have said goodnight to your hostess and gone to your own home. Instead, by spiriting my ward away with you in a closed carriage, you have created a scandal and attached it firmly to her name, where before there might only have been some unpleasant speculation.''

"I suppose it is easy to judge the situation when—"

"When one considers only what is best for the lady's reputation?''

"I meant no harm to Miss Darlington's reputation."

"Whatever you *meant*, you have caused harm," Ian said, "and I expect you to render your apology to General Mayfield within the hour. Send me word when you have put an end to this nonsense.''

The well-shaped mouth of the man standing before him moved as he considered the order. First it tightened, then pursed and finally it opened.

"I can't do that," Travener said. "Not at this juncture. It is too late to back down. I should be branded a coward, and Miss Darlington would be—"

"I shall tell you again that you are not responsible for Miss Darlington. You are not betrothed to her, you are not a member of her family, and *you* are not her guardian. Those are the only conditions which might allow you to act on her behalf. Even if you were any of those things, in this particular case—"

"But it is for that very reason that I did what I did."

"For what reason? What reason can you have for interfering in a situation that is of no possible concern to you?''

"I can understand your reluctance to defend your ward, Major Sinclair, given your own suffering at her father's hands. However, I beg you not to let your personal feelings stand in the way of a quite necessary defense of her honor.''

The silence built between them, strained and uncomfortable.

''Forgive me,'' Ian said, his voice very soft and very controlled. ''I was wrong. You *are* that stupid. Therefore I will make it easy enough that even you can understand, Mr. Travener. Deliver your apology to General Mayfield within the hour or expect a call from my second.''

Travener's eyes refused to quail before the threat, and he made no promises. Finally, he turned and walked across the room to the door. Just before he reached it, Ian added the last.

''Do it, Travener, or I swear before God you'll never see her again. And as Anne's legal guardian, I assure you that is a promise that *is* within my ability to carry out.''

The most galling aspect of this morning's fiasco was that after his interview with Travener, Ian had found himself wanting to discuss the entire situation with Dare. He could imagine his brother's reaction.

He was still standing at the window in the library, looking out at the scene below. His mind was, however, far from what his eyes seemed focused on.

Despite his threats to Doyle Travener, he was aware that there was little he could do if Anne chose to welcome the man's championing. Or if she chose to welcome the man himself.

After all, although the silly bastard was certainly going about it in the wrong way, at least Travener was doing something. *Which is more than I can say.*

''Williams told me Mr. Travener had called on you.''

He turned at the sound of her voice. Seeing her in the doorway, his physical reaction forced him to acknowledge he was as lacking in self-control as he had been the night he had awakened to find her in his room.

It was obvious from her eyes that she had not slept. Their swollen lids gave evidence of tears as well, although her features appeared to be perfectly composed. She said nothing else for a moment, her gaze examining his face as intently as he was assessing hers.

"It was *not* a social call, I assume," she said finally. "I am not sorry to have missed him, then. Especially since I have already received a visit from your godmother this morning. As I understand you did. You have entertained quite a parade of visitors. All my fault, I'm afraid. And you have my apologies. I have apologized to Lady Laud as well. I'm afraid I did not think about the implications of leaving the ball with Mr. Travener."

"It wasn't *your* place to think of them," Ian said.

"I doubt Elizabeth would agree with you. Nor do I, of course. And since according to Lady Laud I am already quite ruined...I have come to thank you for your many kindnesses," she said. "And to say goodbye."

"Goodbye?" he repeated. Whatever he might have expected her to say to him today, it was not this.

"We have both known from the beginning that I am far too old to be your ward. Now that I know the truth about your relationship with my father, I believe there can be no reason to continue with this farce."

"Whatever your feelings, I assure you the courts will not consider my guardianship to be a farce."

The reminder that their relationship, desired or not, was a legality silenced the too-brittle speech she had probably spent most of that sleepless night preparing. Her eyes, however, didn't change.

"I am quite content for you to control my finances," she went on after a moment. "They are, as you well know, nonexistent. I believe that is all the courts will be concerned about. And since I can no longer remain in London—''

''There's no reason for you to leave London.''

''Believe me, I can give you hundreds of reasons. You have only to request Lady Marling's guest list from last night to see them.''

''It will be forgotten in a fortnight. Or at least it will be replaced by...''

''The next scandal?'' she finished for him when he hesitated over using the word. ''Let us at least be honest with one another. Lady Laud was quite forthright. I can only wish that from the first you had been more so. I might have been better prepared then to hear publicly about my father's transgressions.''

''You are not responsible for your father's actions.''

''Perhaps not, but I will be judged by them.''

''Not by me.''

She smiled at him. ''Actually, I find it somewhat comforting to believe that is *not* the case.''

''What your father did has nothing to do with—''

Again he hesitated, and this time he found he could not finish the claim, although she waited. Because what her father had done, of course, had a great deal to do with his refusal of what she had offered him.

And that, too, was something Ian had never intended to tell her. Thankfully, there were very few people who knew the truth about the extent of his injuries. And so she would never learn the reason he had refused a gift he would have given his life, whatever was left of it, to accept.

''Thank you for not completing that,'' she said. ''I should hate to leave with a lie between us.''

An open and gallant heart. He had already told her

one lie, because he had believed it would put an end to what she felt for him. He would not tell her another, especially when the truth, as she understood it, would serve just as well.

"Travener wants to marry you," he said instead. "I shall leave it to you to refuse him."

"There will be any number of men—"

"Believe me, I do not want any number of men. Nor do I want Mr. Travener. I should be bored to tears after our first breakfast together. I'm afraid none of them can compete with the charms of Fenton School," she said, smiling at him. "Chilblains, porridge, running noses, and dragging hems."

"You wanted children of your own."

She had told him that. And her eyes had told him how much.

"I wanted *your* children," she corrected softly. "Will you give them to me?"

For a long time neither of them moved, simply looking at one another across the width of the library.

Then slowly, deliberately, Ian Sinclair moved his head from side to side. There was only that single movement, but it was final enough to break the spell that had held them.

Anne Darlington turned. Opening the door, she disappeared through it, again leaving him alone with the memory of what had been in her eyes.

Chapter Thirteen

"This has gone far enough," Ian said. "Whatever your motives were when you began—"

"My motives were and *are* still exactly the same."

Doyle Travener didn't look at Ian as he said it. His eyes remained on the dueling pistols his cousin was preparing.

"To defend Miss Darlington's honor," Ian said, not bothering to hide his sarcasm.

"Of course. Someone must."

Despite the seriousness of his before-dawn errand, Ian had had to fight not to laugh at the earnest rubbish with which Travener had answered his every objection. With each passing minute, which brought them nearer to the hour of the proposed duel, however, he was losing his appreciation of the absurd.

"Miss Darlington has left London—" he began patiently.

"Driven out by those baying jackals and gossip mongers."

Ian restrained himself from again reminding Travener that it was his insistence on this ridiculous duel that was feeding the current talk. Ian still believed he had been right in his original appraisal. The general's accusations would have been little more than a nine days' wonder without Travener's reaction to them.

"She left because she wished to return to her position at Fenton School."

"Do you really believe that?" Travener asked, his eyes finally rising to meet Ian's.

And he didn't, of course. He knew, if Travener did not, that it wasn't scandal or the fear of it that had driven Anne from London. The general's revelation had precipitated her departure, perhaps, but it had had nothing, ultimately, to do with her decision. His lie about what he felt for her was responsible for that. But he also knew that this separation, no matter how painful it might be, was best for both of them.

"I should feel better if I thought you *did* believe that fable," Travener went on. "I know men can change, and you have certainly had enough to bear that it has perhaps..." He paused and then, thankfully, never finished whatever justification for Ian's lack of action he had begun. "Still, I should never have thought that someone like you, someone I had admired from afar, could be indifferent to Miss Darlington's suffering. Whatever sins may be laid at her father's door—"

"I didn't come to discuss Darlington's sins. Or my feelings about them, which are, quite frankly, none of your concern. I came to tell you that you have no right to presume to act on Miss Darlington's behalf."

"Are you sure of that?" Doyle asked, his blue eyes challenging.

"I have it on the very best authority. That of Miss Darlington herself."

"Don't you understand that she is attempting to protect me?"

"I beg your pardon."

Ian's tone indicated how preposterous he found that claim, but he had recognized shortly after his arrival that attempting to talk logic to Doyle Travener was hopeless. And the conversation seemed to be becoming more bizarre by the second. Of course, he supposed it was equally bizarre that he had come to Travener's house before dawn to try once more to prevent the idiot from meeting Arthur Mayfield's father on the so-called field of honor.

"Anne…" Travener began and then immediately corrected himself with a small, formal half bow in Ian's direction. "Miss Darlington feels that because of her father's actions she is unworthy of the love of an honorable man. And unworthy of a suitable marriage. Those are things to which you and I both agree, I'm sure, that she is perfectly entitled, no matter what Colonel Darlington did. I know of no better way than this duel to convince her that I am quite sincere in my desire to marry her. Despite the scandal surrounding her father."

"No better way than to challenge a sick old man?"

"General Mayfield should never have treated Miss Darlington in that despicable fashion."

"And therefore he should be killed? Because he was embittered to rashness by Darlington's action, which I remind you, cost him his only and much beloved son?"

"I *won't* kill him. I promise you that," Travener said. "And I am *also* a very good shot."

"Then you must be hoping, I suppose, that Mayfield is not."

The blue eyes lightened, and the corners of Travener's mouth slanted upward. "I am indeed. I confess I don't relish getting shot. Despite my lack of the kind of commendations you received, however, I am *not* a coward.

And if I can convince Miss Darlington that I am willing to make any sacrifice for her—''

"A bullet in the heart seems a rather permanent sacrifice to prove the depth of your affections.''

Travener laughed, and despite his exasperation, Ian found his own lips inclined to tilt at the boy's ardently romantic declarations. And it had become very obvious that no matter Travener's age, he was still a boy, much like those who had once served under Ian's command.

"It won't come to that,'' Doyle said confidently. "What makes you so sure Mayfield won't recognize *he* was the one in the wrong and delope?''

"The fact that I knew his son, I suppose,'' Ian said. "Hot-headed and hair-triggered. And I should imagine he inherited those qualities from his father.''

"You liked him.''

"Of course.''

Travener nodded. "I won't hurt his father,'' he promised. "This is all symbolic, as most affairs of honor are these days. You're welcome to join us, if you wish. As a matter of fact, I should be honored if you would accompany me.''

In Ian's experience there was no circumstance in which having a loaded pistol pointed at your heart might be considered symbolic. Of course, he had had far more shots fired at him than this young firebrand, which tended to put things like life and death into their proper perspective.

He glanced up and found the eyes of Travener's cousin on his face. And then, realizing that Ian had become aware of that scrutiny, the man looked down again on the dueling pistols, nested like lovers in their case. These would be the extra set, of course. Mayfield, as the challenged party, would bring his own.

"Have you heard from her?" Travener asked.

And Ian's mind was suddenly, very much against his will, revisiting the sights and sounds and smells of Fenton School. The mental journey had been instantaneous, and its effect was powerful.

The picture of Anne as he had first seen her, little more than a schoolgirl, was too vivid in his mind's eye. And it was only in comparison to that indelible first impression that he realized how much she had changed during these few short months.

The difference involved more than the thin veneer of sophistication and confidence Elizabeth's mentoring had given her, although that was a part of it, of course. When he had met Anne, she *had* been a girl. Now, clearly, she was a woman. A woman who had claimed to be in love with him.

In the two short days since Anne had left, Ian had discovered that his resolve to refuse that love was not strong enough to allow him to think of her. And not strong enough to dwell on images of Anne caring for the "poor Sally Eddingtons" of the world rather than for his children. The physical distance she had put between them when she had returned to Fenton School was not great enough to allow him that indulgence.

"I know that she is doing what she wants to do," he said simply. "And I know that she has always been happy there."

"Happy caring for *other* people's children?" Travener asked, adeptly probing a wound that was still raw. "That's not what a woman like Miss Darlington was created to do. We both know that, I think."

Chilblains, porridge, and running noses. Would it be better for Anne to marry Doyle Travener and bear *his* children? Certainly not better for his peace of mind, Ian admitted, feeling the painful sting of jealousy at the thought.

I should be bored to tears after our first breakfast together. And considering only the few minutes he had spent with Travener this morning, he realized Anne had been right.

That surge of jealousy faded into an amusement he wished he could share with her. She would, he believed, have appreciated a recounting of the discoveries he had made about Mr. Travener's character.

"It's what she wants," Ian said.

"Forgive me if I disagree," Travener responded. "It's all that she believes she deserves. I intend to disabuse her of that notion."

"And you believe that this...symbolic duel is the way to do that."

"We shall see," Travener said, closing with a snap the case that held the dueling pistols. "My invitation is still open, Major Sinclair. If you accompany me, you'll be able to see for yourself that everything is properly done. Perhaps it will put your mind at ease."

They arrived at the Elms before Travener's opponent. Despite the season, the predawn darkness was cold enough that the white fog of the horses' breath was visible in the dim light cast by the carriage lamps. There was even a rim of ice glinting around the edges of the murky puddle that lay in the center of the clearing, the trees that had given this place its notorious nickname looming threateningly above it.

They didn't talk, each wrapped silently in his own thoughts as the slow seconds ticked by. And only when the sound of an approaching carriage disturbed the waiting stillness did any of their party move.

The physician they had picked up on the way climbed reluctantly out of the relative warmth of Travener's coach and walked over to join them. Ian wondered idly how many duels the man had attended and how many of them had ended with a need for his services.

Considering Travener's lack of passion about anything other than convincing Anne to marry him, this one seemed likely to turn out exactly as the young ex-soldier predicted. After all, Ian couldn't believe that in the intervening days since the ball the general had not come to regret his public condemnation of Darlington's daughter.

No gentleman treated a lady in the way Mayfield had treated Anne. And nothing Ian knew about Arthur's father would indicate he was *not* a gentleman as well as a man of honor. Perhaps, as Travener had hopefully suggested, he would delope and put a quick end to this foolishness.

When the old man was helped down from his carriage, he seemed as thin and pale as the first faint rays of the sun, which were brimming over the horizon. Using his cane, he moved carefully across the rough ground, glancing up occasionally at the group which had been awaiting his arrival. Mayfield was accompanied by two men who appeared to be around his age, but Ian didn't recognize either.

As the general drew nearer, his gaze lingered on Ian's face, as if he were trying to place him. They had been introduced once, long ago. However, it would probably be difficult for Mayfield to recognize him since Ian was certain he was the last person the old man would expect to find standing beside Travener. And suddenly he wished he weren't.

"General Mayfield," Travener said, bowing from the waist.

The black eyes left Ian's face to consider Travener's. Mayfield didn't bother to return the salutation before his gaze came back to Ian.

"Sinclair?" he asked, his tone puzzled.

"Ian Sinclair, General Mayfield."

"So the whelp was telling the truth," Mayfield said.

"The truth, sir?"

"That you have taken in Darlington's brat."

"Miss Darlington is my ward. Those were the terms of her father's will."

"And you agreed to them?"

"I didn't feel I had a choice," Ian said truthfully.

"In all honor." The tone was slightly mocking, as were the black eyes. "Arthur admired you a great deal. I find myself wondering why."

Apparently Mayfield had *not* thought better of his accusations. Despite his own very powerful reasons for hating George Darlington, Ian felt his temper rise at the insult. If this was the way Mayfield had behaved at the ball, he had far more sympathy with Travener's subsequent challenge than he had had before.

"Arthur was a gallant soldier, sir," he said. "And I regret his death more than you can imagine. My ward, however, had nothing to do with it."

"Another ardent admirer of Miss Darlington, I see. Admittedly my acquaintance with her was brief, but frankly I failed to see the charms, gentlemen, which might inspire such loyalty. However, since we are now assembled..." He turned, his hand sweeping toward the clearing. His eyes came back to Ian's.

"Surely this can be settled without resorting to that," Ian said.

"Then Mr. Travener is prepared to apologize?"

The black eyes left Ian's face to examine Travener's.

They were still mocking. Or at least that seemed to be his opponent's impression. The flush was back, staining Travener's high, smoothly boyish cheekbones.

"He is not," Travener said.

The general smiled. "Nor am I, Mr. Travener. That woman's blood still offends me. As does your presence here this morning, Major Sinclair."

His eyes had quickly tracked back to Ian's face. And there was little Ian could say in his own defense. Especially since he had himself been questioning the wisdom of his presence, which seemed to imply his approval of what was about to happen.

"Miss Darlington is my ward," Ian said. "She is a woman of unquestionable integrity and great courage. And you have publicly maligned her, sir."

"Are *you* planning to challenge me, too, Sinclair?" the old man asked. "Do you believe that, considering my age, it will require two smitten fools to get this job done? If so, I'm flattered."

Two smitten fools. An apt enough description.

"I am here simply as an observer, sir," Ian said.

"At Mr. Travener's invitation. Not at mine. And yet you were Arthur's friend. At least he thought you were."

"I *was* Arthur's friend. I don't believe you honor his memory, however, by what you did to Miss Darlington."

"Arthur's memory is all I have left, Major Sinclair, and that is the fault of your ward's father. Surely you, of all people, don't deny that bastard's guilt in what happened?"

Ian could not defend Darlington's actions, no matter how he felt about Anne, which was, of course, the greatest irony of Darlington's will.

"Go home," Mayfield advised softly. "Don't lend

your name to this travesty. Your reputation is too fine to
be besmirched by this folly.''

The temptation was there. Ian had known from the start
that this was exactly what Mayfield had called it. A travesty. And a folly. *Two smitten fools.*

Again Anne's face was in his mind. This time the image was from the day he had put his body between hers
and the angry mob, pressing her against the wall to protect her. He would have given his life for her without
thought.

Not that the gift of his life, irreparably shortened by
her father's actions, would amount to any grand gesture.
His unbesmirched reputation, as Mayfield had called it,
would be a far more meaningful sacrifice. Perhaps that
was the same conclusion that Doyle, in his simplicity,
had come to about his own reputation. Whatever Travener's motives, Ian found that he couldn't leave. Travesty
or not, he would see this out to the bitter end.

''I believe my reputation will survive my attempt to
protect my ward's. She is undeserving of your disdain,
sir. Arthur would have admired her courage and honesty.
So do I. She should not be stained with the slander that
will haunt her father's name forever. And that in itself
should be punishment enough for the likes of Darlington.
Please don't let his cowardice claim yet another victim.''

For a moment, the old man's eyes seemed to waver in
their conviction. His mouth moved, but before he could
respond, Travener, his eyes on the rising sun, interrupted.

''The sun is up, gentlemen. It's always possible that
word of our meeting has gotten out. Perhaps we should
begin before the magistrates arrive.''

Mayfield held Ian's eyes for a moment longer before
he turned to Travener.

"The eternal impatience of youth. Are you always so eager to face death, Mr. Travener?"

"I'm always eager to right a wrong."

"And that is what you see this to be?"

"Of course. You insulted Miss Darlington, whom I intend to make my wife. Unless, of course, you are ready to apologize to her. And if that is the case, sir, I must demand that your apology be made in as public a forum as that in which the original insult was rendered."

Mayfield laughed, the sound of his laughter rusty as if from disuse. "Not bloody likely, boy. Let's get on with it."

"As you wish, sir."

Travener bowed again, and then inclined his head to Ian. When he straightened, the blue eyes seemed, surprisingly, touched with amusement. Before Ian had time to interpret whatever was in them, however, Doyle turned away, walking over to where the seconds were examining the pair of pistols the general had provided.

"Did my son die well?"

Ian's gaze returned to the old man's face, and in it he saw again the real cost of Darlington's cowardice. His throat thickened, as memories he had buried long ago crowded his brain. Darlington had held back his own force, watching as Ian's men were cut down before his eyes. And so many of them, like Arthur Mayfield, had been not only comrades but friends. As dear as brothers.

"He died as bravely, sir, as even you could have wished," Ian said softly.

The black eyes glazed briefly with moisture. And then the old man nodded once before he, too, turned and walked across the clearing toward the group examining the pistols.

Ian turned toward the rising sun, blinking back an answering and unwanted moisture. Each of their lives had been touched in some way by the long-ago actions of one man. A daughter he had never known. A fellow officer whose life he had shattered to protect his own. An old man whose only son he had sacrificed. And a smitten fool, who would never have the woman he loved. *Two smitten fools.*

"...very sensitive, sir. I beg you to be very careful."

The sound of Travener's voice brought Ian's wandering attention back to the center of the clearing. And he realized that he had been reliving the events of that final battle far longer than he had been aware. The principals were already in position, pistols raised.

Unconsciously Ian held his breath as he watched the ancient ritual played out. If Mayfield deloped, then Travener would follow suit. In honor, he would have no other option. And Ian had at least made the old man think about what he was doing. He could only hope—

They turned, and Mayfield fired first. The ball sailed harmlessly to the left of Travener, striking one of the elms with a small explosion of bark. It was not the admission of regret on Mayfield's part that Ian had been hoping for, but it could hardly matter. No harm had been done, and surely Travener—

Except he wasn't, Ian realized, continuing to watch in growing horror. Instead of deloping, Mr. Travener was lowering his pistol, aiming it very deliberately at his target, which appeared to be the center of Mayfield's chest.

The old man obviously believed the same thing. He straightened, lowering his now-useless pistol so that it dangled from his fingers. His thin lips were arranged in a sardonic smile and the bristling brows lifted arrogantly above the hooded eyes. And then, frozen by courage and dignity, he simply waited.

Ian's gaze flew back to Mayfield's opponent. Travener's face was set. The beautiful blue eyes seemed cold as he lowered the pistol until the muzzle was pointed straight at the general's heart.

For a breathless eternity there was no movement at all in the clearing. Then, by some infinitesimal change in his posture, Ian knew that despite his promise, Travener's finger was about to close over the trigger.

"Travener," he shouted, taking a step forward. Toward the two men silhouetted against the rising sun.

Ian Sinclair's voice had never lost that unmistakable tone of command. And apparently it was one Doyle Travener had never forgotten.

Responding to it now, the ex-soldier turned, his whole body moving as his shocked gaze swung toward the man who had shouted his name. As he did, the hair-trigger pistol he held discharged, firing prematurely.

Chapter Fourteen

"Bloody hell," Ian said, involuntarily flinching from the last of the surgeon's seemingly endless probing.

"Almost," the man said, the fingers of his left hand wrapped like an iron band around Ian's upper arm. In his right were the forceps with which he was attempting to extract Travener's ball. "One would think if one can see the blasted thing…"

Ian's gasp coincided with the surgeon's exclamation of satisfaction. "There now," he said, obviously relieved. He held the ball, firmly grasped between the metal tongs, up to the light. "Hardly damaged. Lucky you weren't standing any closer."

Dr. McKinley stepped around the surgeon to place a thick pad over the wound, which was bleeding again. He began to wind a strip of clean linen around the lint to hold it in place.

"Major Sinclair's luck is well-documented," McKinley said, gesturing with his chin toward Ian's chest as he worked.

"So I see," the surgeon agreed, his own eyes examining the scars that marred it. "Shrapnel?"

"And grapeshot."

"Nasty business. War was once a gentleman's game. Knights on horseback. England and Saint George, and all that. Now…"

The surgeon's eyes traced once more over Ian's chest. He laid the forceps and ball on the table, and using the tips of his fingers, which were still covered with his patient's blood, he lightly touched the piece of metal that still lay, clearly visible, beneath the skin.

"Lodged between the ribs. You *are* lucky. If this had penetrated half an inch deeper, I should not be digging this morning's souvenir from your hide. Bloody lucky, I should say."

"Major Sinclair's surgeons have warned him there is always the possibility that fragment may shift and endanger the heart," McKinley said.

The surgeon's mouth pursed as if he were thinking about that. And he again touched the obscene ridge, which lay just to the left of Ian's breastbone.

"Given where it lies, *I* wouldn't be willing to probe for it. More likely to do you harm with trying to remove it than with leaving it alone. Eventually the cartilage will simply incorporate itself around this, I should imagine. That one's a souvenir you're destined to keep, I should think, Major Sinclair, whether you like it or not."

"What does that mean?" Ian asked. "What you said about the cartilage."

"Have you ever seen a spike driven into a tree? Over the years the trunk closes around the iron until it becomes a part of the wood itself."

"There's no guarantee of that," McKinley warned.

"Oh, no, of course not. And no guarantee that it won't either. I have seen it happen."

"Have you?" Ian asked McKinley.

"Not personally."

"But...it is possible?"

"*Anything* is possible," the physician said. "I told you I'm a firm believer in the ability of the human body to heal itself. Given that we meddlers get out of the way."

"Do you want to keep that?" the surgeon asked, nodding toward the ball he had put down alongside the forceps on the table. "If not, may I take it? Morbid, I know, but I have a collection of these from the affairs I've been called upon to attend. Few of them in as good a shape as this one. I tell you again, Major Sinclair, you're a lucky man."

He smiled at Ian, one brow raised in inquiry.

"Take it," Ian said.

"Thank you. I shall send you my bill."

He wiped his hands on a stained cloth he pulled from the bag he had brought with him to the Elms. Then, after rolling down his sleeves, he carelessly threw the instruments he had used back into it. Their metal clanged against whatever else was inside. The bullet he dealt with more carefully, placing it into a small drawstring pouch, which he then dropped into his jacket pocket.

"Did *you* think he was going to shoot the old man?" Ian asked, as he watched.

The surgeon looked up, his brows lifted in surprise. "Of course," he said, as if there had been no question about Travener's intent.

Then he put on his jacket, picked up his bag and bowed to his colleague. Neither Ian nor McKinley said anything else until he was out of the room.

"I don't suppose you would care to explain how you came to be shot during a duel in which you were not a participant," the physician said.

"Not particularly," Ian said.

"I didn't think so. May I ask if your ward was involved?"

Ian laughed. "Are you already planning your report to my brother, Dr. McKinley?"

"I ask simply for my own edification, I assure you. You are quite the most interesting patient I've ever had, Mr. Sinclair. I like to keep abreast of your adventures. I should imagine, however, that so would your brother. Have you sent him word about this one?"

"No," Ian said, looking down at the neat bandage the physician had just finished tying around his arm.

"And you don't intend to, I take it."

"No," Ian said, raising his eyes to the doctor's again. The direct hazel stare left McKinley in no doubt about his feelings on that point.

"Then may I suggest that you take care, sir," the physician said. "You have had more than your share of close calls of late. I wonder what the odds would be of so many dangerous accidents happening to one gentleman. Especially to one who professes to be... What was the term you used? Living sedately?"

There was a short silence, McKinley's eyes refusing to release Ian's without an answer. And when it came, it was at best an oblique one.

"You will probably be relieved to learn that my ward has returned to school."

"A much safer situation, I suspect. Have you told *that* to your brother?"

"My brother and I are presently...estranged."

Ian wondered if it would be safe to reestablish communications with his brother, now that Anne was safely back at Fenton School. He wasn't completely sure, however, that he trusted Dare's contrition at having overstepped the bounds of their relationship.

"I see," McKinley said. "Then I shall hope for the earl's sake that this estrangement will soon be mended. He cares a great deal about you."

"Thank you. And thank you for your services today. May I ask how you knew I had need of them?"

"I believe your brother's butler had been given instructions to send for me in case you were again... indisposed. I assume he felt that being shot qualified."

McKinley, too, picked up his bag and turned toward the door. Before he reached it, he stopped and looked over his shoulder at Ian. "That reminds me. He asked me to give you a message when I came upstairs. Slipped my mind until now."

"Dare?"

"The earl's butler," McKinley corrected. "It seems there is a man downstairs who insists he must see you. He says it's quite urgent."

"Did Williams give you his name?"

"A Mr. Smythe, I believe. Which doesn't tell you much. Something to do with an estate, I think he said."

"I don't believe it," Ian said, his eyes still scanning the documents the solicitor had handed him as his brain tried to make sense of them.

His arm hurt like hell. Williams had helped him into a fresh shirt and had then fashioned a sling from one of his cravats to support the injured member.

Considering the papers he had just been handed, he was very grateful that McKinley had not insisted on administering a dose of laudanum. Even with his mind free of the effects of the drug, he was having a hard time coming to terms with this.

"Frankly, Mr. Sinclair, we found it difficult to believe

ourselves. However, I do assure you that the information contained in those papers is quite correct. We went to a great deal of trouble to verify it before we approached you.''

''But…how can this be?''

''What prevented him from gaming this away, too, do you mean?''

Ian looked up, realizing that Mr. Smythe knew his former client very well indeed. ''You wondered the same thing.''

''We believe he simply forgot he owned them. These were virtually worthless ten years ago. The idea of using gas for light was the merest speculation then. That was the kind of investment Darlington loved, of course. The more far-fetched the better. The more risk involved, the greater the reward, he believed, *if* one won through.''

''As it seems he did in this case,'' Ian said, still studying the documents.

''Luckily for his daughter, he never realized what he had. Or this, like the rest, would surely be gone.''

''How much are the shares worth today?''

''The value has gone up rapidly in the last year, and it continues to rise. Gas is already being used to light factories in the north and certain streets of this very city.''

''A rough idea will do.''

''The current value is listed on the third page, I believe,'' the solicitor said.

And when Ian had found the place Mr. Smythe had referred to, his eyes quickly came back up.

''Per *share?*'' he asked.

The solicitor nodded.

''And Darlington held…?''

Since he was managing the documents with only one hand, Ian awkwardly turned back to the first page. He had vaguely remembered that the total number of shares Anne's father had purchased more than a decade ago had been listed there.

"Good God," he said, when he had found the figure.

"Exactly." Smythe's voice seemed to hold a note of satisfaction over Ian's shock. "Your ward is a very wealthy young woman."

"So it seems," Ian agreed absently. He was doing a calculation of just how wealthy in his head, just to be sure he hadn't made any mistake.

"And I can't see anything happening that would bring the price down," Mr. Smythe went on. "Quite the reverse, if you want my opinion."

"Who knows about this?"

"I beg your pardon?"

"I am wondering whom you have told about my ward's fortune," Ian repeated patiently.

The lawyer looked taken aback by the question. "I'm not perfectly sure I understand you, Mr. Sinclair."

"It's very simple. I should like to know who in your firm has been made privy to this information."

"My associate, of course. Our clerk as well, since he drew up the papers you are now holding. But surely, Mr. Sinclair, you don't believe you can keep this sort of thing secret?" the solicitor said.

Ian wasn't sure what he heard in the tone of that question. Suspicion of his motives? If so, Ian found that he didn't care. If word of Anne's fortune got out, every bounder in the country would come courting, despite the scandal that had been attached to her name.

"I would like to protect my ward from the attentions of those who are interested in *only* this," he explained, lifting the documents.

"I understand your concern, of course. I am very much

afraid, however... With the plans to use gas to light the whole of London, the newspapers will doubtless go public with the information about the company's investors very soon. You'll find yourself tilting at windmills if you hope to keep it quiet, Mr. Sinclair. Granted, this can only make your job more difficult, but I'm afraid that can't be helped. News like this will get out. Can't be helped,'' Smythe said again, shaking his head.

He was probably right, Ian acknowledged in disgust. With the circulation of this information, his role as Anne's guardian would, of necessity, expand. Not only would he be protecting her, he would also need to guard the fortune her profligate father had left.

Which would, he realized belatedly, also make quite a difference in Anne's desirability to the gentlemen of the ton. To men who might be legitimate prospects for husband. Thus far, no one other than Mr. Travener—

No one other than Mr. Travener... Who had returned from Portugal shortly after Darlington's death.

Which might, Ian acknowledged, have nothing to do with what Mr. Smythe had just discovered. Despite his self-admonition to fairness, Ian found himself thinking about Travener's connection to everything that had happened since they had been in the capital. He had been there, rather conveniently there, on the day of the riot. He had also been there the night Mayfield had publicly insulted Anne. A chance meeting. And yet...

Ian had wondered at the time how the old man had recognized Anne as Darlington's daughter. She looked nothing like her father. Not in the shape of her face or her features or her coloring. There was nothing about her that should have identified her as a Darlington. And yet, according to what he had been told, Mayfield had bumped into Anne at a crowded ball and had immediately made that identification.

Or, Ian wondered, a slow trickle of ice slipping down his spine, had Anne been pointed out to the general? Deliberately identified as the daughter of the man who had killed his beloved son? If so, for what possible purpose?

Almost unconsciously, Ian touched the wound on his arm, which throbbed with the slightest movement. McKinley had questioned the number of close calls and accidents he had suffered lately. Admittedly, for someone who had deliberately chosen to live "sedately," he had found himself in situations that were not only potentially dangerous...

He took a breath, knowing that he was right. Too many situations that were not only dangerous, but strangely suspicious. As if they had been arranged. Even this morning, the substitution of pistols in the duel now seemed irregular. Not by itself perhaps, but in context with the rest. And certainly in context with the outcome.

Too many close calls and dangerous accidents...

"Mr. Sinclair?"

Smythe's voice interrupted that unwanted realization. Ian's eyes lifted to the solicitor's face, although his mind continued to work on those possibilities as his visitor talked.

"I take it you agree that we shouldn't sell the colonel's shares. Sell them for Miss Darlington, I mean. As her guardian, the management of her resources is completely in your hands. *Legally* in your hands. As her father's solicitor, however, I should advise against—"

"I don't intend to sell them. I do, however, wish you to determine who knows about this," Ian said, indicating the packet of papers he held.

"Who else knows about those shares? Only those people I mentioned."

"How did you find out about this investment?"

"It was in going through the colonel's belongings, which came straight to us from Iberia, that our clerk found a letter that made reference to it. And when we began to investigate—"

"So someone else might have seen that same letter?" *Someone in the army, perhaps?*

Smythe shrugged. "Someone had to pack his kit. His batman, I suppose. An orderly. Some subordinate, in any case. We could query the colonel's commanding officer if it's important. Of course, that will take a while, even if we send our request through the dispatches."

"Would you do that, please, Mr. Smythe? I think it might be important."

"Indeed?" Smythe said, his tone skeptical and his brows lifted again. "Then...of course, I shall, Mr. Sinclair. If you think it important."

Ian nodded, his mind already running ahead. And it was certainly time, he acknowledged. He had been very slow to understand what was going on.

Of course, until he had had this, the last piece of the puzzle, which had made everything else fall into place, he had had no reason to be suspicious. No reason to have any doubts at all, except his own feelings of jealousy. And even now...

He looked down at the papers he held, papers which made Anne Darlington an incredibly wealthy woman. And suddenly, the feeling so strong it was almost a premonition, he knew, despite the fact that he couldn't yet prove anything, that he wasn't wrong in what he was thinking.

Desperate men adopt desperate measures. And it

seemed there could be little more desperate than the murder Travener had attempted this morning. Actually, Ian realized, he could think of only one thing—

The thought brought him out of his chair so rapidly that, given the blood he had lost, his head spun sickeningly. He groped for the table, knocking the documents to the floor.

"Mr. Sinclair," the solicitor said, his voice shocked. He also stood to place a steadying arm under Ian's elbow.

Ian shook his head, trying to clear away the gray void that had threatened. When he looked up, Smythe's eyes were on his face, wide with concern.

"Find out who packed the colonel's belongings. And on your way out, ask Williams to have my brother's curricle and his grays brought round at once."

"Surely, sir, you are in no condition to undertake—"

"A quite necessary journey, I assure you. Else I should not attempt it…at this particular time."

Smythe held his eyes, concern growing in his own. Finally, at whatever he read there, he nodded.

"Then Godspeed, Major Sinclair. I shall pray you arrive safely at your destination."

"You have a visitor."

Anne pulled her unfocused gaze from the scene outside the second-story window to find Margaret Rhodes standing in the hallway, watching her. In the days since her return, Anne had become accustomed to being watched, at least by the girls who had known her before her brief sojourn in London. She wasn't sure what they found so interesting, but whatever it was, it was enough to provoke uncounted hallway discussions, all quickly shushed into whispers when she approached.

"*Not* the one from before," Margaret added.

"Not my guardian," Anne clarified, feeling her heart rate slow in disappointment and with something that felt strangely akin to gratitude.

"But a gentleman nonetheless," Margaret assured her. "Top of the Trees and even more handsome than the last, if you fancy my opinion."

Of course, when you are Margaret's age and living in an all-female institution, the visit of any handsome gentleman is an event, one sure to cause romantic speculation. Anne herself had certainly been guilty of *that* in the past.

"He's waiting in Mrs. Kemp's parlor."

"Thank you, Margaret," Anne said, unfolding her legs from the window seat on which she had been curled.

After her weeks in London, Anne had been far more aware of the chill that seeped through the stones of Fenton Hall. And the spill of afternoon sunshine coming in through the tall windows of the upstairs solar had been too inviting to resist.

Her hours-long daydreaming had done nothing for her attire, she realized. She shook out her skirt, smoothing her hands over the deep wrinkles that had resulted from her position. Not a very ladylike position, Elizabeth would have chided.

As she worked, Anne was thankful the Countess of Dare couldn't see her poor hands, already reddened again across the knuckles with the cold. With that thought, those hands hesitated, still hovering over the fabric of her skirt.

Even more handsome than the last, Margaret had said. Dare? Was it possible that her caller was the Earl of Dare? And if so, why would he have made this long journey?

Again, quite against her will, her heart began to race.

Determined not to provoke further gossip among the girls, she tried to hide that sudden trepidation when she looked up to smile a dismissal at Margaret.

"Shall I go down with you?" the child asked, obviously not interpreting the smile in the way it had been intended.

"I'm sure you have lessons," Anne suggested briskly. "And I *do* know my way to the parlor, Margaret. Thank you for bringing me the message."

"Do you think he's the one?"

"I beg your pardon?" Anne said, imbuing her voice with a touch of adult disapproval, her exact tone borrowed from the headmistress.

"The one you're in love with. Do you think this could be him?"

There were a dozen responses Anne might have made. Six months ago, some teasing comment would have leapt from her tongue, guaranteed to evoke laughter in her audience. Now, however...

"Do you think this could be *he,*" she said, correcting the girl's grammar instead. "*Not* that it would be any of your concern, Margaret, if he is or not."

And make of that what you will, she thought, sweeping past Mrs. Kemp's messenger with as much an air of dignified elegance as even Elizabeth might have managed.

"Why, Mr. Travener. How delightful to see you again."

Anne had paused before she entered the room, surveying the tall, handsome figure standing in the same patch of sunshine she had recently been enjoying upstairs. And as soon as she had recognized her caller, she mocked the runaway emotions that had carried her down the stairs at a near run.

There had been no reason to believe Ian's brother might visit. That was nothing but wishful thinking. Mr. Travener's ardent courtship would have been a much more likely explanation for a gentleman caller, and yet remarkably, that this visitor might be Travener had never occurred to her.

He turned, and Anne knew immediately that something terrible had happened. His expression was…tortured. It was the only word that came to mind.

He walked across the room and took the hand she had unthinkingly held out to him. Instead of raising her fingers to his lips, however, he held them in the palm of his left and put his right hand over hers, squeezing it tightly between the two of his.

"I'm afraid I am the bearer of bad news," he said softly.

Her heart stopped, the blood within it suddenly cold and congealed. She could read the reality of what he had said in the solemn blue eyes. She had never seen them like this, and their unaccustomed seriousness frightened her.

"Ian?"

He nodded, a muscle working in his jaw.

"Is he…" she began, and then her throat closed against the utterance of the word.

He said nothing, simply holding her hand and her eyes, as she tried to read his expression.

"Please tell me, Mr. Travener," she commanded, gathering her courage to face what must be faced. "Is he dead?"

"Not yet, but… In truth, they do not expect him to live out the night."

That same cone of soundless isolation that had surrounded her when General Mayfield turned his back on her formed around her again.

"And it is my fault," Travener added.

Somehow the soft, anguished words broke through the shell of horror his first had created.

"*Your* fault? How can this possibly be your fault?"

"We used my pistols. Mayfield's were ancient and clearly uncared for. Most unsuitable for dueling, I promise you. Both seconds agreed to the exchange. There was nothing irregular about it."

"What are you talking about?" Anne demanded, following almost nothing of what he had said. The few words she had absorbed, like *dueling* and *pistols* and *Mayfield,* only added to her fear.

She jerked her hand from his, clasping hers together to keep them from shaking. She pressed them hard against the growing agony in her chest. She had been imagining Ian felled again by a sudden sickness, perhaps another bout of lung fever. Travener's words seemed to imply that something else had happened. Something—

"My duel with General Mayfield. Major Sinclair insisted on accompanying me, and then in the middle of it, he shouted. When, naturally, I turned toward him…" He paused, shaking his head in disbelief. "I swear to you, Miss Darlington, the pistol discharged on its own. I had warned the general about the sensitivity of the triggers, but I never dreamed—"

"You *shot* him?" she asked, finally making sense of Travener's muddled explanation. "You were dueling with General Mayfield and…you shot Ian?"

"Everyone has assured me that I am not in any way responsible, but I'm afraid I shall always feel the burden of that guilt. Especially if…"

They do not expect him to live out the night.

"You *shot* him," she said again, unable to move past her incredulity over that.

She had had a few days to come to terms with the idea that Ian's injuries were her father's fault. If her guardian had fallen into a fatal illness, that would have produced a guilt she would always be forced to bear. This insanity, however...

The thought that her rejected suitor, this lovesick Romeo, had shot Ian, even by accident, in a duel that he had undertaken to defend her honor was unbelievable. And unbearable.

"He startled me. I turned toward him, and the pistol discharged. You must understand, I beg you—"

"Why are you here?" she asked, breaking into excuses she had finally understood and had no desire to listen to again.

"To take you to London, of course. I thought you would wish to see him before..."

And since she did, she realized she would have no real choice but to let Doyle provide her with transportation. The school's ancient chaise might not survive the journey, and even if it did, it would take hours longer to reach the capital in it than in Mr. Travener's smart, fast carriage. And it was possible, it seemed, that she did not have those hours to spare.

"Will you tell Mrs. Kemp what has happened, please, Mr. Travener. I shall get my things."

"Say that you forgive me, Miss Darlington. I know you admired Major Sinclair a great deal. I cannot bear it if this unfortunate...accident should come between us."

But she *did* hold Travener responsible. He had evidently issued a challenge to the general, although he certainly had no right to presume to do so on her behalf.

And this unfortunate accident, as he called it, had been the result.

She longed to lash out at him, but when she thought of the miles that lay between her and Ian... And even now...

"I am sure you never intended to harm anyone, Mr. Travener," she said, remembering the lesson of charity her guardian had taught her. "And now, please, I beg of you—"

"Of course," Travener said, his voice relieved.

The blue eyes seemed as eager to please as those of the youngest child in Anne's charge. And as he hurried off to inform Mrs. Kemp of the arrangements, she found she had no regrets over the absolution she had just offered him.

Doyle Travener would get her to London as quickly as it was humanly possible. And to accomplish that, she would willingly have told any number of lies.

Chapter Fifteen

"Surely we must be almost there," Anne said.

Night had fallen long ago, and although she had no way of telling time, it seemed to her that they had been traveling forever. Far longer than the journey to London should take. Of course, the very nature of this particular journey could be responsible for her oppressive anxiety over its length.

Mr. Travener straightened in the opposite seat, fingering his watch out of its pocket. It was far too dark inside the carriage to read the face of it, however. Acknowledging the impossibility of doing so, he replaced the watch and with gloved fingers lifted the shade that had been drawn over the window.

Trying to evaluate the depth of the external darkness? Anne wondered. Or perhaps hoping to see some evidence that they were indeed approaching the outskirts of the capital?

"Soon," he said reassuringly, allowing the covering to fall.

She could not tell if that estimation had been based on something he had seen, or if it had merely been intended to placate her impatience. If the latter, it hadn't succeeded.

Despite the fact that they had been racing along a well-maintained thoroughfare for hours, she had a terrible sense of foreboding that they were already too late. It was a feeling she had tried to deny. And when she couldn't, one she had determined not to give voice to.

After all, she could not fault Mr. Travener's efforts. Since they had left the school, they had stopped only to change the horses. Mrs. Kemp had warned that no matter the circumstances, it would not do for Anne to be seen alone on an extended journey in the company of a young man who was not of her family, and so she had not descended from the carriage at any of the coaching inns.

The headmistress had fretted about letting her go with only Mr. Travener's escort. Since it was the end of spring term, however, there was no other teacher at school whom Mrs. Kemp could send with her at such short notice. And yet she was naturally reluctant to disobey what might be the dying request of Anne's guardian. Finally, the urgency of the situation and Mr. Travener's repeated assurances of Anne's safety had secured the headmistress's permission, if not her approval, of the plan.

Doyle had offered to bring refreshment out to the carriage at every stop they'd made, but Anne had refused, knowing she could not eat. At the last inn, however, he had insisted she drink a cup of mulled wine to "strengthen" her.

She *had* felt the better for it, Anne admitted, although its potency had put her to sleep. She had no idea for how long, but when she had awakened, still dazed from the effects of the strong wine, the feeling that something was very wrong had welled terrifyingly up in her breast.

"I don't remember the journey to London taking so long," she said aloud.

"We are making very good time, I promise you," Mr. Travener said. "I was quite surprised to discover exactly how good when last we stopped."

Several times during the course of the journey she had considered asking him for more details of the duel and especially more about Ian's injury. She had refrained because she did not want to be forced to comfort Travener's professed guilt again.

After all, he had given her all the pertinent information in that first breathless confession. *They do not expect him to live out the night.* And now more than half that night had passed. Those despairing thoughts were interrupted by a recognizable slowing of the horses' breakneck pace.

"Are we stopping?" she asked, lifting the shade away from the edge of the window.

By that time it was quite obvious they were. As the driver pulled the horses up, Anne saw through the crack she had created what appeared to be a torch wavering out of the mist-shrouded darkness and making its way toward the carriage. Given her previous encounter with the highwaymen, she felt a frisson of unease at the sight.

Another inn? Surely it had not been long enough since the last that they should need to change teams.

The carriage came to a complete stop, and almost before it did, Mr. Travener threw open the door, showing not the least sign of trepidation about whoever was approaching them. He jumped down, turning and holding up his hand to her.

"Come, Miss Darlington," he said.

Eager to descend, now that the journey was at an end, she stood, perhaps too quickly. Her head swam and her vision seemed blurred, and she wished again that she had not drunk the wine he'd brought her. She placed her fingers in his, grateful for their support, and stepped down.

The scene that greeted her was not anything like what she had expected. Not an inn. Nor were they at the door of the Earl of Dare's elegant town house. They weren't in London at all. Or in any civilized environs, it seemed.

And it was very clear that the two men who stood beside the coach, one of them holding the smoking torch, were not gentlemen. At least not by the standards of English society.

She turned her head, meeting Doyle Travener's eyes, which were focused on her face, apparently awaiting her reaction.

"Where are we?" she asked.

"I regret to inform you that we are presently in Scotland, Miss Darlington."

"Scotland," she repeated disbelievingly.

The repetition was little more than an attempt to buy time. Head swimming, she realized that the wine she had consumed was making clear thinking difficult. Yet if Scotland was indeed what Doyle had said, there was, of course, no doubt what he intended. No doubt at all as to why he had brought her here.

"And my guardian?" she demanded, praying that the story he had told about Ian, like that concerning their supposed destination, had been a lie. "What of Major Sinclair?"

"I knew you would never forgive me for what I had done. And I could not bear the thought of it."

"So you have *abducted* me? Do you expect me to forgive you for that?"

"I had hoped you would not consider our journey in that light."

"How should I consider it? You have deceived me,

Mr. Travener. *And* deceived Mrs. Kemp. At least tell me the truth about Ian.''

''The truth about *Ian*,'' he repeated softly, the inflection clearly suggestive. Almost…mocking.

''Major Sinclair,'' she amended.

''Forgive me if I am wrong, Miss Darlington, but it seemed that just now, as you spoke your guardian's name… It seemed to me there was something… improper, perhaps, in your voice.''

''What you heard in my voice, Mr. Travener, was concern,'' she said, still fighting the strange lethargy the wine had produced. ''A quite *proper* concern. Major Sinclair is my guardian. Should I not be concerned about his well-being? You told me he would not live out the night, and then, instead of taking me to him, you have brought me here.''

She looked around, her eyes again encountering the men who had met the carriage. They appeared to be listening to the exchange, but in the flickering light cast by the torch, she couldn't really gauge their reactions. And as much as she would have liked to believe otherwise, she doubted Travener would have brought her here if he had thought there was the slightest chance they might intervene.

''Tell me the truth,'' she demanded again, her gaze coming back to his face.

''I have told you the truth about everything, including my feelings for you,'' he said earnestly. ''Major Sinclair was injured in the duel this morning, just as I told you. It was a tragic accident, but I could not let what had happened to him come between us. It truly was not my fault.''

''And this? Is this, too, not your fault?''

''I am in love with you, Anne. I have been since the

night I first met you. I knew that you didn't return my feelings. Not yet, in any case. And then, when you left London so abruptly, I was terrified I'd never see you again.''

"Take me back to Fenton School, please."

She turned, preparing to climb back into the carriage. She raised her foot but when she put it down, incredibly she missed the bottom step entirely. Travener took her arm, ostensibly to steady her, but his fingers bit painfully into her flesh, despite the layers of clothing she wore.

"I can't, my darling," he said. "Believe me, I have thought long and hard about what is best for us. Best for both of us. If I take you back now, I shall never be allowed to see you again. And to me that would be…unthinkable," he said, his voice low and intense.

"I am not in love with you, Mr. Travener."

"I can make you love me."

"You can't *make* someone love you," she said.

No more than you can make yourself not love someone, she thought, picturing Ian's face. She spoke from bitter experience. If there was anyone who had ever tried—

"I shall try," Travener said. "Just as I shall try to make you happy, from now until my dying day."

She took a deep breath, attempting again to clear her swimming head. Her words were obviously having no effect on Mr. Travener's surety. And whatever was wrong with her brain seemed to be getting worse rather than better, despite the bracing cold of the night air.

Her eyes returned to the men who had met the coach. In the light of their torch she could barely make out a building in the darkness behind them. It appeared to be a small inn, little larger than some of the cottages she was accustomed to seeing in England, but perhaps there would be someone within it who possessed a shred of human decency.

"Will you not help me?" she asked, pitching her voice so that it would carry to where they stood. "This man has abducted me against my will."

At her question, Travener turned to look at them, too, although he didn't release his grip on her arm. It appeared he had no fear that they might answer her plea in the affirmative. After a moment, a small smile began to play around the corners of his mouth, as his eyes considered the silent Scots.

"Actually, my dear, they have been paid quite handsomely to help *me*. I doubt you will convince them to switch their loyalties."

She ignored him and addressed the men again, although her words had seemed to have no effect on those set faces, ruddied by the glow of the torch or by the habitual harshness of the climate.

"If you will help me, my guardian will see that you are generously rewarded," she promised.

"Since Miss Darlington's guardian is in London, he is hardly in a position to make good on her pledge," Travener said. And then he added, his voice so low it was obvious it was intended only for her ears, "They don't seem to be interested, my dear. I don't think I should waste my breath on them any more if I were you."

"My guardian will give you twice whatever this man has paid you if you will take me to London," Anne said, her eyes moving from one face to the other, searching for some spark of sympathy.

"He might," Travener agreed, obviously unworried about her ability to convince the Scotsmen. "*If* your stalwart guardian were here. But of course he *isn't* here, is he? He's in London, having a gunshot wound attended to. And who knows? By now, any promises you make to these gentlemen concerning what he would do to get you back might very well be moot.''

She turned on him then, staring him full in the face and no longer bothering to hide her contempt. His fair head tilted in mocking inquiry, blond brows arching over those guileless blue eyes. His lips twitched minutely and were then carefully and too obviously controlled.

He's enjoying himself, she realized. He was relishing both her pleading and the fear she was trying desperately to hide. All along he had been playing with her, as a cat will play with the unfortunate mouse he has captured.

What an apt comparison. Travener was simply playing with her by allowing her to imagine there was any hope at all of rescue. He had lied to her to get her into the coach with him, and then he had continued to lie throughout the journey.

And there was no one, she realized, who could know where they were. Not Mrs. Kemp, who believed she was on her way to London. Not Ian, who even now…

She took another breath, fighting the tightness in her chest that the thought of Ian evoked. But if Travener had lied about everything else, and she knew now that he had, then he must have been lying about Ian's condition. Nothing in the story he had told about the duel made sense. If she could only keep her head…

Keep her head? She couldn't even seem to think any more. She was alone in the wilds of Scotland with a madman, and by the time anyone suspected something was wrong, it would be too late.

''I won't marry you,'' she said to Travener. ''And I don't believe that, even here, brides can be *forced* to the altar.''

''I wouldn't imagine you are the first reluctant bride

to be carried across the Border. Or even the first who must be convinced to speak her vows. I hope, however, it won't come to that. You would be very foolish to imagine that you can resist my will.''

Despite the threat that might be more proper on the stage at Covent Garden, Travener's voice was almost caressing. And chilling. As if the thought of resistance excited him. The threat of violence was implicit in them, no matter the tone.

Screaming or fighting him would probably make no difference to his determination. He sounded as if he might even like it. And, she had finally been forced to admit that it would probably make no difference to the Scots either. *They have been paid quite handsomely...*

''I will not marry you, Mr. Travener, no matter what you say. You have proven yourself to be both a liar and a cheat. There is nothing you can do that will make me.''

He laughed. ''Oh, believe me, my darling, before we return to England, you will be eager to exchange vows with me. And very grateful that I am still willing to marry you. And I will be, never fear.''

And yet she was increasingly certain that love had not precipitated this abduction. ''Why are you doing this?'' she begged, hating the note of despair she heard in the question.

''Shall we simply say I have developed a passion for you that will not be denied. I'm sure your headmistress has warned you about man's baser nature. Or your guardian, perhaps?''

It was as if she had left Fenton School with one person and arrived in Scotland with another. There was nothing of the charmingly diffident man she had considered little more than an engaging boy. A boy who believed himself to be in love with her. A boy she had dismissed as harmless.

And at last, far too late, she had been forced to realize that Doyle Travener was neither. Neither harmless nor in love with her, no matter what he claimed. And that, she found, was the most frightening thing of all.

"Little more than a hour ago, I should say. Less perhaps. I didn't see the lass, mind you, but he took a cup of mulled wine out to the coach while the hostlers changed out the teams. And he'd been pushing them hard, I can tell you."

Not as hard as I have pushed mine, Ian thought, feeling a surge of triumph. Apparently the demands he had made on his teams had paid off. He was less than an hour behind his quarry and given the advantage Travener had enjoyed...

Of course, the ex-lieutenant had also, of necessity, spent far more time at Fenton Hall. Ian had been inside only long enough to ascertain that Anne was not there and that Mr. Travener had indeed come for her. After that, he had not even delayed long enough to make the explanation Mrs. Kemp had so desperately pled for.

Instead, as he had emerged from his two-question interview with the headmistress, he had simply thrown his promise to bring Anne safely back over his shoulder. And then he had encountered a small knot of little girls almost blocking the front hallway. Their eyes had been wide and frightened, their thin faces pale, but they had parted before him, like some biblical sea, opening a path to the door.

From that point on, he had shown no mercy in his demand for speed from the horses he'd hired. And he had spared no expense in procuring the best the posting inns along the North Road could provide. His brother's coat of arms, emblazoned on the fast, open carriage he was driving, had been an extra prod to the hostlers' efforts. As had the money Ian had spread with a generous hand to reward them when they had finished a lightning exchange.

As he had driven northward through the night, the countryside and the temperature had gradually changed. Despite its many capes, the woolen greatcoat he wore had long ago been penetrated by the dampness of the cold, rain-filled wind and his hands, covered by leather driving gloves, had gone numb from its chill.

But he had come alone on this quest, of course, and he had no regrets about that decision. He could not know what he would find at the end of this journey, although he feared the worst. Whatever the situation that awaited him in Scotland, he had vowed there would be only three people who would ever know it.

And only two of them would survive to see tomorrow's dawn, he swore grimly, urging the new team on with a crack of the whip. Although Ian Sinclair had not taken time to send for his brother, Dare's pistols resided beside him in their case, both of them primed and ready for the task that lay ahead.

Chapter Sixteen

"I'm looking for a woman," Ian said.

When he had opened the door, the wind had blown the misting rain like a curtain into the public room of the small inn. The gust disturbed the even draw of the chimney, so that black smoke from the peat fire on the hearth swirled outward into the room. It mingled with the white that came from the clay pipes of the men who sat at the table in the center of the room, a game of draughts before them.

"There be no women here."

The player who had spoken was not the oldest, but he was undoubtedly the largest. And it was obvious by his readiness to answer a stranger's question that he was in some fashion their leader. Ian addressed his explanation directly to him.

"The woman I'm looking for is my ward. She was kidnapped and brought north. I have followed her abductor's progress through the changing of his teams. However, since they did not reach the next inn on the main road, the owner there directed me here."

"A fair clever bit of tracking you've done, then," the

man said. "But I've told you. There be no women here. Not your ward nor any other."

As he made his denial, he had lifted a beefy hand to scratch within his reddish-orange beard. Then, as if disinterested in further conversation, his mud-colored eyes left those of his uninvited guest and returned to the game.

"If she is not here, then tell me where she is," Ian said.

He raised the pistol he had hidden between a fold in the wide tail of his greatcoat, hoping that the dampness from the rain would not keep its powder from firing if he needed it.

However, he had no intention of leaving until he had answers to his questions. And watching the eyes of the other men seated at the table, surreptitiously shifting between him and the man with the red beard, there was little doubt in Ian's mind that someone here knew them.

As soon as he displayed the pistol, a breathless stillness settled over both the players and the watchers. After a long moment, the one who had spoken before again lifted his eyes from the board and focused them once more on the man in the doorway.

"*He* said he was her betrothed. How are we to know which of you is telling the truth?"

"Perhaps you should simply believe this instead," Ian said softly.

He extended the pistol until his arm was perfectly straight, its muzzle directed at a lock of greasy hair that fell over the spokesman's forehead. The man's eyes didn't react to the threat, but they did remain fastened on Ian's, almost unwillingly, for a long heartbeat.

"Clever tracking and all," he said finally, his voice almost sympathetic, "you be come too late to do the lass any good."

Ian's heart lurched and then began to hammer. The air thinned around his head, but the hand that held the pistol never wavered.

"I am not too late unless she's dead," he said. "Is that what you're telling me? That he has murdered her?"

The man's eyes reacted to that, their porcine smallness widening in surprise. "She ain't dead, not as far as I know, but if you be planning to take her back to marry off to someone of your choosing... Well, then, she might as well be. Her prospects be dead, *if* you take my meaning. You needn't worry though. He plans to marry her all right. Just as soon as he can convince her to agree."

There was a snigger from someone in the shadows by the fire, but Ian never looked up to seek its source. His eyes remained steadfast on the man with the red beard.

"Take me to them," Ian said.

"She said you'd pay."

"You didn't believe her. What a shame."

"Bird in hand," the Scot said. Beneath the drooping mustache that covered them, the fleshy lips tilted in amusement.

"In the years to come you should think about how much more you might have profited if you had chosen to protect a defenseless woman rather than aid a lying cur. And I hope he has already paid whatever he owes you. You'll find it difficult to do business with a dead man. And whether it's one dead man or two I leave behind tonight matters very little to me."

Ian gestured toward the door with a small movement of the pistol. After a second's hesitation, the red-haired man pushed the chair he was sitting in away from the table and stood up. He towered a good six or seven inches over Ian's own six feet, and his weight would be almost double that of the Englishman.

"I'll take you to them, but I tell you straight out, I'll have naught to do with murder in my house."

"You don't, however, draw the line at abduction and rape?"

The man said nothing. Nor did anyone else watching this scene unfold. It would be hard to argue that every man in this room hadn't known exactly what Travener was about.

"Or do your scruples, such as they are, apply only to your own women?" Ian continued, feeling an overwhelming bitterness that none of them had attempted to help Anne.

"I keep *my* women safe," the Scot said. "It's not *me* who claims to be that lass's guardian."

Sickness stirred in Ian's stomach. Because it would be equally hard, of course, to mount a convincing argument against the validity of that accusation. After all, it was one he had made against himself countless times in the course of tonight's journey.

The innkeeper had unlocked the door of the second-floor bedroom and then disappeared into the darkness of the hall. And when, after a long moment's hesitation, Ian had pushed it open, there was no gust of wind to warn the inhabitants that their privacy had been invaded.

The fire that burned on its hearth was so low that the room was as cold as and far darker than the hallway in which he was standing. Inside the bedchamber's musty squalor, no candles had been lit, or if they had, they had long ago guttered out.

It took another minute or so for Ian's eyes to adjust to the dimness. As they did, he held the pistol out before him, waiting for his target to materialize.

The flickering firelight first illuminated a private supper, laid out on a small table that had been set before it. An untouched joint of meat lay on the platter, the grease in the congealing juices that were pooled around it iridescent. A loaf of bread had been broken into two portions, neither of which had been removed from the trencher they had been served on.

Ian's eyes were drawn next, unwillingly, to the bed. They moved slowly across the flat, white expanse of its mattress. It was not until they had made that same journey twice that he could allow himself to acknowledge that it had no occupants. And acknowledge that his finger had closed over the trigger in anticipation of doing exactly what he had told the Scotsmen he had come here to do.

Had Travener been sharing that bed with Anne, he would by now have been a dead man. Ian Sinclair, an officer and a gentleman, both by birth and by the royal decree of his King, knew he would have had no compunction in shooting the bastard in the back.

Only when he had verified that the bed was empty did Ian remember to breathe, drawing air into lungs that had been starved for it by his sense of dread. And only now did the hand that held the pistol begin to tremble.

In relief? Or in fear that he might yet discover something even worse than that which he had been expecting when he had opened the door of this room?

Again his gaze began to move, carefully examining the thick shadows around the room's perimeter, even as his mind refused to contemplate what he was looking for. And what he found there was nothing he could ever have imagined. Not in any of those long hours during which he had relentlessly whipped his teams through the cold night and the rain.

As his straining eyes focused on the scene that slowly

emerged from the corner beyond the bed, the hammering of his heart, lodged now in his throat, threatened to choke him. Two motionless figures stood in the darkness, their postures painting a narrative of what had happened, one more vivid than if it had been told.

The firelight turned Travener's hair to gilt. Perhaps that brightness was what had attracted Ian's eyes. They moved over the muscled width of Travener's bare shoulders and back. And then his gaze edged downward, over the pale buttocks, following the line of Travener's legs into the shadows that covered the worn, uneven planks of the floor.

Drawn by a puddle of white that lay near Doyle's feet, his gaze moved again. And by fearfully tracing that pale spill of cloth upward, he found his ward.

Anne was pressed into the corner, clutching against her breasts the other end of the sheet that trailed onto the floor. Above it, her exposed shoulders gleamed like pearl.

Her right arm, the one not holding the sheet, was bent at the elbow, and held out awkwardly in midair. Finally Ian realized what she held in that hand. Her fingers were wrapped around the handle of a knife.

The point of its blade was not directed toward her abductor. It was pressed instead against her own throat, the tip embedded so deeply that the smooth flesh was dimpled with its pressure. A trickle of blood, black in the firelight, seeped from the wound. It ran down the slim line of her neck and onto the swell of her right breast, clearly visible above the sheet with which she had tried to cover her nakedness.

Frantically, Ian's eyes lifted to her face. It was as colorless as the cloth, marred by the marks of blows, which had already begun to darken. Her lip was swollen where it had cut against her teeth, and there was a spot of blood at the corner of her mouth.

Her features were as rigid as if they had been carved from stone. Even with the noise of his entry, her eyes had not lost their concentration on the man standing less than three feet in front of her.

Travener, too, was unmoving, both hands raised, their palms toward Anne. His fingers were spread as if, given the slightest opportunity, he was prepared to grab the knife she held. The firelight caressed the floss of golden hair on his forearms. And despite the pervasive chill of the room, it also glistened on a rivulet of sweat making its slow way down his spine.

How long they had been like this, frozen in place by the sheer raw courage of the woman who held a knife to her own throat, Ian couldn't imagine. Nor could he guess what Anne might have said to convince Travener to stay away.

It was possible that words alone had not accomplished that. The small stream of blood on her neck might well be the result of Travener's first attempt to take the knife from her. The fact that he was keeping his distance proved that, whatever had happened before, by now he fully believed her resolve.

"Anne?" Ian said softly, reluctant somehow, despite his horror, to break her concentration.

Travener did not turn, but at the sound of his voice, the girl's eyes shifted toward the door. The knife did not falter, nor did the pressure she was exerting lessen. Only by the widening of her eyes did she acknowledge the presence of a third person in the room.

"I've come to take you home," Ian said, knowing the words were terribly inadequate to convey his intent.

Her eyes moved back to Travener's face and then returned quickly to Ian's. This time they glazed with tears as they held on his. He knew he must seem only another part of this nightmare. A figment of her strained imagination. Someone she had conjured out of the shadows with her prayers.

"It's over," he said reassuringly. "Put down the knife and come to me."

He saw the depth of the breath she drew. The strength of its movement sent a shimmer of light running along the keen edge of the blade. And then another. And another.

The hand with which she had held a madman at bay, ready to plunge the knife into her own throat, began to shake. She pulled the point away, and another surge of blood spilled from the wound as the tension on the fragile skin was relieved.

Even after it was removed, her arm did not fall. It stayed in place, seeming locked in position. With a visible effort of will she forced her elbow to straighten and her fingers to uncoil, allowing the knife to drop to the floor. Then, with the hand that had just released it, she gathered up the trailing sheet as if it were a ball gown.

She ran across the room and threw herself against Ian's body. His left arm, the one that had received Travener's ball yesterday morning, closed around her. He ignored the pain, pulling Anne tightly against his side.

He could feel her trembling, the vibrations as strong as those of someone in a hard chill. Without taking his eyes off her abductor, Ian lowered his head until his face was near enough to the tumbled curls to breathe in their subtle fragrance. And as he did, Travener finally turned around to look at him.

"The gallant Major Sinclair," he said. "Again."

Despite the pistol pointed at his heart, the blue eyes

were derisive. The beautifully shaped mouth slanted sardonically, no longer arranged in the boyish smile he had worn like a badge of innocence through those weeks in London.

"I suppose I should have known that when my ball didn't kill you outright, I could expect you to show up here. I wonder what it will finally take to put an end to your miserable existence."

"Something more than your efforts, it seems."

Travener laughed. "It *would* be the height of irony, I suppose, if your noble ride tonight to rescue your ward were to lead to your much-delayed demise."

"The sweep and the mob were your doing, of course," Ian said, ignoring the other. "The highwaymen, as well?"

"Whatever you're imagining, there was nothing sinister about those. Simply drama. A bit of masquerading. I had arranged to rescue Anne from both. Unfortunately, your interference left me with far too little to do. The second attempt was perhaps the more effective, but was damned difficult for me to appear heroic before Anne when you were doing such a masterful job of it."

"And Mayfield?"

"The story of Darlington's cowardice would have come out eventually. I simply gave it a small, timely nudge. I needed to speed things along."

"To this?" Ian asked, his eyes falling to the trembling woman he held, before they rose again.

"To our marriage," Travener said. "That was always my intent, I assure you, but... Things were not moving as quickly as I had hoped. Anne had proven to be most uncooperative, even after my public defense of her. She really left me no choice. Neither of you did."

"And you couldn't afford to wait. Because there was

another story about Darlington that was also bound to come out. One that would certainly have upped the stakes in your matrimonial race.''

Travener laughed again. "So you *do* know. I had wondered. Even the proudest of the Sinclairs can be convinced to forget and forgive, it seems, if enough cash is on the table. A family tradition perhaps? After all, I heard that your brother also married a whore.''

Despite the innkeeper's warning, when Ian had seen the empty bed and the knife, he had allowed a fragile hope to form within his heart. And now...

He blocked the images, concentrating instead on the still dangerous man before him. "Don't," he cautioned softly.

"Your noble rescue *this* time, major, has come too late, I'm afraid. Even now Anne may be carrying my child.''

I am not too late unless she is dead. And she was not. That was all that mattered. That and convincing Anne of that truth.

He felt her stir against him. She turned her head, looking at Travener over her shoulder. Her arms were still wrapped around Ian's body. Automatically, his hand soothed down her upper arm, the soft skin like silk beneath his palm.

She flinched under the small caress. Bruised? Or repulsed by a man's touch after what she had endured?

"*My* child," Travener said again, his voice softly taunting. "You may marry her to preserve her honor, of course. And given your reputation, I should expect no less. But what ever will you do with my bastard? Raise him as *your* son?''

Ian wondered why he had not already killed Travener, which would, at least, have shut his filthy mouth.

"Of course, she is a very rich woman," Travener went on. "Having control of that fortune will, I'm sure, make up for a great deal. I wonder if it will make up for watching my son inherit it. And watching him bear *your* name. Such a proud name. Such a noble sacrifice. But after all, what are guardians for?"

"To slay dragons," Ian said softly.

"Do you plan to slay this one?" Travener asked, his voice amused.

"Give me one reason why I shouldn't."

"I am unarmed."

"So was she. At least when you began this."

"Taking the knife from the table was rather clever. I confess, you surprised me, my dear."

Still smiling, Travener bent. Ian's eyes and the muzzle of the pistol followed the motion. And although his heart jumped with a sudden hope, he couldn't believe Travener would be that stupid.

"I should never have considered this a viable weapon," Travener went on, retrieving the knife from where Anne had dropped it. He continued to talk as he straightened, bringing the weapon up with him. "The edge is too dull to be effective against an opponent. Of course, only the point need be sharp to do what you threatened, my dear. Had you come at me with it instead, that would have been another story entirely. As it was, however…" Travener shrugged, his thumb caressing the tip.

"You couldn't afford to let Anne kill herself. Not until you had her vow *and* her signature."

Travener hefted the knife's weight lightly, holding it out on the flat of his hand. "I would eventually have gotten both."

"I think *you* would have given up before she did," Ian said.

"I don't suppose we will ever know, will we?"

Travener stretched out his hand toward the bed, as if he were about to drop the knife onto it. It was the move Ian had been waiting for. As soon as the hand that held the weapon shifted from handle to blade and begin to lift, its motion obviously designed to bring the knife above Travener's head and into a throwing position, Ian's finger closed over the trigger.

Doyle Travener deserved to die. It was the only way out for Anne. The only way out for either of them. The threat of the knife was the impetus Ian had needed to allow him to put an end to this.

Before he could complete the motion his finger had begun, Anne moved. She jerked away from the hold of his damaged arm and threw herself in front of him, positioning her body between his and the knife Travener held.

Distracted, Ian delayed a fraction of a second too long. Only when the firelight, glinting off the movement of the blade, drew his attention back to Travener did he fire.

In that split second, however, the long tanned fingers had already released the knife. It flew end over end across the room, its target Ian's heart.

The throw was skillful enough that it might even have found its aim, had it not been for the woman who had thrown herself between Ian and the blade. The point struck Anne's bare shoulder with an impact that was communicated through her body to the man who held her.

Travener had already staggered backwards as if he had been jerked by a rope, a small dark blossom forming in the center of that smoothly muscled chest. He fell against the bed and then slid off it onto the floor. One hand lifted to claw at his chest as the handsome face contorted in agony.

And even as Anne slumped in his arms, her weight pulling against the damaged muscles in his arm, Ian's eyes held a second longer on Travener. And despite the room's dimness, it seemed he knew the exact moment when life left the wide blue eyes.

It was the innkeeper who directed him that dawn to the doctor's house. Ian had poured out onto his huge palm most of the coins that remained in the leather pouch he'd filled before he'd left London. It was more than a sufficient payment for the directions and for the clandestine burial of the stiffening body they had left upstairs. And even enough to see that he would keep his mouth shut about both.

As he had held Anne in the curricle, Ian could feel his fever building. His breathing was becoming increasingly strained as fluid slowly and inexorably filled his lungs. And in spite of his belief that the wound Anne had sustained was minor, he also believed that he could feel her will to live seeping away.

Just as her blood continued to seep out and stain the sheets of the high bed on which the doctor had directed him to place her. Obediently, he had laid her down on it.

He was almost reluctant to release her, however, afraid that if he did, he might never get her back. Steeling himself to that inevitability, he finally stepped back, moving out of the doctor's way.

He heard the Scots physician's soft gasp as he unfastened the greatcoat Ian had wrapped her in and then turned back the bloodstained sheet, revealing what had been done to her. No matter what he was thinking, the doctor began to work, quickly and competently, staunching the flow of blood from the wound in her shoulder.

Then he bathed her other injuries, as if he were unaware of the man who stood in the shadows behind him, watching every move of his hands. And finally, when everything that could be done for her had been, the doctor mixed several drops of laudanum in a small amount of water. Lifting her head, he helped Anne swallow the mixture before he laid her down against the pillow and tucked the blankets around her.

"I need your help," Ian said, when the doctor straightened at last. The physician took time to put the glass down on the table beside the bed before he answered, his voice cold.

"My help for what?"

He laid his hand on Anne's brow, and as a father might, brushed the tangled strands of rain-stiffened hair off her temple. Her eyes were closed, the blue veins in their thin lids visible in the lamplight.

"I want to marry her."

"Are you responsible for this?"

"No," Ian said softly.

The doctor turned, his eyes for the first time considering his face. "You understand—"

"I understand everything," Ian said.

Still the physician hesitated, his gaze considering.

"I'm afraid we don't have much time," Ian warned.

"Time enough to wait for her permission. None of her injuries is life-threatening. The wound in her back is superficial. And the other..." He shrugged.

"Forgive me. I didn't make myself clear. *I* don't have much time. And I will need your help to be sure she is protected."

Again the physician's eyes evaluated the man standing

in the shadows. Then he crossed the distance that separated them, looking closely into Ian's face. He put the back of his fingers against his brow, and his eyes widened.

"This morning," Ian warned.

And this time, without question, the doctor nodded.

"Anne?"

She opened her eyes and knew that she must be dreaming. Ian was bending over her, his face very close. She lifted her fingers, which seemed detached from her control, to touch his cheek. His skin was hot against the trembling coldness of hers. He was unshaven for the first time since she had known him, making him...vulnerable, somehow.

The abrasive texture of his whiskers beneath her fingertips was incredibly sensual. And only with that realization did she remember that touching Ian was forbidden, a luxury of emotion she could not afford.

She closed her eyes and took a deep breath. Which hurt. And although she tried, she couldn't remember why it should. She felt as if her mind were separate from her body. Almost as if she lacked the will to think.

"Look at me, Anne," Ian commanded softly.

The wine, she thought. There had been something about the wine Travener had forced her to drink—

Travener. With remembrance of his name, everything came flooding back. Everything.

She opened her eyes to find Ian's face still above her. Incredibly, despite what had happened, he was smiling. The same infinite kindness, which had been there when she had looked up and found him in the doorway of the room where Travener had taken her, was in his eyes.

As soon as she had seen the knife on the platter the

innkeeper had brought into the room, she had known what she had to do. And she had been more than prepared to do it.

Prepared until she had seen Ian, standing in the doorway, looking at her exactly as he was now, without judgment or condemnation. He had called her to come to him, and instead of doing the one thing that would have freed them both...

With the pad of his thumb he touched the skin under her eyes, wiping something away. Only when he brought the moisture to his lips to kiss it off did she realize she was crying.

He smiled at her again. And the movement unplanned, her own lips lifted in response, their torn flesh pulling against the crust of dried blood.

"Say yes," Ian said.

"To what?" she whispered.

The smile she had always loved widened, relaxed and very assured.

"To me, of course," he said. "Say yes, my darling, and then I'll let you sleep."

"Will you stay with me?" she asked, her tone as hopeful as the voice of the smallest of her charges, pulled from the throes of nightmare and afraid to close her eyes, lest she fall back into it. "Promise me you'll stay."

"As long as I can," he said. "That I will promise you on my immortal soul."

Her eyes held his, seeing nothing but truth in them, just as she always had.

"Say yes, my darling," he commanded again. Inexorably.

"Yes," she whispered because she trusted him. She had from the beginning.

He nodded, smiling his approval. She felt like a clever

pupil who has finally, after a great effort, satisfied a demanding tutor. He took the hand that was still touching his cheek and gently folded her fingers before he kissed the backs of them.

Although she wanted to continue watching his face, exhausted by the small exertion of talking to him, her eyelids fell. She was vaguely aware of droning voices in the background, but she was far too tired to think about what they might be saying.

And whenever she opened her eyes, Ian was always there, just as he had promised, his head bowed as if in prayer against the hand he still held, tightly enclosed in both of his.

Chapter Seventeen

"Had I known you were in such a hurry, I could have procured you a special license," the Earl of Dare said. "Or perhaps your ward found the thought of an elopement more exciting. I believe we have agreed she suffers from a tendency to romance."

Ian looked up from his chair to find his brother leaning against the frame of the library door. Despite the teasing tone, the look in Dare's eyes said he was well aware there was far more to his brother's runaway marriage than a "tendency to romance." And of course, although Ian had no intention of telling him so, there had been nothing remotely romantic about the weeks he and Anne had spent in Scotland.

As soon as they had returned to London, he had sent his brother word of their marriage, and he had been expecting this visit since he'd dispatched that message. Now that it was at hand, however, he found himself surprisingly unprepared to answer Dare's questions.

"Is Elizabeth with you?" he asked instead.

"She's gone upstairs to find Anne. Don't get up," Dare said, as Ian started to rise. "You look far too comfortable to be disturbed." He walked across the room and sat down in the facing chair, his eyes studying Ian's face. "You've been ill."

And how bloody tiresome that it's always obvious, Ian thought, but he said aloud, "The climate in Scotland is uncertain in the spring."

"Then why go? You knew I would help you with the license. After all, I believe I was the first to suggest you should marry the chit."

"Actually, Elizabeth was the first. I should have taken her advice," Ian said, thinking about all that might have been prevented if he had.

"You might at least have avoided the gossip."

"I can imagine what they are saying."

"You don't care two figs what they're saying. If you had, you would never have eloped with your own ward, who, it has now been disclosed, is heiress to a considerable fortune."

"I didn't marry Anne for Darlington's money."

"I never imagined you did. However…"

The hesitation brought Ian's eyes up from their focus on his hands, which he was annoyed to find were clasped together too tightly in his lap.

"I came to wish you happy," Dare said.

"Then I hope you will," Ian said.

"And yet for some reason, looking at you now—"

"Don't," Ian said softly, just as he had once before. "There is nothing you can do here *except* wish us happy. And forgive me, if you can," he added, smiling at his brother for the first time.

"Forgive you for what?"

"For sending you away. It seems your instincts were better than mine."

"I confess I'd be interested in knowing what changed

your mind," Dare said. "You seemed quite adamant at the time."

"One may be adamant and wrong."

"That's true, of course. You discovered you were wrong?"

"I think that should be obvious."

"Why do I feel there is more to this than I'm being told?"

"Because you are suspicious by nature?" Ian suggested.

"You *are* in love with her?"

"Of course," Ian said.

"And she is in love with you."

It had not been a question, but Ian answered it. "Yes."

"Then…"

"Then I think you may wish us happy with a clear conscience."

"Well, *I* certainly shall," Elizabeth said from the doorway. "I couldn't be more delighted. I feel quite like a successful matchmaking mama."

Ian and Dare stood to face the feminine invasion. Elizabeth was glowingly with child, the thickening of her waist cunningly hidden with an embroidered cashmere shawl, which had been draped around her shoulders, the ends crossed in the front.

Ian's eyes, however, after their first cursory examination of his sister-in-law, had gone immediately to the woman who stood behind her. Anne was dressed in a gown of bronze sarcenet. The color brought out the natural luminescence of her skin and added copper highlights to her hair and her eyes. And to him she had never been more beautiful.

She smiled at him, that same enigmatic tilt of her lips with which she answered his every expression of concern since their marriage. Far too self-contained. Especially since they had returned to London.

Throughout the long days and nights they had spent in Scotland, Anne had slept on the floor beside his bed, his hand held tightly in hers. Sometimes she dreamed. And when she did, she would come into his arms like a child, her cold body sheltered against the fever-ridden heat of his. Half-delirious, he would hold her as she trembled with the force of her memories.

And even then, knowing the thing she feared, in his baseness he had wanted her. He wanted her now. She was his wife, and yet she was not. And he had finally been forced to acknowledge she might never be.

At first, he had told himself that the horror of the night he had rescued her from Travener would gradually fade. Together they would rediscover the easy friendship they had once shared. He had even dared to hope that, as long as he was patient, moving from that to the kind of relationship Dare and Elizabeth had would one day be possible. And now...

He pulled his gaze from Anne's face and found Dare's on his. The earl's eyes fell to the too-revealing line of the skin-tight pantaloons Ian wore. And when they rose again, they were alight with brotherly amusement.

"You may congratulate yourself later, Elizabeth," Dare said, his gaze now carefully confined to his brother's face. "I had forgotten we're interrupting a honeymoon. My apologies. We came to welcome Anne into the family. Rogues and scoundrels all."

The earl's voice was touched with some emotion, nostalgia perhaps. After all, those were the same words with which Ian had once welcomed Elizabeth to the family.

"Now you are one of us," Val continued. "And you will find that whatever our other faults, the Sinclairs always defend their own, even unto death.'' There was a small awkward silence, and it was the earl, ever sensitive to nuance, who broke it. ''I demand the traditional bridal kiss, and then we shall be on our way.''

''Nonsense,'' Ian said, because he had no choice. And because he was forced to admit that it might even be better if they had guests. At least there would be something to distract Anne from that which loomed unspeakably between them. ''I'm sure Elizabeth is tired from your journey.''

''Of course you must stay,'' Anne said, crossing the room to take Dare's hands. She leaned forward, and smiling, pressed her lips against his cheek. ''I insist upon it. I shall be most disappointed if Elizabeth and I don't have time to visit.''

''Wifely secrets to share, no doubt,'' Dare said. ''Now I'm sure we should leave.''

With the resulting laughter, the earlier tension seemed to ease. The conversation turned to the social events of the summer and then to news of the war and of Sebastian, the youngest Sinclair, who was still with Wellington. Gradually, Ian began to relax, hopeful that their deception had been and would continue to be successful, at least through the course of this visit.

It was less than an hour later that the countess pled fatigue and was escorted by both her husband and her hostess to her room. Anne didn't come down again. He would see her at dinner, where they would once more be protected from having to really talk to one another by the demands of entertaining their guests. And perhaps, he thought again, it was even better that they were.

No way out, Anne thought, as she must have a thousand times in the last two months. No way out.

She paced away from the window, her palms soothing down her upper arms, which were crossed over her breasts as if she were chilled. And she couldn't be, not in the middle of summer. She shivered, however, before she turned restlessly and recrossed the wide expanse of her bedchamber to stand once more by the window she had just deserted. *No way out.*

He had not loved her before. And now... Now there was so much more that lay between them. Her father's guilt. Travener's betrayal. The manner of his death.

She had hoped it would make a difference in their relationship when she had gone to Ian with the news that she was not, after all, to bear Travener's child. It had to her, of course, the relief so great that she had been faint with it. Yet for almost a week she had not found the words to tell her husband. When finally she had, he said only, "Now you need never think of it again."

And she really had tried not to. Until today, when she had seen his eyes on Elizabeth. They had touched on the small bulge of the countess's pregnancy, before they had lifted to find hers, their hazel depths carefully cleared of what she had seen so briefly within them.

Envy? Did Ian feel the same deep jealousy she felt each time she was forced to watch Dare's hand touch Elizabeth, whether unthinkingly straightening her shawl or placing steadying fingers under her elbow? Did he, too, feel the same emptiness when the earl's eyes caressed his wife's face? Or when he teased Elizabeth, laughing about her unabashed joy in their marriage?

Their marriage. Which was no marriage at all. Ian never touched her, not if he could possibly avoid it. He hadn't since those long nights in Scotland when she had clung to him as desperately as if he were her only hope of redemption. And perhaps he was.

Her eyes were attracted by some movement on the grounds below. Almost without her conscious volition, her hand pushed aside the draperies to reveal the moon-dappled expanse of lawn beneath her window.

Two figures moved slowly across its smooth green sward. It took a moment for her to realize who it was and what they were doing. The Earl of Dare and his countess were dancing.

Elizabeth's slender white hand was on the dark shoulder of her husband's jacket, her face turned up to his. Even with the distance and the moonlight, it was clear what was in her eyes. An intensity of love, so powerful it had overcome all the barriers that society and the past had thrown in its way. The same kind of love...

The same kind of love. The words echoed not only in her heart, but also in her brain. Perhaps Ian *hadn't* loved her when he had married her. Perhaps he never would, but what was in her heart for the man who had made that sacrifice was enough for both of them. Far more than enough.

The slow, silent waltz on the moonlit grounds below continued, and smiling, Anne watched the graceful glide and sway of the lovers. And it was only after she had watched them a long time that she realized Dare was barefoot.

Her lips lifted, her irrepressible appreciation of the ridiculous breaking through her unhappiness. Every romantic fantasy, even one as beautiful as that which was being acted out below, had about it some element of illusion, which hid its less-than-perfect reality. Like the Earl of Dare dancing barefoot in his evening clothes with his awkwardly pregnant countess.

It was not the illusion that was important. Not the silvered moonlight. Not the beauty or the fantasy. All that mattered was the strength of the bond that had brought two such disparate people together, despite all the things that conspired to keep them apart.

How well that applied to the illusion of her own marriage. All her life she had wanted the fantasy. A man who trembled when he touched her. A man whose eyes looked at her with a love so strong it would color whatever he saw—age or imperfection—with beauty. A man who would always be there, holding her hand through the darkest hour of any night.

Reality and illusion. And if she could have only one...

Hot tears veiled the scene below. Her fingers released the drapery, letting it fall over the glass, as if she could no longer bear to watch. Because if she could have only one—illusion or reality—she knew now which she would choose. And if the other never came, at least she would never have to endure the blackness of any other midnight alone.

Whatever Elizabeth had hoped for when she had agreed to take Anne under her wing, Ian thought, she must have been very satisfied tonight with the results. The girl he had fetched from Fenton Hall had during these short months become a beautiful, self-assured woman, fully prepared to take her place in the society to which she had belonged since birth.

Watching Anne at dinner, however, he knew he would far rather have had the laughing hoyden Travener had destroyed than the self-contained stranger who graced his table. And he feared that the girl he had fallen in love with had disappeared forever.

He removed the onyx stickpin from his cravat and dropped it on the top of his dressing table. Despite

Anne's performance, and even despite his own, Ian knew his brother had sensed something was wrong.

Val could never imagine the truth, however. And if he asked, Ian would continue to do what he had done from the beginning. He would conceal the horror that had brought them together.

As he began to loosen his neck cloth, his eyes caught the movement of his hands reflected in the mirror. They stilled, as he considered the face of the man the glass revealed.

What did she see when she looked at him? A reminder of an event that was too painful to remember? Or—and the thought was bitter as gall—did she see him as a threat? Simply another Travener, biding his time until he, too, would make demands.

He turned away from the mirror, forcing his fingers to complete the task they had begun. The cravat joined the discarded stickpin, and then he unfastened the top button of his shirt. He turned his head from side to side, trying to work out the stiffness produced by the strain of the evening.

He walked across the room, throwing open one of the tall windows that looked out on the gardens below, breathing deeply of the rose-laden air. He stood there a long time, watching the slow drift of cloud-dappled moonlight across the garden.

Gradually, the noises in the great house stilled, as the servants finished their duties and made their way to their own quarters. And yet he was not surprised when the soft knock sounded on the door to his room.

He had known he couldn't escape Dare's questions. Val saw too much and understood him far too well. Without bothering to close the window, Ian turned and called out permission for him to enter. He had already braced himself for the coming interview when the door opened, revealing not his brother, but the slender, nightgown-clad figure of his wife.

The last person he had expected to see, Anne realized as Ian's eyes widened. And then they fell, just as they always did. After a heartbeat, he raised them again to smile at her.

"I should have known Dare would come as soon as I wrote him with our news," he said. "My apologies."

"For having a brother who loves you? I confess to being jealous of that, but you certainly owe me no apology for it."

She stepped inside, closing the door behind her. She stood in front of it a moment, the knob still in her hand, before she forced her fingers to release it. She walked across the room until she was less than three feet away from him.

Through the open window, the scent of the roses wafted upward from the garden below. She wondered if Ian had seen the dancers, although the slow waltz she had watched had taken place several hours before. Hours she had spent marshaling her arguments and gathering her courage until she had found enough to bring her here. And now that she was...

She took a calming breath and realized other scents were as pervasive in the room as the heavy fragrance of the roses. The same masculine aromas she had always associated with Ian were also here: expensive soap, the starch in the fine lawn shirt, even the subtle, totally masculine smell of his skin.

And tonight there was a whiff of brandy underlying the others. She envied him its fortification. She wished she had been wise enough to think of that.

"Is something wrong?" he asked.

She looked up to find his eyes on her face, the kindness she had learned to depend on through those long days and nights in Scotland within them again.

"I had thought…" And then she hesitated, unsure, despite the hours she had planned this assault, how to begin it. "I had thought we might dance," she said softly, the image of that slow waltz in the moonlight stirring within her heart.

"Dance?" Ian repeated, as if he had never heard the word before.

"We did once. I don't know if you remember—"

"I remember," he interrupted.

His face was still, the lips she longed to feel against her own almost stern. And in his eyes…

"I remember everything," he added, and the hope that had begun to grow at what she believed she had read in that hazel intensity faltered.

And then Ian held out his hand, exactly as he had in the ballroom that day. The intricate steps of the courtly charade they had acted out then was not, however, what she had come here for tonight.

"A waltz," she said softly, placing her trembling fingers over his. And just as it always had, the steady warmth of his hand under hers comforted and welcomed like a fire on a winter's night.

Tonight he made no disavowal of his skill. Instead, he lifted her right hand into position and then laid the fingers of his left against the small of her back. She could feel their hard masculinity through the sheer fabric of her rail.

The distance between their bodies, however, remained exactly the same as that prescribed by society's dictates. And with that realization, she knew with a surge of bitter disappointment there would be nothing about this dance that would echo the intimate connection evident between the couple she had watched on the grounds below.

"Shall I hum?" Ian asked, his lips carefully arranged now in a smile.

He had hummed that day. *That* day. When what she felt for him was new and unexplored and her anticipation of its fulfillment was a tantalizing expectancy that existed only in her own heart, secret and guarded. And in the intervening months, instead of the fulfillment she had hoped for, there had been nothing between them but betrayal.

The caustic knowledge of her father's. And then Travener's. And if she did nothing to break the hold those had taken...

Ian was still waiting, she realized, her left hand resting lightly on his shoulder and her right trembling in his. He was waiting for permission to hum. Waiting for her to take the first step. Waiting to do, once again, whatever she asked of him.

Reality and illusion... And she knew with a sudden and blinding clarity that this was not the way. The waltz she had watched had been Dare and Elizabeth's illusion. Their reality. It was not hers. Nor was it Ian's.

Theirs was more down-to-earth. More practical. It was the strength of a good man's hand, always there in the terrifying darkness. It was forgiveness. Endurance without complaint.

From somewhere within the cherished memories of each moment she had spent with Ian Sinclair came the reminder of her own beloved reality. *Chilblains, porridge, running noses, and dragging hems.* And if she did nothing...

She freed her fingers from his and stepped back, putting even more distance between them. He made no effort to hold her, releasing her hand at its first movement. And still he waited, with nothing but compassion in his eyes.

"I saw how you looked at Elizabeth," she said.

His eyes narrowed slightly as his head tilted. "Elizabeth?"

"She is carrying your brother's child." She wasn't sure why she had begun this way, but now that she had… "And I know that eventually you, too, will surely want sons of your own."

She watched his face, trying to gauge his reaction. He was so controlled, especially since they had returned from Scotland, that she had known she would see only those involuntary physical responses no one could hide. The slight dilation of his pupils. The reactive working of the muscle in his throat as he swallowed against an emotion he wouldn't express. And they were all there.

She let the silence build again, hoping he would fill it, but when he did, it was nothing she had expected.

"I told you that you need never think of that again."

Never think of sons? She, who had confessed how much she wanted them. And then she realized that wasn't what he meant. He meant never think of what Travener had done. And yet…

"I don't know what to do," she said. "I don't know what you want me to do."

"About what?" He reached out and took her hand, holding it in both of his, just as he had throughout that first endless day and night they had spent together. "Anne?"

"About this. About our marriage. You have to tell me what I must do."

"What you must do?" he repeated, watching her face. "You must do nothing. You don't have to be afraid."

"I'm not afraid. Travener's dead. He can't hurt us again. I know that."

The sudden stillness was brittle. And painful.

"I meant of me."

Of me. For a fraction of a second those words made no sense. It was only when she put them together with what he had said before...

"Afraid of you? You think... You think I'm afraid of *you*?" His eyes answered her, and at what was in them, her heart began to beat too fast. "How can you think I'm afraid of *you*?"

That was exactly what he believed, she realized, her eyes searching his again. And as she did, hope began to grow.

"You thought I was afraid, and I thought..." She shook her head, fighting tears.

"What did you think?" he asked, his voice still kind.

"That you couldn't forget."

The question moved behind his eyes. "Forget Travener?"

"What he did. You were so..." She shook her head, a hundred images running through her brain, all of them requiring a reinterpretation in light of this revelation. "You never touched me. Never looked at me. *Really* looked at me. I thought that was because when you did, that room—and what happened there—was all you saw."

"No," he said, the word abrupt. And unequivocal.

"No?" she repeated softly.

"What I see in that room is only my failure. You were entrusted to me, and I failed to keep you safe."

There was no doubting the guilt in his eyes or in his voice.

"And how long must you be punished for that?" she

asked, understanding him enough to know that nothing she could say would convince him that what had happened that night hadn't been his failure, but Travener's. "How long must I?"

"This isn't—" he began, and then he stopped the words, his eyes still holding hers.

"What Travener did has nothing to do with you. And nothing to do with this," she said, her hand tightening over his. "I know you don't love me. And the reasons you married me are very far from those on which a real marriage should be based, but we *are* married. And there is nothing now we can do to change that."

She hesitated, giving him a chance to refute what she had said. He said nothing, his face very still, his eyes on hers.

"What I feel for you," she went on, forcing the words past the emotion that crowded her throat, "what I have always felt for you, is enough to sustain any marriage. If you will only give me a chance. I know that you think—"

"You have no idea what I think," he said.

And there was something different in his eyes. Not kindness. Not even compassion. Or comfort.

"I know…what you told me."

He nodded, and then he brought her hand to his lips, his mouth brushing over her fingers. "And what I told you…"

She waited, almost afraid. "*Is* there someone else?" she asked finally. "Was that a lie?"

"Not that."

"Then…"

"Another failure. Forgive me. I have proven a most unsatisfactory guardian, it seems." His voice had lightened, and the stern lines in which his face had been set seemed at odds with what he said. "I promise you I shall endeavor to be a better husband."

Her throat tightened with the promise of that, and with what was in his eyes.

"And you must never believe I didn't love you," he said. "Nothing could be further from the truth. It seems as if in trying to protect you…" And instead of finishing that equally promising revelation, his voice trailed off.

"I don't understand." She didn't. She had come to offer him a compromise. And instead…

He smiled at her, and then he pulled her to him. Whatever doubts she had died as his mouth closed over hers. There was nothing tentative about his kiss. And nothing within it of pity or compassion. Or even of compromise. This was desire, decently denied, and only now, with her permission, given expression.

Despite her experience with Travener's perverted version of this, Anne responded, pushing aside whatever trepidation she might have felt at placing herself into a man's control. This was Ian, and there was nothing to fear in his arms. It seemed she had always known that.

Whatever dark memories she had brought to this embrace would be denied, buried and eventually forgotten, in the tenderness with which he treated her. A tenderness she knew she could trust not to be overwhelmed, not even by his passion.

His tongue pushed against her lips, and she opened them, welcoming its invasion. He held nothing back, his mouth demanding, his hands on her upper arms, holding her on tiptoe as his mouth ravaged.

Almost in wonder, she finally understood that this was

not a man fighting the ghost of another man's possession. This was a man claiming that for which he had hungered.

His mouth released hers to trace across her cheek and then along her neck, trailing heated moisture in its wake. Her head fell back as her eyes closed, savoring his touch.

His hand flattened against her back, urging her body into closer contact with his. She put her arms around his neck as his tongue found the slight depression of her collarbone, sending a frisson of sensation spiraling through her body.

Her head tilted to give him greater access to her throat and at the same time, she felt his fingers working deftly at the closure of her gown. They slipped inside its high neckline, their masculine roughness moving abrasively against her skin, and she shivered again, this time in anticipation.

His hand stilled, and for a moment she didn't understand why he had stopped. She turned her head, her mouth moving against the fragrant softness of his hair.

She put her hand over the fingers that had halted, their movement frozen. Her mouth breathed the word she had once only dreamed about saying to him. And now, finally, she could.

"Yes," she whispered.

Instead of returning to that caress, however, his hand slipped beneath her knees, and he bent, lifting her into his arms. Looking down into her eyes, he carried her across the room to the bed where he had slept alone. And where tonight…

He would never again sleep alone, she pledged, although the words were only in her head. Neither of them would ever again be alone in the darkness, not as long as they lived.

* * *

Despite what she had told him, she had thought at some point she might be afraid. Surely there would be some residual anxiety, if not in her brain, which welcomed his touch, then in her skin and muscles, branded with the memory of that other pain. And now, with thanksgiving, she knew there was not.

She wondered if the slow, sensual glide of his hands had been deliberate. Or was this the way he would have made love to her, even if what had happened in that inn in Scotland had not been between them?

His movements seemed completely unstudied. He touched her as if he enjoyed touching her, whether his palm was sliding over the slight convexity of her stomach or trailing slowly down the outside of her thigh. He had explored her body with a skill that left her breathless and shaken.

And she had denied him nothing. Because at last she had understood what he had feared and because she had told him the truth. The depth of the love she felt for him was itself more than enough to see them through this night. More than enough.

He had touched her a long time before his lips and his tongue had joined the sensual worship of his hands. And she had known then that what he had said was truth as well. He did not find her sullied or stained. If he had, he could not caress with his lips the trembling flesh that had once been torn and bloodied by another man's brutal lust.

Even in her innocence, she knew this was not lust, despite its power. That, too, she had needed to learn. There was daylight and there was night. There was what had happened before. And there was this.

This wonder, for which she had no words. No guides.

No rules. Only that she was his, to do with as he wished. And what he wished...

And what he wished, she had discovered, was nothing that she, too, did not crave. The quickly spiraling desire had come as a surprise to her. She had been prepared to endure.

What he had given her first was a shimmering anticipation, created by the slow secret movements of skin against skin. Heat to heat. Moisture to moisture.

His lips brushed the sweat-dampened hair at her temple and then he raised his chest, propping above her on his elbows. He smiled at her, his eyes tracing over her face.

She knew he had watched her. And she knew why, of course. Now, however, his eyes on her face were simply a part of what was happening between them. No more and no less.

He found joy in watching her. And she had found it in letting him. *Joy.* He had given her joy. Or rather he had given her back the sheer joy in being alive that had always been an integral part of who she was.

"Why?" she asked, expecting denial or avoidance.

His thumb touched her cheek, following the line of bone up to the temple he had touched with his lips.

"Why?" he asked, his voice completely relaxed.

As much as she hated to destroy that tranquillity, she needed to understand this, the last of all the things that had stood between them. Understand and then destroy, as they had tonight destroyed the rest.

"When I came to you and told you I loved you—" she said, and watched his eyes change. "You said that Dare had been wrong. And now... Forgive my arrogance," she said, smiling at him, "but it is obvious, even to me, that you lied about what you feel. I need to understand why.''

''Because I'm a fool,'' he said, answering the smile.

''Whatever else you are, my love, you are not a fool. Was it the money? Because you were afraid of what people would say?''

''I didn't know about the money. It had nothing to do with that. And nothing to do with you.''

''Then…'' *Nothing to do with you.* ''It must have had something to do with you.''

As the silence stretched too long without his answer, her smile faded, as did the tranquillity.

''Ian?''

''I wanted your life to be only joy,'' he said.

She shook her head, still watching his eyes. ''No one's life is 'only joy.'''

''I wanted yours to be,'' he said.

''And you thought it would be without you? You thought that by denying you loved me—'' She stopped because there was no logic in that. ''I don't understand.''

His lips tightened, and then he took her hand, guiding her fingers over a ridge on his chest. She had seen the scars, and known again her father's guilt, but this…

''What is it?'' she asked, her fingers exploring the shape and size of whatever lay beneath the skin.

She felt the depth of the breath he took before he said, ''Something I brought back from Portugal. Something they tell me may…move. Become dislodged and shift its position.''

''What would make it shift?'' she whispered, trying to make sense of what he had said. ''Why after all this time…''

''Physical exertion. At least that's what McKinley has warned me about.''

''Exertion? Such as in fighting off a highwayman?'' she asked. ''Or a mob?'' Her voice rose on the last, remembering those things with a sense of horror she had not felt then because she had had no idea what had really been at stake. ''You did those things, knowing that it was possible—''

''Nothing happened,'' he said, his thumb again moving over her temple, his voice soothing. Reassuring. ''Nothing at all.''

It hadn't, she realized. He had survived both of those battles. *And* being shot by Travener. He had even survived that terrible fever in Scotland, an illness brought on by that injury and his reckless drive to rescue her.

Survived. Even Travener had recognized the tenacity with which Ian Sinclair clung to life. Which must mean…

She put her fingers against his cheek, thinking about how long he had lived under the shadow of this death sentence. A sentence which, given all that had happened to him since she had known him, she found she could not believe.

''McKinley could be wrong. He *must* be. If that were ever going to happen, it would have by now.''

His eyes held on hers. Wanting to believe.

''I refuse to allow it,'' she added softly, smiling at him. ''I refuse to believe whatever they told you. I refuse to allow you to believe it.''

''You were made for joy,'' he said again.

''I was made for this,'' she said sharply. ''However long it lasts. *No one* has guarantees. Not of anything.''

That was another illusion. That there would be years

to savor. Sometimes there were. And sometimes there were not.

The only thing sure was this moment. This second. This heartbeat. And she knew she wanted all of them, as many as were left, against hers. That was the reality of loving someone. That inevitable and terrible price.

"I want *this* joy," she said. "I want your sons. And most of all, I want you."

Far more than enough... And however long or short it was, she knew that it would be.

* * * * *

GAYLE WILSON

Four-time RITA finalist and RITA Award winner Gayle Wilson has written twenty-five novels for Harlequin. A former high school English and world history teacher to gifted students, she writes historical fiction set in the English Regency period and contemporary romantic suspense. She has won numerous awards, including both the 1998 and the 1999 Kiss of Death Awards for Outstanding Romantic Suspense, the Texas Gold Award in 1999, the Laurel Wreath Award for Excellence in 1998 and 1999, and the 1999 Dorothy Parker Award for Category Romance, given by Reviewers International Organization. Gayle was a RITA finalist in the category of Best First Book in 1995 for her first historical, *The Heart's Desire*, and a RITA finalist in Romantic Suspense in 1999 for *Ransom My Heart*. In the 2000 RITA competition, she was a finalist in both the Short Historical category for *Lady Sarah's Son* and in Romantic Suspense for *The Bride's Protector*, for which she won the RITA.

Gayle still lives in Alabama, where she was born, with her husband of thirty-two years and an ever-growing menagerie of beloved pets. She has one son, who is also a teacher of gifted students. Gayle loves to hear from readers. Write to her at P.O. Box 3277, Hueytown, AL 35023.

Travel back in time to America's past with wonderful Westerns from Harlequin Historicals

ON SALE MARCH 2001

LONGSHADOW'S WOMAN
by **Bronwyn Williams**
(The Carolinas, 1879)

LILY GETS HER MAN
by **Charlene Sands**
(Texas, 1880s)

ON SALE APRIL 2001

THE SEDUCTION OF SHAY DEVEREAUX
by **Carolyn Davidson**
(Louisiana, 1870)

NIGHT HAWK'S BRIDE
by **Jillian Hart**
(Wisconsin, 1840)

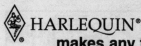